Revolution

DAEMONS & LUMENS SERIES

BY S. D. PAINE

ASIN ebook: B0F82S5LFK

ISBN Paperback: 979-8-9997972-0-9

Cover Design & Print Formatting: Miblart

Editor: Andrea Halland, Editing by Andrea

Ebook Formatting Nicole Kincaid, Naughty Nook PR

DAEMONS & LUMENS SERIES

Retaliation

A Daemon's Alliance

Resurrection

A Lumen's Surrender

Revolution

Aut inveniam viam aut faciam
I shall either find a way, or make one.

Hope is the thing with feathers that perches in the soul.
- Emily Dickinson

Never fear the darkness within you. Embrace it.
Find your happiness and let the rest burn.

AUTHOR NOTE

This book contains dark themes and the characters make questionable decisions. Tropes and triggers include graphic violence, torture, physical and mental assault, BDSM-related scenes, and explicit intimate scenes.

For more information about this book and future books in the series, visit my website and sign up for my newsletter!
www.sdpaineauthor.com

NOVELLA PLAYLIST

Find me on Spotify to listen to this Daemons & Lumens playlist!

Wake Up by Llunr
Superpower by X Ambassadors
Chains (The Tower) by Fame on Fire
Bulletproof by DIAMANTE
wonderland by MVSSIE
Riot by Hollywood Undead
Unstoppable by Disturbed
The Unknown by BONNIE X CLYDE
Watch the world burn by Falling In Reverse
Revenge EP by Mike's Dead
All My Life by Falling In Reverse
Bad Guy by Falling In Reverse
F*ck by Mandrazo
Wait For You by Myles Smith
Half God Half Devil by In This Moment
Obsessed by Henri Werner
Fighter by Christina Aguilera
Demon Mode by Stileto, AViVA
Stuck In My Head by Sleep Theory
How Can I Live by Ill Niño
WOOF by FKA Rayne
Judgement Day by Five Finger Death Punch

The Emptiness Machine by Linkin Park
It Ain't Right by Jessie Murph
Blood by In This Moment
Dead Memories by Slipknot
Revolution by Bishop Briggs
Any Other Way by We The Kings
Confident by Demi Lovato
Fall In Line by Christina Aguilera, Demi Lovato
Hail the Apocalypse by Avatar
Bloody Angel by Avatar
Far Away by Breaking Benjamin, Scooter Ward
Painless by Fozzy
Made For Me by Muni Long
Awaken by League of Legends, Valerie Broussard
Shadow and Soul by Red
Not My Fault by Reneé Rapp, Megan Thee Stallion
No Good by KALEO
Skin And Bones David Kushner
Higher by The Score
Sail by AWOLNATION
Girlfriend by Icona Pop
Can't Remember to Forget You by Shakira, Rhianna
Rise Up by Sum 41
Sweet Dream by Bohnes, Underoath
Throne by Bring Me The Horizon
Novel Blood by Tommee Proffitt, Fleurie
Limits by Bad Omens
Formaldehyde Footsteps by Houndrel

White Widow by Crown the Witch
Doomsday Blue by Bambie Thug
To The Wolves by Stitched Up Heart, Escape the Fate
Let the Flames Begin by Paramore
Superhero by Kim Dracula
Bite Marks by Ari Abdul
Counting Bodies Like Sheep by A Perfect Circle
Evergreen by Arankai
What It Takes by Adelitas Way
Follow You by Bring Me The Horizon
Everything's Burned by Michael Malarkey
Blow Me Away by Halo, Breaking Benjamin

THE V.I.P. LIST

Seraphina Valdis Bronwen - Daughter of Aurora Valdis, alias Sara Braun

Aurora Valdis Bronwen - Mother of Lailah, Seraphina, and Michaela, Deceased

Joseph Bronwen - Husband of Aurora Valdis, Father of Michaela, Deceased

Lailah Valdis Bronwen - Oldest daughter of Aurora Valdis, sacrificed, Deceased

Michaela Valdis Bronwen - Youngest daughter of Aurora and Joseph

Andras Blackbyrn - Prince of The Obscuritas, son of Laszlo
Typhon "Ty" Radnor - Prince of The Obscuritas, son of Darren
Leviathan "Levi" Delano - Prince of The Obscuritas, son of Samuel
Devon "Dev" Parrish - Prince of The Obscuritas, son of Ezekiel

Laszlo Blackbyrn - King of The Obscuritas, Leader
Darren Radnor - King of The Obscuritas, Enforcer, Deceased
Samuel Delano - King of The Obscuritas, Seducer
Ezekiel Parrish - King of The Obscuritas, Technician, Deceased

King Corson Ormaenus - King of Caligo and all daemons
Prince Belial Ormaenus - Oldest son, Prince of Caligo and loyal to the king
Prince Morax "Mor" Ormaenus - Middle son, Prince of Caligo
Prince Phenex "Phen" Ormaenus - Youngest son, Prince of Caligo

PAWNS & PLAYERS

Belfegor - Daemon, King of the Novo Mountain Tribe, Deceased

Gremory Cerravaux- Daemon, once Commander of the Daemon Army, mate of Delphine & Tabitha

Delphine Bellinor - Powerful witch, of The Mal-Regia

Nuriela Ramas - Lumen, mate of Lailah Valdis

Leona "Lo" Rigby - Human, rescued by Nuriela

Foras - Daemon, loyal to Belial

The Malefica - Akin to witches, living in Tellisa

The Mal-Regia - Royals of The Malefica

Adriel Uthra - Father of Lailah Valdis, family is part of the Lumen Council, Deceased

Aleya Danai Kel - Goddess who resides beneath Mount Monkara, the all-knowing power worshipped and feared by all who live on Stella Terra

Scribe Lahabiel (Lay-ha-Bee-el) - Scribe of the truxen daemons, half witch, known for knowledge of ancient prophecies

Elgo - Soldier, truxen daemon

Halphas - Lumen, alliance unknown

Deccaria - Truxen daemon, loyal to Belfegor's heir

Jophielle - Lumen, slave working in Zamina Castle

Jormund - Truxen daemon, loyal to Belfegor's bloodline

Mihra - Truxen daemon, cousin of Seraphina

Mr. Edward Kingston - Father of Audrey Kingston, potential Obscuritas member, Deceased

Ryan Lancing - Lead Bartender at Noircoeur, Obscuritas member

James "J" Azer - Gym Manager, close friend of Ty, Umbra Noctis member

Dominique - Owner of Noircoeur, Obscuritas member

Otis Redford - Operations Manager of Noircoeur, Obscuritas member

Josie and Lottie Hayes - Twins, Dancers at Noircoeur, friends of Sara Braun

Jade Dawlish - Professional boxer, employed at Ty's gym, allegiance unknown

Xavier Saladino - Fireman at firehouse, member of unnamed gang, allegiance unknown

IMPORTANT PLACES

Vespertine Hall - Estate located just outside city of Boston, owned by The Obscuritas

Blackbyrn Manor - Estate located near Asheville, North Carolina, owned by The Obscuritas

Noircoeur - Burlesque club beneath restaurant in downtown Boston, owned by The Obscuritas

The Towne House - Home of Andras, Typhon, and Leviathan, located near Harvard University

P4 Fitness - Gym owned by Typhon, located near The Towne House

Stella Terra (Stel-uh Tare-uh) - Planet of the daemons and lumens

Tellisa (Teh-lee-sah) - Country of the daemons and lumens

Caligo (Cal-ee-go) - Capital city of the daemons territory

Caelum (Kay-lum) - Capital city of the lumens territory

Dariava Palace (Dar-ee-ahvah) - Once home of the Valdis family, last rulers of Caelum

Zamina Castle (Zah-me-nuh) - Home of the Ormaenus family, rulers of Caligo

WORDS & PHRASES

The Obscuritas - Exclusive cult seeking otherworldly power

Umbra Noctis - Shadows of Night, secret sect of The Obscuritas created by the Princes

Daemons - Monstrous creatures of myths and legends, varying degrees of magic/power relating to the elements

Lumens - Ethereal creatures of myths and legends, varying degrees of magic/power relating to the elements

stellatium (stuh-lay-tea-um) - a rare metal created from a dying star, powerful enough to kill a daemon or lumen

luxenite (lux-eh-night) - rare stone, magically charged to harness the power of a lumen's essence

tenebrite (teh-neh-bright) - rare stone, magically charged to harness the power of a daemon's essence

Vis-el (Veez-elle) - elemental power of the daemons and lumens, different from the spells wielded by The Malefica

truxen daemon - type of daemon with the ability to shift into any creature and communicate with animals

Cancatier (Can-kah-tee-air) - A rare power giving the creature the ability to control other creatures with their voice

Mae domina - my lady/master

Diabla - (she) devil

Mi diosa - my goddess

Belle femme - beautiful woman

Mera dil - my heart

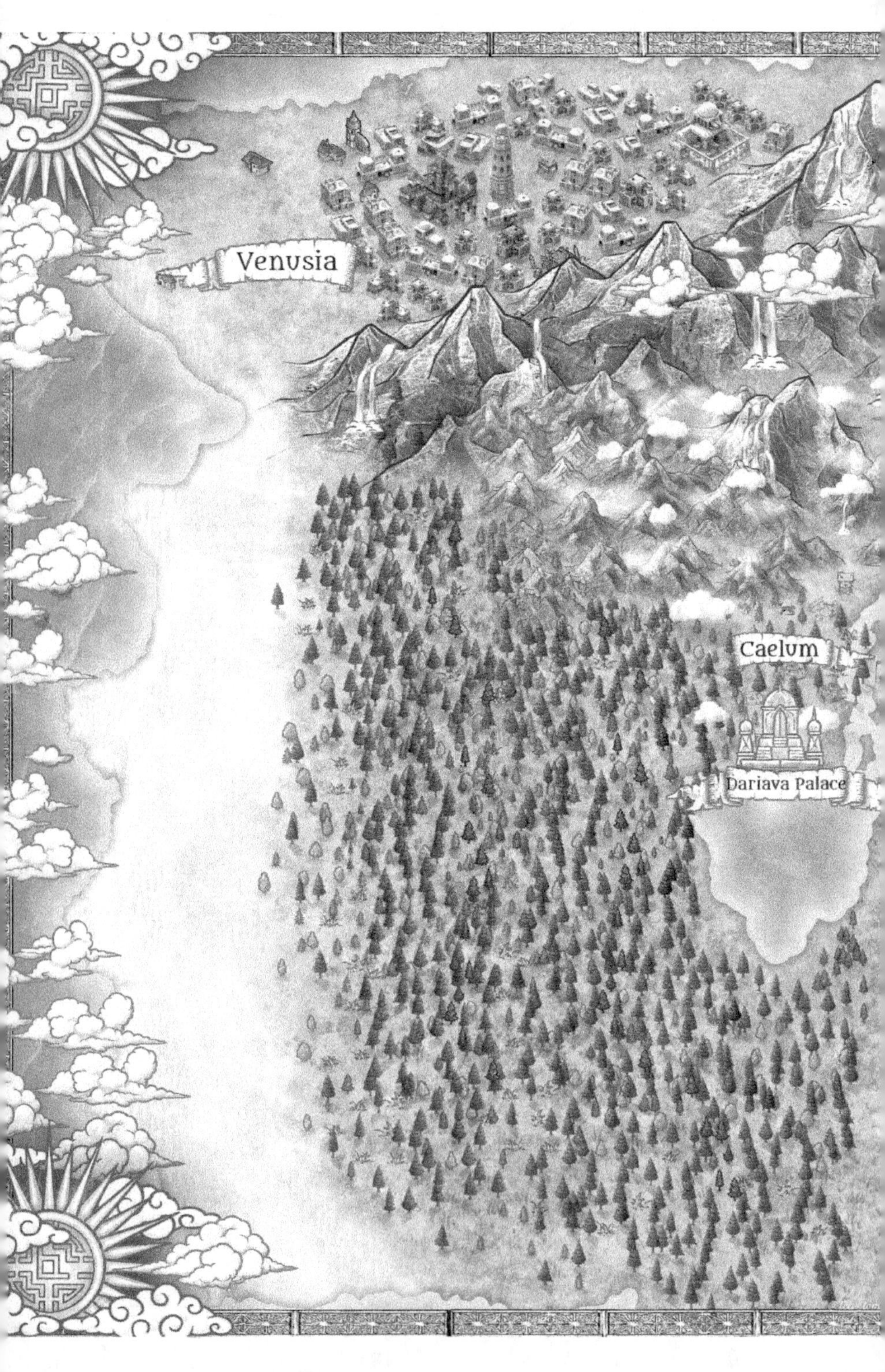

Venusia
Caelum
Dariava Palace

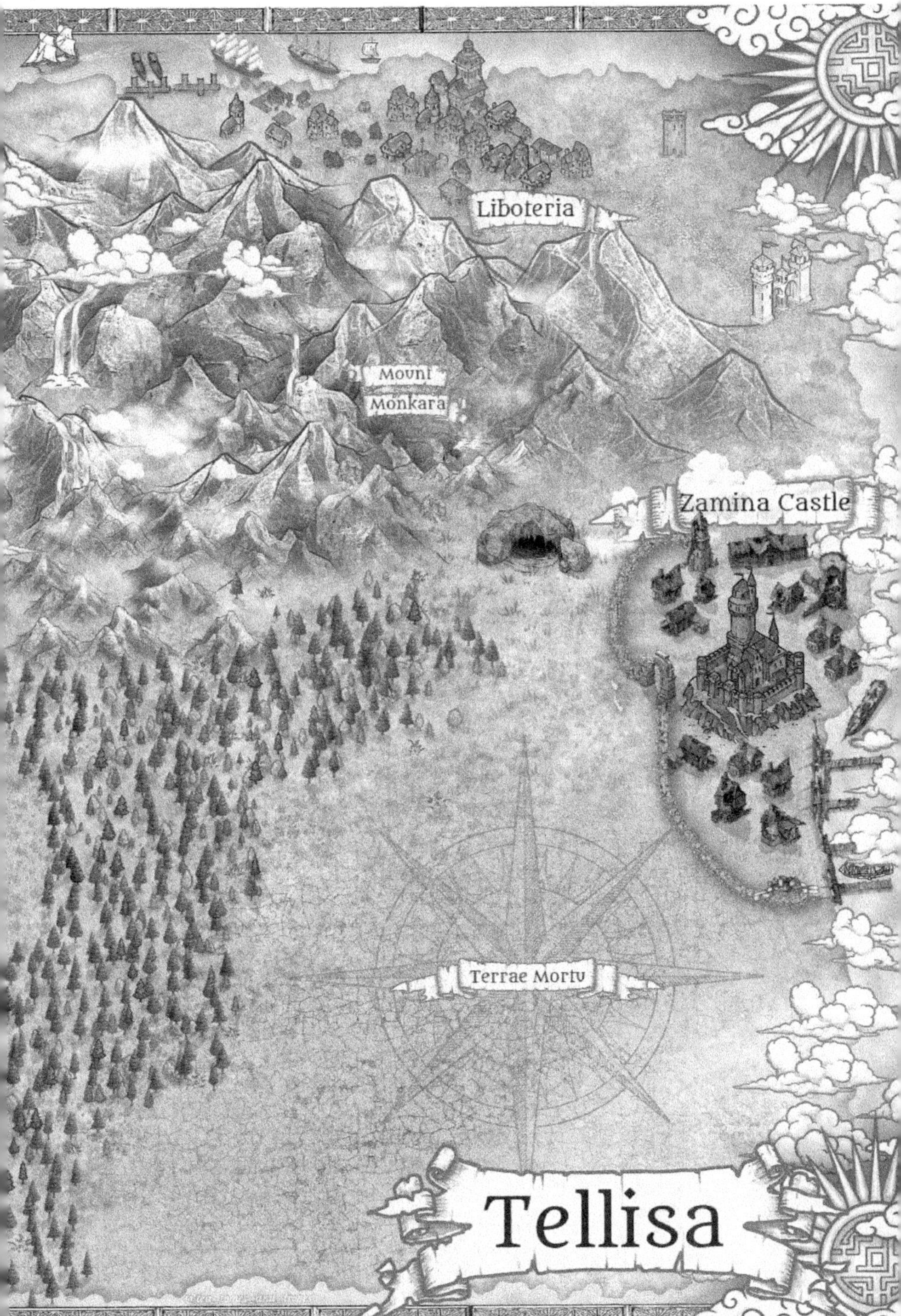

Liboteria
Mount Monkara
Zamina Castle
Terrae Mortu
Tellisa

PROLOGUE

Lailah

I thought dying would hurt, but it was the humiliation that caused me actual pain. The Obscuritas Kings dressed me in a simple white dress, the fabric so thin I knew my body was on display. Hooded figures escorted me to the massive room they'd readied for the ritual. The lecherous cult members reached out with grubby hands as I passed through to the center of the room, touching me, pinching my skin and pulling my hair. They whispered vile taunts about my family and friends. I swallowed my fear and continued on. The Kings waited for me. My family was still locked in cells on the lower level, for now. My mother said she would come, though, before the end, and that they would be safe, free, because of what she and I were preparing to do next. Until that time, I was on my own.

Several guards behind me shoved me to the floor, and I winced as my knees slammed into the marble. *Assholes.* I wasn't much for foul language, but Nuri used words as weapons. The thought brought a smirk to my face. She and my sister, Seraphina, would spar often in the future.

My wrists were bound in front of me, and a cloaked figure attached the metal cuffs to a heavy chain embedded in the floor. They weren't made of stellatium, only steel. It was a mistake I intended to take advantage of when the moment came. One of the Kings came forward. I knew instantly who he was, having seen him, and how he would hurt my sisters, in my visions. He was massive, a monster of a human with evil lurking in his eyes. He crouched down in front of me, cocking his head to the side.

"You're a pretty one." Dark intent laced his deep voice. "If only I had more time, we could have had real fun together."

The King reached into his pocket and pulled out a small knife. He flicked the blade open and swiftly cut down the center of my dress, revealing my breasts. He traced the cold steel along my bare skin, flicking my nipple with the sharp edge. I remained still, frozen, and willing my body not to react. He wanted my fear, but I would not give it to him. The Kings would gain nothing from me, or my death.

He chuckled. "Yes, it would have been a real treat to break you. But don't worry, I'm going to take my time with your sisters. The little blonde one is to be mine."

Rage threatened to bubble out of me, but I bit my tongue, tasting blood. He wanted to provoke me, wanted me to show him how much his filthy words affected me. I. Would. Not. Give. In.

Instead, I smiled up at him, pushing my power over The Sight out just enough to make my eyes shine. My voice changed to a deeper cadence laced with the power of destiny. "I've seen your death, Darren Radnor. And it's going to be glorious."

The King snarled, fear clouding his gaze, and slapped me across the face, knocking me to the side. "Little bitch." He turned to the other Kings. "Can we wait for the next full moon? This one needs to be properly broken in."

"No, Darren," the King at the top of the circle snapped. "It must be tonight."

A third King stepped forward, his face cloaked in shadow, but I could feel his poisonous smile when he spoke. "I have another idea."

"Make it quick, Samuel." The King who appeared to be in charge snapped at this one, too.

The creepy one slipped behind me, and I resisted the urge to shiver in revulsion when his fingers danced down my spine. "Let your wings out, lumen princess."

No. I shook my head slightly in refusal.

The creeper pressed his hands to my back, and I nearly cried out. It felt like needles digging into my skin as he whispered words beneath his breath. There was nothing I could do in this moment to stop him, and my wings wooshed out. At least they knocked the creep in the face.

My moment of satisfaction quickly died when the foul King grabbed my left wing and held it wide. Bile rose once more at the inappropriate touch. Our wings were sacred, meant only to be embraced by our mates. Before I could even blink, the big one was there, sawing my wing in jagged cuts. The scream I uttered was like nothing I'd ever heard from myself. The pain was excruciating. I coughed and sputtered as my voice gave out completely. When they started on the second wing, my voice was gone, and the croaks of agony leaving my being were hideous and humiliating. The Kings laughed as I writhed, chained to the floor.

My eyes had glazed over when The Sight took control, sending me into the future.

My wings were pinned to a wall in Zamina Castle. Nuriela stared up at them with fury. And yet, beneath her rage, I felt her love. We gave our hearts and souls to each other, and that was it for us. A young mortal behind her screamed at the daemon trapped on the far side of the room. I knew what would come next. "Nuri. Help Her."

Pain rushed through my body as I recovered. Blood poured from the open wounds where my wings had been, and the four Kings moved as one, dipping their fingers in my blood and drawing a star on the floor, with me at the center. Darren dug his fingers into the wound, and I groaned in pain.

"Fuck, that sound is delicious. I want to paint my cock in your blood before I fuck you with it." Darren's cruel voice was miles away.

Or at least, it felt far away. My mind was beginning to shut down, protecting me from the pain. I latched on to the love and strength my mate had radiated in my vision. If she could survive, I could too. Long enough to do what must be done.

When the bloody star was completed, the candles sprang to life, and I felt my power seeping out of me and into their spell.

They chanted faster, eager for my death and their own rise to power. But greed would be their downfall. I lifted my tongue and plucked the small stone from my mouth. My mother gave it to me before I was brought here, and I knew what I needed to do next. With every single ounce of my strength, and every shining piece of my soul, I surrendered my magic to the stone. It was called luxenite, and this particularly rare stone was the only one of its kind with the power to hold a lumen's soul, the source of our Vis-El.

The crux of it was, when a lumen chose to do this, their soul was lost to the endless darkness, unable to rest among our ancestors amidst the stars. But it was worth it. I sent my heart away to Nuri, begging her for forgiveness, for I would not meet her in the next life. And yet, it was the only way. The only way for my sisters to win this war. Michaela would need my power. With this sacrifice, I could save them all.

The chanting cult members carried on, but I was strong enough to resist, I would be strong enough for this. One of the Kings shouted angrily, realizing something wasn't working. The power drained from me, but not to them, into the stone.

Movement to my right nearly broke my concentration, but I didn't look away. I knew who had come.

"How the hell did she get out?" the creepy king shouted. "Seize her at once!"

But these fools could not contain Aurora Valdis. In the next moment, her voice rang out, power spilling from her in waves. Her words grew louder, the light emanating from her blinding to the humans. Several screamed in agony, and their deaths fueled me. I chanted the final words of my own incantation, feeling the last of my Vis-El slip away into the stone. It was gone, and I was mortal.

"You did well, my angel." My mother's soft voice was suddenly close. "My brave, beautiful daughter. I love you. You will find peace."

Her voice soothed my aching body. The tip of her finger touched my temple, and I moaned as a spark of power seeped beneath my skin, setting the delicate beam of purest magic alight within my soul. Tears sprang from my eyes as I slumped to the side, unable to thank her for this gift, or tell her one last time how much I truly loved her. The final words of Aurora Valdis had passed. A sonic boom echoed in the room, knocking out everyone within the walls of the manor. Utter silence descended.

My mother, the most powerful creature I'd ever known, was gone. She didn't tell me all, though, when we made this plan to save our family. She hadn't said her final act would be to save my soul and see hers lost instead. For there was only one other way to gift a mortal the chance to live on among the stars. The last ember of her power went into me.

The silence was deafening, enough so that the quiet footsteps of someone approaching echoed like a snare drum. He knelt beside me. Ezekiel Parrish. It took all my strength to open my enclosed fist and present the stone.

"For Michaela." The words croaked out of me, and I could only hope he understood. That he was truly trustworthy in this task. I'd seen it briefly, the love he had for his son would ensure his loyalty.

He nodded, bright eyes filled with devastating sadness. "It shall be done. Rest now, brave child," he murmured, his voice so unlike the others. The voice of a father who loved his children.

Nothing else needed to be said. And in the next moment, he was gone.

CHAPTER ONE

Seraphina

My feet smashed into the ground heavily, and my knees buckled. The weight of what I'd done to save my princes, my sister, all of them, started to creep beneath my skin. Laszlo's influence over me was a writhing, toxic thing. But that wasn't the only power thrumming through my blood. The foreign air around me suddenly sucked in on itself, as if it were alive, sensing me, and in the next second, raw power erupted in my veins. I gasped, unable to keep the feeling of it to myself. Laszlo's influence faded, and for a few blessed seconds, I was myself. And fuck if I wasn't going to use those seconds to cause absolute fucking carnage.

"Seraphina—" Laszlo started, but I was already moving.

The blade strapped to his ankle was in my hand, and I shoved off the marble floor, leaping onto Samuel. I brought the blade down swiftly. *Stab. Stab. Stab.* He screamed, and the high notes were music to my ears. *Stab. Stab. Stab.* My biceps burned with the constant movement. Blood splattered my face, dripped down my neck, and soaked my clothing. *Stab. Stab. Stab.*

"Stop this!" Laszlo shouted, his voice booming in the empty room.

His command was dulled beneath my bloodlust and the power humming in my veins. I grinned down at the King dying beneath me. *Stab. Stab. Stab.*

"Belial," Laszlo snarled, his voice shaking with anger. "Stop her. Now."

Belial's deep laughter seeped through the haze of red. "Oh, you humans do spoil all the fun, dying so easily."

Strong arms wrapped around my middle and ripped me away from my enemy. I scratched and clawed at him, to no avail. Belial was easily twice my size in his full daemon form. He dropped me to the floor in a heap, and I heaved several breaths, glaring at him.

He cocked his head. The movement reminded me of Phen. The three daemon princes—Belial, Morax, and Phenex—shared similar features. They all had tanned olive skin, midnight black hair, and strong jaws. They were each muscular, having spent years training for battle and growing up under a tyrant.

That's where the similarities ended. Morax was stoic, reserving his outward emotions for only my sister, Michaela. And Phenex, my wild man, he was chaos embodied. He made me feel alive. Belial, well, this brother was harder to read. His face betrayed little emotion, and his eyes were dark and clouded with a sadistic edge. He would not be so easily manipulated.

"Seraphina, hold out your arms. Now." Laszlo's command sank beneath my skin, and my arms lifted obediently. He smiled, satisfied, and snapped cuffs around my wrists.

I hissed in pain the instant the metal touched my skin.

Laszlo's eyes heated at my discomfort. "Stellatium. Quite uncomfortable for your kind. Mutes your powers as well."

Samuel groaned, interrupting what I am sure was a speech I didn't want to hear. Laszlo stomped toward the man, spitting orders at anyone within shouting distance. Daemons and lumens rushed to his aid, taking the Obscuritas King away.

He would likely survive. The Kings were filled with power, stolen power, and aided by traitorous daemons and lumens loyal to Belial. And somehow, Belial had gained more power than any other daemon had access to. The eldest brother was wicked strong, and I'd need more than my stellar skills with knives to defeat him.

He was watching me, the oldest son of Corson Ormaenus. I could feel his eyes scrutinizing every inch of body.

"A true hybrid," he mused, red eyes glowing with power. "There hasn't been one in ages. And they rarely lived long enough to attend their Vis-El Ceremony."

The ceremony he mentioned was something every daemon and lumen went through upon reaching maturity, and it awakened the true potential of their powers.

"Score one for me, then. And I never had a fancy ceremony." My words were clipped and sassy. I needed to get a rise out of him, find his weaknesses.

Belial nodded, stalking to a chair near a massive fireplace. Since we arrived, I'd been more focused on stabbing and less on my surroundings. We were definitely inside some *Beauty and the Beast* type castle. Not the nice one after the beastie fell in love, the creepy one when he was still all grumpy and growly. Personally, I would've preferred the Beast. He was like a cuddly, deadly teddy bear, and I would always choose the bear.

A fire roared within the stone fireplace, creating shadows around the room. The ceilings were hundreds of feet tall, with windows covering the walls on the far side of the room. Outside, a full moon glowed high in the dark sky.

"It is curious that you should feel so connected to your power without an awakening." Belial crossed his legs, scratching his chin as if he gave a damn about anything.

"Maybe I'm just *that* talented," I taunted, hiding the bite of pain from the cuffs every time I moved.

"Unlikely." He spoke without enthusiasm, but there was a hint of something in his eyes. "Perhaps if we put you through it, something new would emerge."

"Something like…The Sight?" I smirked, seeing my words finally affect him.

Nuri told us of Belial's obsession with Lailah and her power to see the future, to affect the very fabric of time. She never mastered it, but with effort, someone with this power could do great or very terrible things.

Belial snarled, standing abruptly from his chair and charging toward me. He snatched my neck between his massive clawed hands and lifted me off my feet. I didn't move. Didn't speak. Waiting to see what the beast would do when provoked.

"You know nothing of real power," he purred, eyes glowing red. "But you could. I could show you, train you. That oath could be broken."

Suddenly, it was me becoming affected by his words. I would give fucking anything to break the oath I made with

Laszlo. Belial's eyes glittered with triumph as he read that very thought on my face. Fuck, I needed to work on my poker face.

His hand squeezed around my neck, cutting off my air supply and holding me aloft as if I weighed nothing. Black spots started to appear at the corners of my eyes.

"When you've had enough of that false king's hold over you, come to me. I will make you a queen with powers beyond your wildest imagination." His voice was low and so close to soothing, attempting to draw me in.

"Belial," I murmured, and his eyes lit with something akin to hope, but for evil monsters. He leaned in, enticed by my tone, and I whispered against his lips. "Eat shit."

I kicked out, managing a swift hit to his balls, and the daemon dropped me with a roar of fury.

"Enjoy your torment, then, hybrid. I will not offer this again." He spat the words, stalking out of the room just as Laszlo returned from his aiding Samuel.

"Seraphina, my new toy. Come along," Laszlo snipped, turning on his heel.

There was nothing I could do now but follow.

CHAPTER TWO

Seraphina

It was always difficult to guess what type of torture evil men enjoyed most. Every vile soul was different. Darren Radnor, Ty's father, preferred the desecration of the flesh. He made that very clear with both of my sisters. It pained me that I wasn't the one to kill him. Alas, Morax received that honor. At least with his power he was able to show me the memory. Seeing that fucker's body explode into bloody pieces was practically orgasm material. The thought that he was able to touch Michaela the way he did before his death brought a pulse of power into my veins.

I stopped suddenly, the rush of magic flowing through me enough to quiet the blood oath. Laszlo turned sharply and hissed in irritation. Two guards grabbed my arms, and he forced my chin up to stare into his eyes.

"Seraphina." He snarled my name like it was his favorite word and biggest regret. "You. Are. Mine. Let the power rush you're feeling go. To please me."

My eyes blazed with fire power, but I wasn't strong enough to control it. His words pressed into my skin, and the power drifted away, settling out of reach within me. If only I was strong enough to channel my power, I was certain I could beat him. Belial's words slithered through my mind, and I gritted my teeth, forcing the allure of his offer from my thoughts.

There had to be a way to escape without breaking my bonds to the princes. Just thinking of them sent a rush straight to my clit. I was fucking horny for those assholes. Every moment I spent with them was pure bliss. And I loved them, damnit. It seemed impossible that someone like me could feel so much, so deeply.

Laszlo's guards shoved me into a chair, and he circled me like a predator, searching for weaknesses within his prey. One of the guards handed him a knife, and the sharp edge glinted in the low light of the room.

"Tell me, Seraphina," Laszlo drawled, stopping in front of me. "How many times did you stab Samuel?"

I scoffed. "Not enough."

"Answer," Laszlo snapped.

The need to obey surged through my veins. "Eleven glorious stabs."

He smiled, and I hated that the pleased look on his face made my blood sing. Laszlo extended his arm slowly, offering the dagger to me. "You will stab yourself, eleven glorious stabs."

My hand trembled as I took the knife. In my soul, I wanted to turn the blade on him and end this here and now, but the oath burning in my veins refused. Instead, I turned the fucking thing on myself, stabbing into my left thigh. Each stab brought my screams closer to the surface, but I refused to give him that satisfaction. He would not have my cries.

Laszlo Blackbyrn snapped at the guards to leave the room after the fourth time the blade pierced my flesh. As soon as they were gone, his pants dropped and he fisted his cock, stroking.

"Again," he groaned. "Shove the blade into your pretty thighs for me like a good little toy. Now just below your navel."

Tears burned the backs of my eyes as I stabbed myself again and again. I could feel the power within me swirling and sizzling, healing even as I stabbed myself once more. The pain was fucking awful, but still I refused to scream. A single moan escaped my lips, and Laszlo's answering groan of pleasure brought bile up my throat, threatening to spill over.

His stupid cock throbbed and pulsed as he came, mixing with the bloody mess on my thighs.

After the eleventh stab, I dropped the blade and let my body slump in the chair, closing my eyes. A shadow hovered over me, and I cracked one eye open to stare up at my captor.

"Pathetic." I spat the word at him.

Laszlo slapped my face hard enough to sting, but not nearly enough to hurt. He was trying to humiliate me, but I'd already been at rock bottom and his games wouldn't work on me. I refused to let them.

My smirk irritated him, and his next strike across my cheek was hard enough to bust open my lip. And yet I grinned, blood coating my teeth. "There is nothing you can do to me, Laszlo. You will not break me. Anything you demand from me comes from that fucking oath. You will never have my submission willingly."

The Obscuritas King snapped his teeth in my face, rage etched into his features. "We shall see."

I may have spoken too soon. It was now hour three of being chained up to a saltire cross, completely naked and at his mercy. Laszlo's preferred method of torture wasn't just physical assault, it was humiliation. He hadn't touched me since slapping my face earlier.

His guards brought me to a series of rooms with a multitude of torture devices. The cross was located in the corner of a room with only one small window and zero cozy furniture. Laszlo commanded me to strip and step up to the cross, where the guards fastened stellatium chains to my wrists and ankles. Stellatium was the only metal that could truly harm a daemon or lumen. It dampened our power and burned like a bitch.

Once I was in position, Laszlo took a seat in a chair that resembled a gaudy-as-hell throne and ordered the guards to masturbate. Sticky cum clung to my legs where one guard unloaded himself. The other, well, he had stage fright. Unfortunately, my laughter was not welcomed, and Laszlo allowed him to piss on me instead. My body was essentially a fraternity house floor at this point. When it was over and the guards left and my unbothered smirk remained, Laszlo stabbed me in the abdomen with a slim blade and stalked out of the room. It was regular steel, and the wound closed by the time night fell.

And so I remained, weakened by blood loss, bound and gross, but blessedly alone. My senses were heightened, even dulled by the stellatium, and I could make out muffled voices and several heartbeats somewhere nearby. It was strange, having all this power, these new abilities. The fact that Lailah was able to grow up with her power while Michaela and I were left in the dark was more than a little irritating. The memories of my time in this world were more like dream sequences. Flashes of soft, white sand and bright-blue ocean. A forest with lush trees taller than skyscrapers. This world was mine, my home. And yet it was foreign.

I sighed. My arms ached and my skin itched, but the chains wouldn't budge. What I needed was sleep, to let my body rest and maybe gain enough strength to fight back. Because if there was one thing I knew about Laszlo Blackbyrn, he was only just getting started with me.

CHAPTER THREE

Seraphina

The sound of footsteps woke me from a restless sleep. My muscles fucking ached from being chained to this fucking cross for so long. It was going to drive me mad. Perhaps that's how Laszlo would finally break me, by driving me insane on cross. It had now been five days since I was chained up. Each night, I watched the moon wane further, the new moon nearly upon us. The moon was larger here, similar to the one I knew, and yet different. The night sky held more stars here, and they twinkled with colors, unlike the muted stars I grew up whispering my hopes and desires to.

Laszlo's guards opened the doors, their gazes lingering on my naked flesh. How they could find me even remotely attractive covered in this much dried piss, blood, and cum was beyond me. One fucker even squirted into my hair. I was cutting his dick off first, mark my words.

"Time to get cleaned up, my dirty little toy," Laszlo mused, eyeing me with his stupid haughty smile. "Tonight, the creatures of this ridiculous planet will come together and pledge allegiance to their new leaders."

A stunted laugh escaped my dry lips. "If you think Belial is going to share his throne with you, you're an imbecile."

Laszlo, to his credit, barely flinched at my words. "Belial knows the importance of our alliance. He rules Stella Terra, and I rule Earth. Together, two worlds of slaves, two worlds of power. With our combined efforts, we will take on every planet and bring the universe to heel."

"Oh, so not your normal, take over the world plot." I rolled my eyes. "Go big or go home, as they say. I stand by my previous statement. He will never share power with you. In the end, you will be just another pawn in his game."

Laszlo toyed with his cufflinks, a simple outward sign of his annoyance. Seeing him dressed like this reminded me so much of Andras, my dark prince.

"And if you think I blindly trust that daemon without my own plans, you're a bigger fool than I expected." Laszlo stalked closer to me and scrunched his nose. "You smell, Seraphina. Get cleaned up for the party. As the honored guest, we must have you looking your best."

He brushed his thumb across my mouth, pressing in on the wound he made earlier today. While the physical violence was minimal, whenever my mouth delivered a sassy comment, which was often, he slapped me hard enough to draw blood.

But pain was an old friend, and I didn't flinch when my lip split under his hard touch. He smeared the blood across my lips and leaned in as if he meant to kiss me. Laszlo's body pressed into mine, his erection poking my stomach like some horny frat boy who couldn't find a clit if it was shoved in his face.

I glared up at him. "Rub that cock on me as much as you want. But it will never be as good as your son's. Fuck me, oh douche king. Take your pound of flesh and know that there is nothing you can do to me that I won't overcome."

Laszlo stepped back, crossing his arms, wrinkling his tailored suit. "I am not going to fuck you, Seraphina. No. I'm going to let every creature in this army take you in every way they want. And all the while, I will watch. Your body will be used again and again and again. And you will do this, because it pleases *me*."

Rage burned through me, and a flicker of power sizzled just out of reach.

He smiled, greedy eyes taking in my anger. "And when your sister comes, I will do the same to her. By then, you might even help me."

I screamed at him, spitting curses and every threat I could come up with. My skin burned where I pulled against my restraints. "I will fucking kill you before you touch her."

His dark and hateful eyes pierced mine triumphantly. "And when I have severed your ties to my son, when I have broken your mind so completely that all you crave is my touch, I will make you beg for my kiss. My cock. You will moan for me and only me. And all those who stood for you will bow to me."

Bile rose in my throat as I continued to struggle against my bindings. "I will die first."

Laszlo patted my cheek and stepped back, a satisfied smile on his smug face. His words rattled me, and he knew it. "It has begun."

He walked out of the room, head held high, and I screamed profanities at his back.

There is another choice. Belial's enticing voice wrapped around my mind like an inky cloud.

Two idiot guards stepped forward, and the one to my left immediately stuck a needle into my neck. My body dropped forward as I lost feeling. The larger guard carried me through Laszlo's rooms into a massive en suite bathroom. A small female in a gauzy shift dress stood in the room, waiting.

The guard lowered my body into the bath already filled with warm water and stepped back, turning to the woman. "Laszlo's orders are to clean and dress her. No talking. You will have one hour, and we will be waiting outside the rooms."

She nodded but didn't speak. I groaned, unable to move due to the drugs and my unbelievably sore muscles. Never in all my days had I missed my ability to heal rapidly until now. Lying in the steaming bath, I watched the woman walk toward the doors and wave her hands in front of them, muttering words I didn't know. A thickness suddenly coated the air around us, and she turned back to me with a smile.

"We can speak freely now, but we don't have much time." She smiled, her green eyes glowing. "I am Jophielle."

"Who are you, exactly?" I mumbled, unable to be courteous when my mind and body were so fucking exhausted.

Jophielle smiled again. "An ally." She knelt beside the bath and slid her arms into the water. Her soft hands brushed against my arms, and warmth spread through my body.

I gasped as the pain receded and my body finally began to heal. My eyes darted around the room, searching for an escape, when Jophielle squeezed my arm, drawing my attention back to her.

"No." She shook her head. "Now is not the time to flee. You'd be caught instantly, and the protections to keep us out would double. You must remain for now, but know, we will pull you out soon."

My shoulders slumped back into the water. "How soon?"

Jophielle smiled sadly. She picked up a cloth and delicious smelling soaps and began washing away the grime from my hair. I grabbed another cloth and scrubbed my body, ridding my skin of the soon-to-be-dead guards' fluids.

"I cannot say too much now, just in case others are listening," she finally spoke. "When the new moon rises, be ready for us."

I paused my ministrations. "How will I be ready? What creature are you, exactly?"

Jophielle giggled, her bright eyes twinkling. "So curious. Your mother was that way, too."

My head whipped around in a blink. "You knew my mother?" I scrutinized her further. This woman did not look nearly old enough to know my mother. Time moved differently here, though. Morax said something about daemons and lumens living for centuries, their youthful looks lasting for just as long.

Jophielle nodded. "I am a lumen. I lived in the palace."

We both continued cleaning my battered body as I let her words sink in.

"How did you end up here?"

She dunked me under the water, scrubbing her nails into my thick hair for several minutes before letting me up. At least some of my power was coming back, otherwise I'd have drowned. She smirked at me, and I grinned back.

"Queen Aurora only kept a small circle of us close after Belfegor was killed. My family was loyal to the crown and to the Valdis line for hundreds of years. We remained at her side until the end." Jophielle sighed, her eyes downcast and clouded with hurt. "Most of my family was killed, but one of my powers is the ability to project a mirage of sorts, and I made those who came believe I was dead, too. I was entrusted with a task. To be here, in this place, when the daughter of Aurora and Belfegor returned."

My mind whirled with the implications of her words. There was so much more to this story, so many things my mother put into place without us knowing. "I'm sorry your family was killed."

Jophielle nodded. "As am I. But we all knew the parts we would play in this."

I shook my head, brows scrunched in confusion. "But why? Why is this all happening?"

She stepped away from the bath and held out a robe for me before speaking. "Because you are the one who will end it."

A startled laugh escaped my lips. "No pressure."

Jophielle cocked her head up at me. I wasn't tall, and she was still at least a few inches shorter than me. She might be a lumen, but the female was giving me major pixie vibes. She reminded me of Tibby, in that way, but with dark curly hair instead of bright blonde.

"A millennia before even Queen Aurora was born, the old gods sent down a prophecy," she began. I aimed to interrupt, but Jophielle held up a hand to silence me. "No time for questions. This prophecy foretold the greatest battle, one all creatures in our world and beyond would have to fight. And the one to end it would be born of a great Seer and a prince of old with a tainted soul. This child would be a perfect blending of light and dark, lumen and daemon, life and death."

This was insanity. I shook my head vigorously and stepped back from her. "There is no fucking way I am that…creature. I have power, but I am not all that."

Jophielle clasped her hands in front of her and sighed. "Not yet, young queen. But you will be."

A sigh escaped my lips. I wanted to believe her.

A guard pounded on the door, shouting for us to hurry along.

She squeezed my shoulder. "*Illegitimi non carborundum.*"

I cocked my head to the side. "What does that mean?"

Jophielle smirked down at me. "Don't let the bastards get you down."

CHAPTER FOUR

Seraphina

While I wasn't back on the stupid fucking cross, this cage was not much better. The entire thing was made of stellatium, of course, and while Jophielle had given me some strength back, it wasn't enough to escape the cage waiting for me just outside the doors of Laszlo's rooms. Plus, according to her, it wasn't the "right time" to go. So here I was, a pretty toy to be gawked at. It almost reminded me of the burlesque club I sang at back in Boston. Those days seemed a million miles away now.

The dress Laszlo left for me to wear, if these tiny pieces of gold fabric could be called a dress, was meant to tempt. Showing off my body didn't bother me. My curves and toned muscles were something I prided myself on. Hours and hours spent at the gym to get this fucking figure meant I would absolutely show it off. If he thought dressing me like a high-class whore was going to add to my humiliation, he was sorely mistaken. What did surprise me was the second dress laid out for me. It was just as slutty, but more dazzling, with silky black fabric that dipped low in the front and back. My initial reaction was to go for the black, until my fingers traced a tiny silver B on the curve of fabric that would cover my breast. Belial was still playing games, and I needed to be clever about which devil to anger in this moment. Being that the eldest Ormaenus brother was new to me, I chose Laszlo's dress.

My cage was lifted into the air via some creature's power and slowly moved about the massive ballroom. There were hundreds of daemons and lumens in the room, and I wasn't the only one in a cage. Unfortunately, the other caged creatures were having less fun. While I seemed to be off-limits to touch, they were not.

Males and females were stripped of clothing, poked with knives, groped, and assaulted in various horrible ways. Some took the abuse without responding, while others snarled and tried to fight back. The fighters were quickly brought to heel with pain, and tortured screams filled the giant ballroom throughout the night. And no one batted an eye. It seemed the sounds of torture were common. I scanned the room for Belial, but he hadn't arrived yet. Laszlo was also missing. Perhaps they were killing each other.

A horn blared, announcing the arrival of the Obscuritas Kings, and my hopes and dreams of Laszlo's demise turned to ash. He walked in with added arrogance, and to my great disappointment, Samuel was at his side. The memory of stabbing him over and over would hold a special place in my heart. Hopefully, I'd be doing it again soon.

Samuel's eyes darted to my cage, and the hesitation I saw in his gaze brought a smile to my face. I gave him a little wave, and he huffed, turning away. It seemed the memory was on his mind as well. Laszlo narrowed his eyes at me, and I gave him a thumbs-up. His eye twitched in what I hoped was severe irritation as he made his way to a dais. My own gaze followed his path as he stopped just to the left of the singular throne.

Before I could think better of it, I cupped my hands around my lips and shouted at him. "Did your new bestie forget to make you a fancy chair, oh mighty cult leader?"

The room went silent at my outburst, and I glared at all of them, enjoying their discomfort. Sure, most of them just looked mildly curious, but a few uncomfy looks gave me some satisfaction.

Laszlo ignored me, his head held high, but that wouldn't do, so I sang out a few bars to one of my favorite Rhianna songs. "You look so dumb right now…"

Several people snickered, and Laszlo's eyes narrowed on me. Before I could goad him further, the damn horn blared again, announcing the arrival of Belial, eldest of the Ormaenus brothers. Phenex, the youngest, belonged to me. And Morax, the middle son, was mated to my sister.

Phenex was my mate, but it didn't quite feel the way it should. At least, it seemed like our connection was missing something. Watching my sister and Morax, I knew this was true. Sure, we fucked like horny devils, and the greatest fuck fest of my life included him and my princes, but there was still…something missing. Phen's confidence in us, in the bond between the six of us, gave me confidence as well. Whatever that thing was, we would find it, together.

The thread connecting my soul to Phen's pulsed with life, tugging gently. I closed my eyes, feeling him, feeling them, buried beneath Laszlo and that fucking blood oath. They were still with me, even now.

"Come find me, my princes." I whispered the plea to the universe, hoping somehow, wherever they were, they would hear me.

It didn't take long for Belial to release me from the cage, his eyes flicking over my body and the dress that wasn't his.

"The black would have suited you better," he murmured, forcefully guiding me to the open dance floor.

He was, unfortunately, quite handsome. Belial shared the same sharp jawline as his brothers, but with a long, slightly hooked nose. His black hair was twice as long as Phen's and braided down his back. He wore an all-black ensemble, with a silver tie that matched the beading on the dress he'd chosen for me.

Everything about him oozed power and lethal grace, but his eyes gave him away. This monster cared for nothing and no one, only power. And even glowing red as they did now, there was no light, no spark of feeling. Belial was a walking plague, a bringer of death. How these people could willingly follow him, I couldn't understand.

He pulled me into his arms as the song changed and led us into a slow dance around the room. I could feel Laszlo's greedy eyes on me from his position near the throne.

"Laszlo's oath compelled me to please him, so I wore his dress of choice," I responded, gauging his reactions.

Belial's face remained bored. "Do you enjoy being leashed? I would've thought the heir of the Valdis line would prefer a bit more freedom. More power."

"Just because a man holds a leash, doesn't make him a master."

He spun me out and back into his arms.

"True power comes from those who kneel willingly. And that, I will never do."

Belial's mouth twitched, but in irritation or amusement, I wasn't sure. "Have you not bowed for my brother, then? I sense him, but the connection is weak. Perhaps he isn't enough for you?"

"Perhaps," I murmured, staring into his eyes.

The elder prince stumbled a single step, recovering quickly, but we both noted it. He expected my devotion to the princes, but I wanted to see what he would do with a different response.

"So, you're succumbing to the blood oath then? Or are you ready to break your bonds and join me?" Belial purred, his voice deep and deadly, meant to entice.

I could not be seduced by him or anyone else, but he didn't need to know that. "If I did break my bonds, how would I do it? Would they need to die?"

Belial smirked, squeezing my waist. "Breaking a mate bond often sends the mated pair to their death, the pain is excruciating, but I'm certain you could handle it."

My own smirk mirrored his. "Oh, I'm sure of it."

The song ended, and a single bell rang out, gathering the attention of the room. Laszlo was clearly feeling left out. He stepped up on the dias, directly in front of the throne. Belial tensed at my side.

"Come to me, Seraphina," Laszlo commanded.

As much as I didn't want to, the call of my blood oath forced me toward my captor. His smile was incredibly unsettling as I walked stiffly to his side.

"While you may know her as a powerful member of the Valdis family, she is nothing more than a pawn, a toy to please and serve me." Laszlo's words grated against my soul, and my fingers itched for a dagger. "And my dear friend Belial, when I allow it." He spoke with effortless calm, staring out into the room of creatures. As a human, he was severely outnumbered and outgunned.

"Belial, I have a gift for you." Laszlo's tone shifted to something sinister and raised the tiny hairs on the back of my neck.

The crowd parted as two men wheeled in a massive glass frame, like a shadow box of sorts. When the murmurs began. I craned my neck to see what was causing the stir. Wings.

My heart cracked, a piece falling away and turning to ash. I'd never seen her wings, or at least, didn't remember seeing them, until now. They were Lailah's. A memory flashed through my mind of Joseph rushing Michaela and I away from the scene of her death. Lailah's wings lay beside her, crudely cut from her body.

And now they were here, in the hands of my enemies.

A whisper of power caressed my skin, and I closed my eyes. *Seraphina.*

Tears threatened to fall at the sound of my name on her lips.

Laszlo's voice brought my attention back to the room. "Lailah Valdis was meant to be yours, but her soul was stolen from your grasp," Laszlo drawled. "I give you her wings, wrenched from her body just before her death."

Belial tapped a clawed hand against the glass, greedy eyes roaming over the bright white wings. "There is power in a lumen's wings. I can almost taste it. These will look beautiful above my throne."

The devil wasn't kind enough to offer a thank you, but his pleasure in the gift was obvious. My vision blurred as rage bubbled out of me. I was seconds away from running at him. I'd claw and bite and punch him to death with my bare hands if I had to.

Laszlo's strong hand was suddenly around my throat. He stepped in front of me, blocking my view of Lailah's wings. "Now, now, my little toy," he cooed. "Calm down. Don't ruin the party. It would please me greatly to hear you sing for everyone."

The blood oath pounded in my veins at his words, urging me to obey. A microphone was suddenly brought out and passed to me. Laszlo caressed my cheek before stepping away and pulled a young female into his arms, forcing her to the dance floor.

A simple melody began to play while I stood there, watching. He didn't specify what song I had to sing, and that was his mistake.

CHAPTER FIVE

Seraphina

If Laszlo thought I was just going to sing some nice song and go quietly into the night, he was very much mistaken. A servant appeared at my side, asking what the band should play to accompany me. I had no idea if these fuckers were hip to pop culture from my world, but we were about to find out.

The servant nodded when I gave him the song, and a few minutes later, I heard the first notes of Billie Eilish's "Six Feet Under." It was a somber choice, a song about loss and love dying. But there was hope in it, that maybe it wasn't truly gone, that love was only lost. As I sang, images of my princes filled my head and the bonds between us pulsed with life. It was the hope I needed, the reminder that this was far from over. That I would find them again.

When the song ended, I opened my eyes to find the crowd mirroring my own melancholy mood. The musicians continued to play, and the guests swayed slowly, their eyes glazed as if in some kind of trance.

Belial watched from across the room, his eyes glowing red, and some emotion I couldn't place crossed his face. Laszlo suddenly snapped his head up and stalked angrily in my direction. He grabbed my arm and shoved me toward the cage.

"Get in," he demanded. "Take off your dress and dance for them. Touch yourself and let them see how much you want to please me."

I snarled at him, my claws extending slightly as my power rushed to the surface. Before the oath could send it away, I slashed at my arms and chest with my claws, blood oozing from the cuts.

"There, I've touched myself," I growled at him. "Next time, be more specific."

Laszlo slammed the cage doors and left without a word. The cuts on my body were already healing. Unfortunately, the stupid oath began coaxing my mind into taking off my dress and dancing as the music continued.

As I did, a male creature approached the cage. His aura felt more pleasant than most of the others, and curiosity had my eyes locking with his dark-green gaze. He dipped his head in the slightest of bows, and my eyebrows shot up.

The male brushed his fingers across his lips. "Don't speak. Just dance as if I am not here."

His eyes darted to Laszlo and back, and I, for some reason, trusted this creature. While I danced, he circled the cage, a bored expression on his face as he watched.

"I am Halphas," he muttered, barely loud enough for me to hear over the music. "A…friend of your father's. They are coming for you, but you must remain strong. Do not give in to Belial."

I scoffed. As if that would ever happen.

Halphas shook his head. "He is more clever than you realize. I can see his influence within you already."

My brow furrowed, but I continued to dance. No, that couldn't be right. My mind was still my own.

"But I don't think even he could have predicted you would be a cancatier." Halphas chuckled. "How curious."

"A what?" I couldn't help asking, the word completely foreign to me.

He smiled, eyes roaming my body in a way that began to cause discomfort. Was this part of his act? "It's quite rare and comes from your lumen blood. Cancatiers are what humans think of as sirens. A creature who can lure others to their call with a song."

Halphas pressed in closer to the bars, his skin sizzling against the stellatium when he got too close. "You can make them feel things, even do things against their will when you spell them with a song."

My feet stumbled at his words. This was most definitely not something I had ever heard of before. Even with the training Michaela and I had begun to do with the Phen and Morax, they never mentioned a power like this. Neither had Delphine. And yet…when I sang, the mood of the people in this room shifted, almost at once. Could I sing them into a rebellion?

"Tread carefully, Seraphina," Halphas whispered. "This is a great power that not even you know how to control."

Before I could respond, the stranger drifted away, his tongue flicking out once as his green eyes lingered on my curves. It was a complete mindfuck. He said he was a friend, but his eye-fucking of my body did not feel friendly.

CHAPTER SIX

Seraphina

Laszlo made certain I was punished after my little rebellions at the party, and this particular round of abuse was difficult to stomach, even for me. For what seemed like hours, Laszlo had me tied to his bed and assaulted my mouth with his cock. The fucking blood oath wouldn't let me bite his dick off.

He stuck a plug in my ass and forced an orgasm from my body with toys. Tears streaked down my face, and my insides writhed with disgust. It felt like a betrayal to my men. It was the first time, in everything he had done to me, that my mind began to fracture. I couldn't escape him, couldn't fight him. My body betrayed me, and my bonds tying me to the princes frayed.

And all the while. Belial's whispers lured me away. Promising freedom from this oath, and fucking hell was I tempted. Pain I could handle, but Laszlo forcing pleasure from me was a boundary I didn't know I had.

Laszlo was gone now, leaving me tied to the bed to wallow alone. When the door handle turned, I flinched, and I fucking hated myself for it.

"It's me," Halphas, the odd stranger from the party, whispered as he crept into the room. "Time to go."

He cut the ropes previously stretching my arms and legs across the bed. I groaned as he gathered my bruised and battered body into his arms. Laszlo enjoyed my pain, and the stab wounds were still healing from his stellatium razors he used to slice me open. My muscles were weak, and all I could do was whimper as Halphas took me from the room.

"Don't let the oath rule you, Seraphina," he murmured close to my ear, brushing his hand against my cheek. "He finally used your body, didn't he?"

Shame colored my cheeks and sharp pain pierced my heart at what I allowed him to do to me. "I wasn't strong enough to stop it."

His light-blue eyes filled with pity. "He has power only because of the oath, and you are untrained. You can be more, Seraphina." The stranger cradled my exhausted limbs as we walked, brushing steady circles against my thigh. "Next time, he will take more from you, violate you in every way he can."

The pain returned, and I knew I couldn't take this torture any longer. I needed to get out from under Laszlo's oath. Even if I broke my bonds, there had to be a way to get them back, right?

"I would lose them all," I whispered, my head bobbing against his chest as he carried me through the castle.

Part of me noted the eerie silence, and the lack of Laszlo's guards, but I was too tired to care.

"And you'd be free. Free to enact the revenge you are so clearly owed." Halphas squeezed my thigh, and I shuddered at his words.

A whisper of pleasure tickled my skin, and I leaned into him. "Take me to Belial."

He smiled, and I was too far gone to notice the smugness of it. As if I'd had any other choice.

My body stirred, a blend of pain and pleasure guiding me back to consciousness. At some point, I passed out in Halphas's arms. That was mildly alarming, considering I trusted no one in this fucking place. There was something familiar about him, though, and maybe on some level, I knew that he was safe. A tiny corner of my mind scoffed at that, raging at me to wake up. But I couldn't. That part of me was locked behind an impenetrable fog. All I could think and feel was Laszlo's pain and the immense pleasure I'd feel when that oath was broken.

My gaze landed on Halphas still holding me in his arms. We were back in the throne room, and several others joined us now, including Belial.

"There she is." Halphas smiled. "Are you ready to break your bonds and take your revenge?"

The girl locked away screamed at me through the fog. Something wasn't right, but I couldn't figure out what it was, not with Halphas holding me and smiling like I was making all the right choices.

I turned from him, steadying my weight but still holding his arm. A soft white robe covered my body, and I watched as other creatures circled around us.

Halphas squeezed my hand, and a giddy feeling zipped through my veins. He produced a blade similar to the one I once had, but with a black onyx stone in the hilt. "For this to work, we must carve a symbol over your heart. It will hurt, but I know you can take it."

A barrage of questions filled my head, slipping into the fog with the screaming girl. "I'm ready."

The circle of creatures began to chant, and Halphas slipped my robe off my shoulder enough to reveal my chest. His touch was soothing, and I shivered, staring into his eyes as blue as a cloudless sky.

Little sister…

Lailah's voice echoed in my head, and an inkling of recognition reached me through the fog. "You have her eyes."

Halphas stopped, the blade poised over my heart. His eyes shuttered, and his face changed with a cruel grin. "My brother's eyes. We always did look alike, although I dare say I'm the more handsome choice. But where I was clever, he was strong. The greatest warrior, until your father murdered him and mated with your whore mother."

A gasp escaped my lips, but I had no time to react to his words. Halphas gripped my arm, and I screamed in pain. He was doing this. The pain and pleasure, his touch clouded my true feelings. The fog lifted, but it was too late. He expertly carved into my skin, and a soul-shattering scream echoed in the room. I barely registered that it was mine.

I could feel them. The bonds of my mates. And they were leaving me.

Laszlo's blood oath lifted away first, and my power surged. My skin glowed with the force of it, but Belial was there with us now, holding me still as Halphas finished carving the symbol.

Levi left me first. Then Typhon and Andras. And suddenly Dev was there in my mind. His scent wrapped around me, and he shouted my name. I tried to reach for him, but the darkness between us grew heavier and heavier. Phen, his bond was still there, barely, frayed, as Halphas finished the mark.

I'm so fucking sorry. I sent the thought down the last thread of my bond to Phen. Because I was wrong. I couldn't get them back. The endless nothing that existed within me was proof of that. There was not a whisper of my princes left in my soul. Laszlo and Belial, of course, knew the consequences of this dark magic. I was alone, broken and instantly racked with regret.

The weight of what I had done settled in my soul just before all hell broke loose.

CHAPTER SEVEN

Michaela

TWO DAYS EARLIER

My wings snapped out to catch the current of air as I curved my body in the sky to match the direction of the wind. Flying was the only time I was able to find peace in the last twenty-four hours since my sister gave herself up to save us.

It killed me that I wasn't with her. Everything happened so fast. The Obscuritas Kings were once again several steps ahead of us. And while we thought the small army we'd gathered would be enough protection with the Princes away on their rescue mission, it wasn't enough at all.

A shadow above me blotted out the sun, and warmth spread from my chest straight to my toes. Morax Ormaenus, my mate. He was strange and familiar all at once. We'd only known each other for less than a year, and yet he felt like home. My heart and soul were blended with his for eternity. I shivered at the feeling of his eyes on me. Turning in the air, I glanced up at the monster flying above me. Morax was in daemon form, dark horns spiraling out of his thick dark hair. Black feathered wings flapped strongly in the wind. His golden eyes glowed with power, captivating me. And he looked entirely too serious. I knew that was partly my fault. I'd been mostly a mess since we lost the fight against the Kings. But the blubbering phase was over. Now it was time to kick some ass.

"Catch me if you can," I called out to him, blowing a kiss before whipping around and diving back to the field below.

You know what happens when I do, little doe. Morax rumbled, his deep voice echoing in my mind.

A whimper of need zipped through to my core, and his answering roar above me in the sky made me giggle. With our mate bond solidified, Morax and I could communicate within our minds, and every emotion, every fiber of our souls, we felt as one. My heart beat only for this creature of mine. And right now, it fluttered with desire.

Morax had a bit of a primal kink, and what happened when he finally caught me was absolutely worth being hunted.

Do not pretend you don't enjoy the chase, too, little doe. Morax growled in my head. *I know your sweet cunt is wet for me already.*

It was impossible to clench your thighs while flying at speed, but my body jerked awkwardly to do so anyway. Morax chuckled, and I scoffed, sending a blast of air back at him. He roared in fury, and my laughter carried through the sky, enraging the monster intent on catching his prey.

I might not be as much of a badass as my sister, either sister, if I was being honest, but poking the beast was too much fun.

My feet hit the ground, and before I could look up, thick arms wrapped around my middle, pulling me into the muscular body that belonged to my mate. His forked tongue flicked out against the shell of my ear, and I shivered.

His claws scraped softly against my skin, tugging up my sweater. "Mine." My mate growled the word, biting down on my throat hard enough to leave a mark.

Morax held me in place, asserting his dominance and making me feel safe all at once. And I loved it. I loved him.

We walked back into Vespertine Hall hand in hand. Daemons, lumens, and witches greeted us as we made our way to the ballroom, now acting as our war room. There were even hybrids among us, creatures like me who were a mix of human and something more. If we weren't planning a literal war right now, I'd be fascinated and asking dozens of questions.

It was insane to me that so many hybrids lived on this planet. But before my mother sealed us off with her sacrifice, daemons and lumens traveled to Earth quite often. And not just our planet, dozens of others, too. That bit of information I was still wrapping my head around. Daemons and lumens weren't the only creatures with power; there were so many others. The gods, according to their lore, split apart and used their varying powers to create all creatures, each as unique as the next. While it was a wild truth to accept, there was a part of me that wasn't shocked. It was arrogant to think we were the only creatures to exist in this multiverse.

The voice of the witch who shared all these fun facts with me caught my ear as we walked down the hall. Since mating with Morax, all of my senses heightened. I was still getting used to that. Blocking out sound was my first task, considering how many horny-as-hell creatures now lived in the manor. Not even ear plugs could block them all out.

Morax pushed through the doors, keeping a possessive hand on my back. With all these new guests, he was extra snarly and territorial. Not that he was worried I'd have a wandering eye, mated creatures were just extra proprietary. I discovered this about myself when the first new lumen appeared and winked at Morax and I nearly drowned her with water magic.

To be fair, I wasn't trying to create a waterfall, but my powers were still new and mostly untrained. It was a constant worry of mine, especially when we were preparing for a battle of epic proportions.

If I didn't get my powers under control, I'd be a liability on the battlefield. And sitting on the sidelines while everyone I cared for risked their lives was not an option. It was past time for me, Michaela Valdis, to become a badass warrior like her older sisters.

CHAPTER EIGHT

Leviathan

Ever since Seraphina was taken from us, my thoughts were always halfway between worlds. I flicked a tiny fireball between my palms, pretending to listen to the witch, Delphine, and her plans for us. Delphine Bellinor was our only shot at getting to Seraphina. Our perfect, feisty mate was alive. The bonds connecting us, while dim, still pulsed with life.

That sliver reassurance was the only thing keeping me, and the others, from going insane. Phen explained how time worked differently there. Several hours on Earth was a day on Stella Terra, which meant Seraphina had been at the mercy of my fucking father for a few days now. The math of it was irrelevant to me. I didn't care how much time had passed. Even a single hour as their captive was one hour too many. And that fucking oath.

We were still furious at her for accepting Laszlo's blood oath. I knew she did it to save her sister, and us, but she would be answering to each of us for that decision when we finally got her back.

"Now that the lovebirds are back." Delphine's voice echoed in the silence. "We can get started on the next part of our plan."

"Which is what, exactly?" Andras snapped from his seat at the massive oak table.

The table was circular, so no one creature had a more important seat than another. No one even got my King Arthur joke after a daemon conjured the thing with his earth power. Phen insisted we watch the movies as soon as we had Seraphina back. He started calling her Princess Gwyn, to which I said she was more like a knight than a damsel in distress. So we called Dev Princess Gwyn instead. He loved it, on the inside at least.

Andras stood, placing his hands on the table and glaring at Delphine. Gremory growled low, his bright-blue eyes glowing with power. Grem was a new friend, and one I enjoyed. He was nearly as sassy as me, but not as unhinged as Phen. Grem was Delphine's mate. And in a crazy plot twist, mated to Tabitha as well.

Tibby, Seraphina's bestie, sat next to him and threaded her fingers with his, calming him. There were entirely too many alpha males at this table.

"We are going to send one of you to Stella Terra," Delphine continued, unphased by Andras. Her curly hair was pinned up on top of her head, and she wore a fitted green dress that complimented her hazel eyes.

Even now, she radiated a power that was impossible not to feel. Delpine was a member of some witch royalty in their world. And what was even more insane, she was less powerful than Aurora Valdis, Seraphina's mother. I suppose that made sense, considering the power she must have possessed to seal off all travel between worlds with her death. Lailah, Seraphina and Michaela's older sister, had inherited Aurora's power as a Seer, which would have been incredibly beneficial right now. If only we could see into the future and know that our efforts would not be in vain.

"I'll go." Ty stood from his seat to the right of Andras. "I will find Seraphina and bring her back to us."

Delphine rolled her eyes. "Simmer down, beefcake. It's not just about finding her. This is a multi-step plan that will take a shit ton of power to get us all back to Stella Terra." Her eyes slid to Michaela. "We are going to need your necklace."

All eyes swerved to the youngest Valdis daughter. Her hand moved over the stone fastened to the gold chain. It was similar to the one Seraphina had, before she used the power within.

Daemons and lumens could make gifts of their souls, their power, placing it within a stone. Luxenite for the lumens, and tenebrite for the daemons. Seraphina's tenebrite stone held the power of her birth father, Belfegor. He sacrificed his place among the stars when he did this, and with his help, we escaped from our fathers and another of their rituals for power was ruined. But not before Seraphina was forced to slit Joseph Bronwen's throat, the man who raised her and Michaela's birth father.

To say things had been difficult for us would be a severe understatement. And we were so close to being happy, whole, when they took her from us.

"You think my mother's soul is in this necklace, and it can help us get Seraphina back?" Michaela asked, her voice hopeful.

Delphine's face was inscrutable. "Perhaps it is your mother. But yes, it will help us get to Seraphina."

Movement to my left caught my eye, and I raised a brow at Nuriela. She was new to me and my brothers, but not to the world of daemons and lumens. Nuriela Ramas was the mate of Lailah Valdis, and she spoke very little to anyone but Delphine and the tiny human she guarded, Lo.

Lo was the only other human at the table besides Tabitha. Seraphina told us some of the story. The girl covered in burn scars marked over with tattoos was the daughter of a pedophile. A pedophile Seraphina killed when she burned his gym to the ground with him inside. Only Lo and her sister were there, too. Lo's younger sister didn't survive, but Nuriela was able to save Lo. They'd been together ever since.

The girl was around Michaela's age, with long black hair and pale skin. Her wide green eyes made her appear naive, but I could see a level of cunning hidden beneath her soft facade. What part she was to play in all this, I wasn't entirely sure. Nuriela trained her to fight, but once we went into battle against creatures with magic, a solid suckerpunch wasn't going to be very useful.

"Let's get going, then," Nuriela chimed in, her curly hair braided down her back swaying as she stood. She flipped a dagger into the air, catching it with ease. "I'm bored with this."

"Feel free to leave then, lumen," Phen purred, a glint in his silver eyes.

I smirked at my newest brother in arms. He didn't have any issues with the female, but Phen was a perpetual shit-disturber. One of my favorite things about him.

Nuriela ignored him, circling the table and tossing her blade with casual grace. Andras flicked his eyes to the lumen, and my instincts told me something was amiss. Unfortunately, none of us would be fast enough to do anything about it.

The blade in her hand slashed across Devon's throat before anyone could move. Rage bled through my veins, and the fireball I'd been toying with grew twice in size as I aimed for the female.

Ty roared, and even Phen shouted curses as he rushed to Dev's side. He was the closest, catching Dev as he fell to the floor, light fading from his brilliant green eyes. The bond between us dimmed, and the pain of it was excruciating.

Before I could kill the lumen who murdered my brother, Morax wrapped his muscular arms around my own, pulling me back. "Stop," he shouted over the panic. "Listen."

We quieted enough to hear chanting and turned to Delphine. She was murmuring words swiftly, magic thickening in the air. A ball of pure energy lifted from Dev's body, and he went limp in Phen's arms. The ball of light grew, shimmering before us.

Delphine stopped chanting. "Phenex. Go. He's your anchor. We'll see you soon."

Phen placed Dev's body gently on the floor, and in the next moment, leapt into the air at the ball of light. Nuri launched the dagger in Phen's direction. A crack like lightning cut through the air, and I shielded my eyes. When I could see again, the light, the dagger, and Phenex were gone.

Anguish squeezed my heart as the reality of the situation sank in. *Dev was gone. My fucking brother was gone.*

"Did you just fucking murder him?" Ty snarled. He might be as big as a tree, but Ty was lethal when he wanted to be. He had Nuriela on the floor, his hands around her throat before she could blink.

Nuriela stared up at him, unphased. "I thought he was the one who betrayed you all, so I figured you'd enjoy seeing him get his throat slit."

Fury boiled through me, and in that moment, I wouldn't feel an ounce of regret if he killed her.

CHAPTER NINE

Michaela

The tension in the room was ridiculous. Nuriela's face was turning purple. Lo punched her dainty fists against Ty's back, but he didn't even flinch. Morax stood in front of me, acting as a shield.

"Delphine, my love." Grem coughed. "Perhaps you should've explained to the princelings that you were not, in fact, murdering one of their bonded brothers before you started the spell."

Delphine smirked. "And where's the fun in that?"

Andras pinched the bridge of his nose, the only outward sign of his inner turmoil regarding the craziness that just unfolded. I swear that man was part statue for all the expressions, or lack thereof, that he shared. But I was also certain Seraphina would not have chosen him for a mate if she hadn't seen something of his true self.

"Explain, now," Andras demanded. "Before I let Typhon squeeze the life out of the female."

Delphine crossed her arms, unafraid. "We needed a soul connection to Seraphina. Not a body, the pure energy of a soul. And I was only strong enough to send one of you with him. Phen knows the land."

Ty roared, and my eyes snapped back to him in time to see Nuriela kick him in the balls and roll them over. She pointed a second dagger directly over his heart. Of course, a cheeky assassin like her would have more than one. *Seraphina would have enjoyed this.*

"Enough," Morax growled, his voice cutting through the tension in the room. "We are all on the same side, and you're behaving like children."

I scoffed at his attempt at controlling the chaos, and Morax elbowed my side, raising a brow. My big, scary mate. I ducked under his arms and stood in front of him, letting him cocoon me against his hard chest.

Delphine's attention turned to me. "Your turn, Michaela. Time to unleash the power."

Nervous energy sizzled in my veins, but Morax kissed the top of my head and sent soothing thoughts down our bond. *I will be with you the entire time.*

It wasn't just the power that I was nervous about, but seeing my mother. Seraphina saw Belfegor when she unleashed her stone. My memories of Aurora Valdis were very few, being that I was so young when she died.

"What do I do?" I asked Delphine, snapping the chain and holding the stone in my palm. It looked similar to a clear quartz and pulsed with powerful energy.

"Smash it." Delphine crossed her arms, and I nodded.

Typhon picked up Devon's lifeless body and everyone in the room stepped away from the table, away from me. Morax stayed by my side as I stepped up to the table. I pulled the slim dagger from the sheath around my thigh. It was strange to wear weapons, but Morax said it was better to be armed and get comfortable with weaponry.

Flipping the blade around, I hovered over the stone and took a breath. "Here goes nothing…"

As soon as the hilt of my dagger cracked the stone, the room vanished and I was alone. The mate bond shimmered within me, alive and intact. I sent a message down the bond that I was okay, hoping he would get it.

Everywhere I turned, puffy white clouds passed me by. Somehow, I floated amidst the clouds without my wings, endless blue skies in every direction.

A presence was coming, but who, I wasn't sure. "Mother?"

The clouds parted, and a figure walked toward me. She had golden-blonde hair and bright-blue eyes that matched one of my own. Her smile was soft and reminded me so much of our mother's.

"Lailah."

She grinned, her pink dress swaying as she drifted toward me. Her figure was similar to mine, slender and long limbs. She reached for me, and when our hands connected, a surge of power rushed through me. Flashes of memories passed through my head.

"Little Kaela." She smiled, squeezing my hands. "You're gorgeous and everything I knew you'd be."

"Knew?" I asked, trying to stay in the moment as the visions kept coming.

She sighed, sadness in her blue eyes. "It wasn't a power I wanted, but in the end, it's the one that would save everyone I love. Now it's yours."

I winced, the visions causing my head to ache. "Does it always hurt?"

Lailah shook her head. "Only if you reject it. This power is so much more than visions, Kaela. Don't let Belial take it."

I nodded, taking deep breaths and trying to let the visions flow through me. "I won't."

She smiled at me. "I know you can handle this, baby sister. Help Seraphina. She's going to need you." Lailah paused, tears threatening to spill over. "And tell Nuri…she's doing everything right. Tell her I'll see her in the stars."

CHAPTER TEN

Morax

The strength of our mate bond was the only thing keeping me from losing my damn mind. Michaela dropped as soon as the stone cracked, and I caught her. Her limp body weighed next to nothing in my arms, and yet she was my everything. Delphine assured me she would wake whenever what was in the stone completed its task.

Michaela's skin glowed, and I could feel some new power burning through her veins. Flashes of visions passed through my head, but they were all too fast to catch. And yet, I knew what this meant. I hugged her close when she started to tremble.

"The Sight," I murmured, kissing her golden hair. "She's becoming a Seer."

"Holy shit," Grem blurted. "Well, that will certainly help our cause."

"As long as she can handle it," Delphine whispered thoughtfully.

I snapped my fangs at the witch. "She is stronger than you know. Michaela can handle anything."

Levi grinned, navy-blue eyes twinkling, and rested his thick arms over the back of a chair. "I have no fucking clue what's going on, but it's all very exciting."

Michaela suddenly groaned, and I pulled back enough to see her face. Her eyes opened slowly, and I gazed into the blue and gold irises of my perfect other half. "Hello, my love. Are you all right?"

She smiled softly. "I think so. It was Lailah."

A thud caught our attention, and everyone in the room turned to Nuriela. She'd dropped to her knees, eyes wide. "Did you talk to her?" Her voice was rough with emotion.

Michaela moved into a sitting position in my arms and nodded. "She said you did everything right and…see you in the stars."

A sob caught in Nuriela's throat, and in the next moment, she fled the room. Lo followed after her.

Michaela closed her eyes, brow scrunching, and Delphine clapped once to get everyone's attention. "Well, now that that's done, you've got three days to figure out how to use all your new powers to get us to Stella Terra."

"What?!" my mate, and I shouted in unison.

Delphine shrugged. "Yes well, if we don't get Devon's body back together with his soul in about three days, he will actually die. I'm confident you'll figure this out before that happens."

"Why me? Why can't you take us back?" Michaela groaned anxiously. I could hear her heart fluttering dangerously fast.

"Because with all that Seer power running in your veins, you're now the most powerful creature at the table, Michaela Valdis." Delphine smirked. "Might even give Seraphina a run for it."

At her words, Michaela sucked in a breath, her eyes glazing over, her Seer power already active. She blinked several times. "Holy hell. I don't think so."

My claws tickled my mate's bare flesh as I nipped at her throat. She moaned, soft and mewling in my arms. The saucy lumen wiggled her ass against my cock, getting it half hard for her already.

After the dramatics of the afternoon, I insisted we rest and take some time to ourselves. We did not, in fact, get any rest. Michaela Valdis was impossible to resist. And sharing her with all those other creatures all fucking day drove me insane. I needed to feel her body submitting beneath mine. Hear her soft moans and take her screams as I filled her with my seed.

Once I had my fill, for the moment, I carried her to the tub where we now rested. She wiggled against me again, and I bit into her neck. The sound of her moans drew a low purr from my chest.

"Naughty little lumen," I uttered in a menacing tone. "Behave or you'll be punished."

"Promise?" she whispered, her big doe eyes captivating me completely.

"Always." I stole a kiss from her plump, pink lips. This perfect creature was my addiction, and I would never get enough of her. "How are you feeling?"

She sighed in my arms, her golden hair piled high on her head to keep it from getting wet. "Like I have been given too many responsibilities and no time to figure out how to handle them."

I was inclined to agree. Delphine saddled Michaela with a heavy burden, and yet, it wasn't really the witch who did this. Retracting my claws, I cupped Michaela's cheek gently and forced her to look at me. "This power was always meant to come to you. If we know anything, it's that your mother put her plans in place before you were even born."

My mate's dual-colored eyes brimmed with tears. "But if she saw so much, how could she not change this fate? If she knew this great evil was coming to us, why couldn't she stop it?"

I brushed a tear from her cheek, wanting desperately to take her sorrow away. "Perhaps she wasn't meant to stop it. Aurora Valdis was a fierce lumen and queen. She would never have put her children in harm's way if there was another choice."

Michaela stared up at me with grief shining in her eyes. "How do you know she was fierce? How could she know I would be strong enough to take this on?"

My mate needed to be reminded of her own strength. She needed to train and gain confidence. The doubt clouding her mind and flowing through our bond was unacceptable. I lifted my little lumen from the tub, and she yelped as I cradled her soft body to my chest.

"It's time to practice," I announced, walking us back to the bedroom. "No mate of mine is allowed to feel inadequate."

I tossed her onto the bed, and a gasp whooshed out of her. The predator in me growled at the site of its prey in such a vulnerable position. Michaela's pupils dilated as she dragged her gaze down my chest to my hard length that was already eager for the feel of her.

"Again?" she teased, clenching her thighs together.

But that wouldn't do. I needed to see her. Every perfect inch of her belonged to me. Using my earth power, I conjured vines to latch on to her ankles and splayed her legs. Her pink pussy glistened with desire, and a purr built in my chest. I stalked to the edge of the bed, my tongue flicking out to taste her desire in the air. Michaela licked her lips, a beautiful blush coloring her cheeks.

"Again," I growled, grabbing her thighs and tugging her body to me. "And again." I dropped to my knees, lining my face up with her perfect cunt. "And again."

Not waiting another second for her response, I drove my forked tongue into her sweet heat. She moaned for me, her legs shaking as I edged her toward another orgasm. The sounds of her pleasure had my cock leaking, eager for her.

"Fuck, my love. My mate," I murmured between her thighs. "You taste absolutely divine."

She whimpered at my words, and I sucked her clit between my teeth. "Morax. Make me come. Please."

The sound of her sweet voice begging me was all it took. I was a slave to her pleasure. "As you wish, mate." Her head rolled back, and I nipped at her thigh with my fangs, bringing her gaze back to mine. "Eyes on me, little lumen. I need to see your face when I ruin you."

CHAPTER ELEVEN

Michaela

My legs ached from the multi-orgasm session Morax insisted I receive before we trained. Who was I to disagree with his decision? The anxiety I felt earlier faded to the back of my mind after experiencing pleasure unlike I'd ever felt. My mate always seemed to know exactly what I needed.

I dropped into a crouch, facing him now, an icy ball of water forming in one hand and a short sword in the other. Morax said we had to train with all kinds of weapons, not just our power. Fighting in a battle against other daemons and lumens would not be like the wars of humans. Daemons and lumens both fought dirty, using every ability they had to unseat their opponent. Our power could maim and wound, but only stellatium could kill a creature like us. The blade had to pierce the heart. The metal being poisonous to our kind and instantly turned our hearts to dust.

Morax circled me now, his golden eyes glowing with his power as he stalked me in the clearing near Vespertine Hall. It was really fucking hot seeing him all monster-like. He also said I had to get used to the forms of creatures. Once we made it to Stella Terra, most daemons and lumens would be in their true forms. Some had horns and tails, some had wings, some had pointed ears and forked tongues. The appearances varied based on their lineage and affinities. Royal bloodlines all had wings. And daemons were generally more adept with earth or fire power, whereas lumens excelled with air and water. The more powerful the lineage, the more power over the elements.

My cunning mate lashed at me with a vine, attempting to draw my attention to his left side as he feigned to the right with his blade. I whirled around, blocking his sword and slicing through his whip.

Morax chuckled, a sexy-as-hell smirk on his lips. "Very good, little lumen." He was also shirtless, which was completely distracting. "Focus, mate. Don't think I can't feel the lust building inside you."

I smiled sweetly then launched my ball of ice at his perfectly sculpted abs, knocking him to the ground. His eyes widened as I leapt at him, my blade poised over his heart. "I can multitask."

Morax's clawed hands squeezed my waist over my leggings. "I can see that."

The sound of someone clapping had my head whipping up to see who had arrived. Morax seemed unphased, as if he knew Gremory was there all along.

"Very good, young Seer." Gremory grinned, wiggling his eyebrows. "But can you do that when it truly counts? When you're on the battlefield and those you care for are in mortal danger."

A massive broadsword appeared in Gremory's hands, and he dropped into a fighting stance. His eyes tracked Morax, and my mate subtly moved in front of me, readying for a fight.

The daemons circled each other, using minute amounts of power to test the other's defenses. Gremory lashed out first, and the sword fight began. It gave me flashbacks to the first time I encountered Gremory, only then, Morax thought he was an enemy, and they fought to kill. So much had changed since then, and now the Commander of the daemon army was here, fighting with us. Although right now, he was attempting to hurt my mate.

I watched intently as they fought, both daemons moving with a preternatural grace. Morax was a beast, lethal and strong, but Gremory was fast, too fast. He landed several small slices of his sword on my mate, and each cut sent power burning through me. Seeing his blood spilled was too much.

A vision flashed before my eyes of Gremory's stellatium blade piercing Morax's heart, and I gasped in shock. Grem would never do that; he was one of us. And yet I saw it happen. The combination of moves in my vision began in real time as I watched Gremory get the upper hand. There was no time for me to intervene, no magic I could think to conjure up to stop this from happening.

And yet, power built within me, pulsing with life and feeling unlike anything I'd experienced before. Just as the moment arrived and Gremory's sword edged toward my mate's heart, I screamed, throwing my hands in the air to unleash whatever was inside me. Time slowed. Gremory and Morax were still facing off, but it was as if their movements were caught in molasses. My own body remained free, so I ran at them like a damn bull, knocking Morax out of the way just as the power faded.

Gremory landed hard on the grass, his sword several inches into the earth instead of my mate's heart. He grinned.

"What the hell is wrong with you?!" I shouted at him, rushing the daemon and intent on causing him pain.

Morax leapt up from the grass and was at my side in seconds, holding me close. "Not exactly the teaching tactic I had in mind, Grem."

Gremory seemed unbothered, crossing his arms, long blond hair loose at his shoulders. "She needed real motivation to see what her new power could really do."

My chest heaved with rage as I absorbed their words. The dangerous edge to my power began to fade. "I saw a vision of you killing him."

The clever daemon smirked, his bright-blue eyes twinkling. "Well, it had to be believable. If I thought it was only a test, you'd know, and then you wouldn't have been able to use your power to save him."

Morax wrapped his arms around my waist from behind and brought his lips to my neck, nipping my skin. "You were incredible, little lumen."

His words sent shivers down my body. "I don't even know how I did it. All I knew was that I couldn't let you die."

My mate squeezed my middle, keeping me close as he nuzzled into my collarbone. "Often our emotions trigger bigger surges of power. Gremory was testing that theory. Perhaps not how I would have chosen to do it, but effective, considering we have little time to get to Stella Terra."

"Now that you've tapped into that power, you should be able to do so again more easily," Gremory added, pulling his sword from the earth and leaning casually on the hilt. "Remember the feel of it flowing through you and start there. You'll be kicking all our asses soon enough."

He walked off, joining the Princes practicing across the clearing.

I sighed, slumping against Morax and feeling for that strange pulse of magic that rushed through me. "Maybe if I'm stronger, I can stop time long enough for us to just snatch your evil brother and the Kings off the battlefield and end the whole damn thing before it begins."

Morax chuckled. "A nice thought, but unlikely. My brother will not be on the field. He will send others to fight for him before he shows his face. And I imagine your cult leaders have a few tricks as well. But your abilities will certainly give us an edge."

I nodded, agreeing. We couldn't take any chances. My sister was locked away by those evil assholes, and I would do everything I could to get her back. "Let's practice again."

CHAPTER TWELVE

Delphine

We were nearing the end of the second day since I sent Phen and Dev to my home. Michaela was stronger already. I wasn't surprised. She was a Valdis, after all. Their bloodline was incredibly powerful, and if anyone was going to pull this off, it was the daughters of Aurora. But not alone. It would take all of us to win this war against Belial. The Obscuritas leaders were not to be discounted either. Laszlo Blackbyrn proved time and again to be cunning, nearly as much as Belial. And his schemes were not solely wrapped up in the daemon prince. I suspected he had far grander plans. That male suffered from grandiose delusional disorder, with a healthy side of narcissistic tendencies.

But what he intended, I couldn't discover. Even now. Sitting quietly in my rooms, I painted a field of daisies, hoping to trigger something. The power of the Seer was reserved for lumens, but witches had ways of seeing the future. We often used a conduit, like tarot cards, runes, and such. For me, I discovered I could get glimpses of what was to come when I painted. Even after a couple decades of practice, there was still no rhyme to it. Sometimes I painted the future, and sometimes it was only a field of daisies.

I pulled a fresh canvas onto my easel and started again. Two pairs of blue eyes formed. One belonging to my daemon mate, Gremory. I'd know his mischievous gaze anywhere. He was my light in the dark. A bright, brilliant thread of color in the endless gray that was my life for nearly two decades.

The other set of eyes was a lighter blue, so pale they were almost white. Her skin was fair, and the silvery blonde pixie cut looked real enough to touch. Tabitha. She was a soul I did not see coming. The goddess did not grant me images of her existence until she fell into my lap, bleeding and nearly dead. Gremory rescued the girl from the Kings, and the horror she endured at the hands of Laszlo Blackbyrn was some of the most horrific I'd ever heard. That prick was going to die for what he did to her. My second love. As soon as I saw them together, I could see the bond between Grem and Tabitha. It was pure and beautiful. The three of us together was a happiness I never knew I could have.

My smile dimmed as I painted them, the backdrop shifting. Tabitha held a sketchbook in her hand. My sketchbook. But I wasn't with them. And from the lights of the city behind them, I knew exactly where they were. Pain lanced through my heart, another confirmation of something to come. At first, I rebelled against it. But the vision never wavered, and I eventually accepted it as true.

A soft knock on the door caught my attention.

"You never have to knock, my darling."

Tabitha's petite frame slipped into the room. She looked stunning in a pale-pink dress. Her perky breasts drew my eye immediately. I smiled at her, and she blushed. The rush of power I felt from her reactions was a heady thing.

"I thought I'd check in." Tabitha sat on the bed, crossing her legs and letting the dress ride up her thighs. Her bright-blonde hair was stylishly tousled, and she wore no makeup.

It gave me immense pride to see her so relaxed. After we nursed her back to health, it took many nights to quell her nightmares. Her mind did not break beneath Blackbyrn's torture, but he came very close. Having a drop of Seraphina's blood in her body saved her life. The pact made between friends years ago preventing tragedy even now.

Grem had worked out quickly that Tabitha must have had something other than human blood in her veins, just as I had. Humans could not handle the blood of a creature, it would drive them insane and eventually kill them.

Hence Laszlo's willingness to work with Belial. While the human cult leader could wield power, he would never truly be as powerful as a daemon or lumen, or even a witch. But I suspected he worked out a way to become something more. It was only a matter of time until I discovered what that was.

"And where is Gremory?" I asked her, arching a brow. Tabitha never went anywhere without him or myself at her side. While she was so fucking strong and healing inside and out, a small part of her soul would always fear others. But when she was with one of us, her nightmares faded.

She grinned, toying with the hem of her dress. "He's fighting Morax, trying to provoke Michaela."

I stood from the chair facing my easel and sauntered toward her. "And you walked back here to me, all alone?"

Her face flushed again, and I traced the rosy color of her cheeks with my fingertips. "I thought I sensed…sadness. I didn't want you to be alone if you were feeling sad."

My heart filled with love for this empathetic little creature. Tabitha was only a handful of years younger than me, but her ability to manage emotions was far superior. "My sweet girl. Always looking out for your mistress."

Tabitha's eyes dilated as I ran my nails across her collarbone and along the sweetheart neckline of her dress. She nodded, and desire pulsed through my veins. I continued down her front, teasing her nipples through the thin fabric with one hand and bringing the other between her soft thighs.

"Cheeky little thing," I purred. "Nothing under your dress? And who was that for?"

She moaned as I brushed my knuckles between her slick pussy. "You, mistress. And Grem."

I extended my fingers and slipped one inside her, feeling her body tighten and shiver with pleasure. "Only us."

She nodded, but that wasn't enough.

"Say it, sweet girl. Who do you belong to?"

Tabitha whimpered when I inserted a second finger inside her dripping pussy. "You. And Gremory."

Leaning down, I kissed her softly, tasting her sweetness and relishing the way her body reacted to my touch. "Good girl."

The door to our rooms opened suddenly. Tabitha gasped, but I knew who was joining us.

"Well, well," Gremory drawled. "Having a pleasure party without me?"

I rolled Tabitha's perky nipple between my fingers, and she moaned. "Never, my love. Now get undressed and lie on the bed."

Gremory followed my commands instantly. In the beginning of our courtship, submission was new to him. But I needed it, needed to be in control and dominate my partner. Our dynamic was based on complete trust, and with Tabitha joining us, it finally felt whole.

My sexy daemon eagerly dove onto the bed, stroking his cock and watching me toy with Tabitha's tight pussy.

I slipped my fingers from her and brought them to my mouth, tasting her sweet essence. "Delicious."

Gremory whined. "I want a taste."

I grinned and pressed my slick fingers to Tabitha's lips. "Suck." And she did, like a good fucking girl. "Now, arms up."

Tabitha obeyed without question, and I lifted the dress over her head, revealing her perfect, pale flesh. She was beautiful. Her body held scars from her time as Blackbyrn's slave, and Gremory and I both took special care with them, marking them with our lips and teeth, claiming her for ourselves.

"Now be a good girl and go sit on Gremory's face." I gave the command, and Gremory groaned, his cock twitching, needy for his mistress.

Tabitha moved up the bed, and Gremory pulled her down for a searing kiss. I watched them, enjoying the view of their naked bodies writhing together. My sweet girl pulled away first, eager to follow my command. She hovered over Gremory's head, leaning forward to press her hands to his chest.

Gremory growled, a guttural, beastly sound. "Gods, you smell fucking delectable, love. Now do as you were told and fucking sit."

Tabitha yelped as Gremory pulled her down. The sound turned into a moan as he began feasting on her sweet pussy. My core heated at the sight of these two perfect creatures. Slowly, I climbed on the bed and straddled Gremory's lean, muscular thighs. I brought the head of his cock to my entrance, and he moaned as I swiftly seated him inside me. He felt divine as I rolled my hips at a leisurely pace.

Tabitha licked her lips, her eyes filled with lust as she watched me fuck our daemon mate. His hips jerked up, attempting to control our movements, and I chuckled.

"Be still, lover," I purred. "I'm going to fuck you slowly. And you're going to make Tabitha and I come before you get your release."

"Yes, mistress," Gremory mumbled against Tabitha's pussy.

I leaned forward and teased her clit, bringing a beautiful moan to her lips.

We moved as one being, gifting pleasure to each other in waves. Tabitha's breathing grew ragged, and my own moans increased as I toyed with my lovers.

"Come for us, sweet girl," I demanded, rubbing circles over her swollen clit.

She cried out, and Gremory latched on to her thighs, keeping her flush against his face and prolonging her orgasm.

His cock throbbed inside me, and I knew he was close. I increased my movements, riding him faster. Tabitha leaned in and latched on to my nipple, sucking and flicking the raised bud with her tongue. I moaned, gripping her soft hair and holding her in place.

"Don't stop," I commanded both of them as the pleasure building within me toppled over the edge and I cried out, my pussy clamping down hard on Gremory. "Your turn, mate."

Gremory snarled, feasting on Tabitha as his hips rocked faster, fucking me from below. Tabitha screamed his name as he brought her to ruin a second time, and I moaned, the magic of our joining building even higher. I could feel the mate bonds singing with power between us. Gremory groaned our names as he unleashed inside me, drawing a second heady orgasm from my body.

We collapsed in a mess of sweaty limbs. Tabitha snuggled between us, her soft whimpers music to my ears. I loved her. I loved him. And I would do whatever I had to do to keep them both safe.

CHAPTER THIRTEEN

Seraphina

The densely wooded forest blurred into a mass of green and black as I sprinted away from the castle. But I wasn't me anymore. The Princes were gone, the bonds of my mates ripped from my soul, leaving a dark void of endless rage and desolation. I felt all of that pain for approximately thirty seconds, and it was enough to last a lifetime.

As soon as the bonds started to fray, chaos erupted in the throne room. Animals crashed through the doors and attacked the daemons performing the ritual. Massive brown bears, eagles with talons as long as my forearm, and many more. I couldn't focus on any of it while my soul was being ripped to pieces, until one of the animals shifted in front of me. One moment, a cheetah was running straight for me, and the next, a female covered in strategically placed leaves crouched in front of my writhing body.

"We don't have time for pleasantries, I need you to shift," she shouted at me over the roar of fighting. Before I could respond, she grabbed my face and forced a blue liquid down my throat.

My insides burned as if I'd swallowed liquid fire. The female vibrated with power, and the cheetah reappeared in her place.

SHIFT.

The command hit me like a wrecking ball, and my limbs hummed with power. There was no time to understand what I had become.

Now run.

The cheetah took off, and I followed. The heavy pain of my bonds dimmed to a dull ache and relief soared through me as I chased after the wild cat racing out of the castle. We'd been running for hours, but my powerful legs showed no signs of slowing. *What had I shifted into?*

You're a panther. And Elgo owes me a new blade.

Huh?

The cheetah slowed, turning her small head back and rolling her eyes at me.

Elgo said you'd turn into a bird so you could fly out, not unlike your father, but I knew you would be a jungle cat the moment I saw you. Big bad pussycat vibes for sure. I won the coin toss, and now he owes me a new blade because that was an epically perfect escape.

My mind was too jumbled to truly focus on the hints she casually dropped about my father. *Who the fuck are you? And how are you in my head?*

The cheetah huffed a laugh, as much as a cheetah could laugh. *A cousin, technically. On your father's side.*

Her revelation had my massive paws stumbling. The truxen daemons, I presumed. There were so few of them left, and what exactly they were capable of was a closely guarded secret, according to Jophielle. She'd left a note that burned up as soon as I read it, telling me to trust the truxens. I knew very little about my birth father, but there was something familiar about this female.

And I'm in your head because the vial I shoved down your throat had a bit of my blood. Your mental barriers aren't as strong in this form, yet, so it was easier to slip in.

The idea of anyone getting in my head was discomforting, but for whatever reason, I trusted this creature. Our pace slowed, and I was able to finally examine my surroundings. There were other animals, truxen daemons, I assumed, traveling with us.

You all came just for me? Did everyone get out of the castle? Jophielle's face flashed in my mind. *Oh gods. Did she get out?*

The cheetah shook her head softly. *I don't know how many were lost. We will assess when we return home. I haven't seen Jophielle. Anyone who lost their life on this mission knew what the price would be. Death is better than capture. If they cannot escape, we were given poison to end it before being taken.*

I stopped hard and snarled in rage, my growl echoing in the forest. *No. I won't leave people behind to die for me like that.*

The cheetah turned to face me, several other animals pausing to watch our exchange. *It's not your choice. Every one of us pledged our loyalty to your father. Your mother. Your family. We all know the prophecy. And if we hadn't got you out when we did, we'd all be dead soon anyway.* Her stern voice boomed in my head, shaming me.

I don't want anyone to pledge loyalty or whatever. None of it matters anyway. They're gone. My mates…the bonds. They're gone.

The pain returned as I spoke, and it was too much. Leaping over the cheetah, I took off into the woods, away from everyone. She called after me, but I shut her out. Somehow, I let my animal nature take over, and bit my bit, my humanity faded. Only predatory instinct remained. No more feelings, no more heartache. No more death.

CHAPTER FOURTEEN
Phenex

The familiar scent of my world overloaded my senses as soon as my feet hit the ground. I shifted immediately, the thrum of power in my veins pulsing in time with the beat of my heart. My claws extended and my wings snapped out, the black feathers glimmering with a silver tint in the sunlight. While I had plenty of power at my fingertips on Earth, Stella Tella was my home, and the elemental magic in my blood called to this land like a lover.

I had two tasks to accomplish: find Seraphina and fuck her brains out. Well, three goals, then. The third being that I had to keep Dev's sweet little soul safe. He was floating around here somewhere. Delphine didn't exactly give me all the details of the spell she performed to send us here, but as long as the mate bonds were intact, we could find our girl and make things right.

The jewel in the dagger hummed with a familiar energy. I patted the thing gently. "Oh hi, Dev. Are you cozy? Don't worry, I'll keep you safe."

The jewel glowed, giving off some kind of irritated vibe. Yep, definitely Dev. From what I could see of my surroundings, I was in the Uada Forest, north of the Zamina Castle. If she was still under the control of my brother and the Kings, she'd be in the castle. I closed my eyes and sensed the mate bonds within that connected me to Seraphina and my new brothers. They vibrated with life, although dimmer. What exactly that meant, I wasn't sure.

It was difficult to not feel some jealousy toward them. Andras, Ty, Levi, and even Dev had connections with Seraphina on a deeper level. They went through some serious shit to get where they are now, and Sera and I…well, we needed more time. At least, she did. I knew instantly she was the one. The one her father spoke of, the one Lailah ordered me to never give up on. She was meant to be mine. Hells, I had more connections with her family members than any of the others. And while I could make her scream with pleasure, feel the weight of our bond when our heated bodies writhed in ecstasy, gaining her trust was something I still needed to do. And I would. If I had to spend every day of our extended lifetimes earning that trust, I promised to do so.

When I turned south, an uneasiness settled in my soul. The mate bond shuttered, as if the threads were being cut. My feet stumbled as pain lanced through my heart.

"Seraphina. No." I groaned as I felt them being torn away from me. Andras. Ty. Levi. They were gone, ripped from my heart, stealing pieces of it as they went. Dev's soul glowed within the dagger. *Would this disconnect kill him?* I had no fucking clue.

My soul was being shattered by the destruction of our bonds. Someone was doing this to her. I roared her name to the skies, begging for the gods to spare her life. Pain flooded my system, and I called to my mate one final time as darkness claimed my soul.

The night sky greeted me as I slowly pried my eyes open. A hollowness settled in my chest where the others should have been. And yet, something remained. The dagger hummed beside me, and I snatched it up.

"Dev! Are you in there?" I whispered to the stone. I couldn't feel my connection to him like I had before, but there was some minute measure of power still linking us.

The mate bond between Seraphina and I was gone, lost. The hole in my soul ached to the beat of a deadly gong, solemn and unending. Something terrible happened to our girl, to us, and I bet my forked tongue it was my shit brother and those fucking cult leaders.

The forest stirred, and my heightened senses caught the gentle huffs of a jungle cat prowling not far from me. The wind whispered with the gentle flap of wings, and I turned to the east just as a massive golden eagle dropped out of the sky. The deadly bird of prey shimmered, and a young male dropped to the forest floor in its place. He was not much younger than me, with olive skin and auburn hair. His hazel eyes glowed with power. While he was unfamiliar to me, I didn't detect any malice.

"Prince Phenex." The male bowed, and I arched an eyebrow.

"While I do love when cute males bow to me, mind telling me why you're worshipping at my altar?" I smirked, crossing my arms and waiting.

The male blushed slightly but kept his back straight. "I am Jormund, a member of the Stella Viri. We are loyal to Belfegor's heir, and her chosen mates."

A grin stretched across my face, and I stomped over to him. "Nice to meet you then, Jormund. Do you happen to know where my beautiful mate is?"

He nodded. "We retrieved her from the castle, but in order to get her away faster, we had her shift. She, ah, ran from us soon after. Elgo is tracking her, but even as a newly shifted panther, the princess is as clever as her father was."

I barked a laugh. "Well, can't say I'm shocked. Point me in the direction she went, and I'll find her."

Jormund nodded curtly and shifted back into his golden eagle. He flew above the trees, and I leapt into the air after him. He was nearly as large as me in this form. Truxen daemons could transform into animals that matched their spirit, and the size of them was often twice that of a regular creature.

The daemon was fast, but I was faster. We flew due north, away from the castle and closer to the edge of the forest. The truxens lived beyond Mount Monkara. Supposedly, the witches that weren't exterminated by my father built a city near the mountains, hidden from the world. Bels was always curious about it, but Mor and I never cared to take up our father's mantle and hunt them down. Why he had such beef with the witches, I still didn't know. He refused to give us answers.

Our father refused us most things. Love, affection, a mother. Her death was a mystery, and it happened when we were all too young to remember her. King Corson Ormaenus was not an affectionate nor sentimental creature. There were no photos of our mother, no letters or books of hers. There were no soft, womanly touches to the castle we were raised in.

Mor and I rebelled against his solitary lifestyle. Bels went full crazy the other direction, viewing females and partners in general as breeders or weaknesses. Mor was more reserved with his thoughts, but we both understood each other in a way Bels never could. He entered his villain era at a young age and never left. Could someone so vile have a soul? Debatable.

A roar reached my ears from the sky, and I grinned. Fuck. Yes. There was some small connection still fighting for life between my mate and I. And I would do everything in my power to bring her back to me and my brothers.

CHAPTER FIFTEEN
Seraphina

Running in this form was beyond exhilarating. All my worries faded to the back of my mind, and pure animalistic urges took over. I could hear prey scurrying along the forest floor, sense the changes in the wind when a bird flew overhead. The colors of the jungle-like forest were vibrant, the exceptional eyesight in this form aiding me as my paws thundered against the soft earth. I let out a roar, enjoying the way the world shuddered around me. A mighty tree with limbs large enough to hold a full-sized jaguar called to me, and I used my powerful hindlegs to leap into it.

Damn, that was graceful as hell.

Apparently, my naturally sarcastic personality persisted even in this form. The sun was beginning to set, and I rested my massive head on my paws, enjoying the lazy evening free of responsibilities. Who cared about wars and evil cults when this life existed? The searing pain from earlier was gone, and I had no desire to feel it ever again. No more guilt for breaking my bonds, no more shame for what Laszlo did to me, no more anything. Closing my eyes, I shoved my humanity down even further, fully becoming the beast.

A sudden thud at the base of my tree caught my attention.

An eagle dropped out of the sky and landed as a young man. He stared up at me uneasily, but his presence didn't bother me. I could crush him easily, if I needed to. The second male, however, was an issue.

Phenex. I shook my head and snarled. *No. I won't go back.*

"Seraphina, my queen," Phenex drawled, reaching out his arm in a casual wave. "Come down and greet your favorite mate."

A deadly purr rumbled in my chest.

"She doesn't seem happy to see you." The young man stepped backward, a bow and arrow materializing in his hands.

Phenex glared at him. "If you launch a single fucking arrow at my mate, I will gut you with my claws. Put. That. Away."

His possessive words stirred something within me, but guilt and shame clouded the feeling. I didn't want any of it. Instead, I leapt from the tree, landed easily, and took off in the opposite direction.

"Now what?" The young man sounded extra grumpy.

Even several paces in the opposite direction, I could hear Phenex clearly, as if he were speaking next to me. "We try a new tactic. Fetch Mirha for me."

A hint of curiosity pressed against my mind at this new name. It sounded like a female's name. I shook my head and growled, shoving the jealous thoughts back into the humanity box.

There was a clearing ahead, and the sound of rushing water reached my ears before I came upon the flowing river. Before I could leap across, Phenex landed on the other side, directly in front of me. He was smirking, his silver eyes glowing with power.

I gazed at him, taking in his more daemonic form. On Earth, the daemons often had their wings and horns visible, but this form was something more monstrous. His grin revealed sharp fangs and a forked tongue. Long, dark claws protruded from where his nails were previously, and shit, did they look deadly. His feet were bare, and black claws extended from his feet, digging into the earth as he crouched in a threatening stance. A menacing purr emanated from my chest, but he didn't flinch.

In the next moment, a female with navy feathered wings dropped out of the sky. She had silver hair, a shade very similar to Phen's glowing eyes.

"Hello, Phen," she cooed at him. "It's been too long since you visited me."

The hair on my back stood up at her seductive voice aimed at my mate.

He grinned, side-eyeing her, then turned his back to me. "Hello, Mihra. Lovely to see you as well. Meet Seraphina." Phen gestured in my direction.

Mihra barely glanced at me, her attention focused on Phen. Her eyes drifted down his bare chest to his muscular legs, visible in the torn, fitted jeans he wore. "A pleasure." She murmured the greeting, her navy-blue eyes filled with lust for *my* fucking mate.

Phenex took a single step toward the female, and just as she reached out to cup his cheek, I hurled myself across the river, knocking the female to the ground. My fangs were inches from her pretty face as a predatory roar gathered in my throat.

"Seraphina, my perfect mate," Phen murmured to my right. He was crouched down next to us with a smile on his stupid, beautiful face. "Probably best not to kill her, she is a cousin of yours, after all. People would be upset."

I snapped my sharp teeth at him and snarled, but he merely chuckled, unafraid.

"Come on now, *mini monstra*. Tell me how you really feel," he taunted me.

That fucking nickname was my undoing. The broken threads of our bond shimmered within me, and my humanity burst through the damn I built in my mind. My jaguar form vibrated, unable to remain with all the emotions flooding my system. My naked body flattened on top of the female.

"Hello, cousin." She smiled up at me, which was enough to earn my wrath. My claws extended, and I grabbed her throat, relieving her of the ability to breathe.

Phenex rushed forward and grabbed my waist with his muscular arms and ripped me off the girl. "As fucking hot as that was to watch, I can't let you kill her."

"She was flirting with you. Touching what belongs to me." I snarled the words, practically spitting mad as the female got to her feet and smirked.

She bowed to me, and I paused, confused. "Well, she certainly is her father's daughter. Good luck, Phen." And with those parting words, Mihra launched into the air and flew out of sight.

Phen walked us to a nearby tree and turned me in his arms, slamming my back into the rough bark. "Fucking gods, you are stunning. I need you, *mini monstra*," he groaned, his nostrils flaring. "And you need me, too."

Fiery heat burned through me as his hands roamed over my naked body. He wasted no time, dropping one hand between my legs and sliding two fingers inside me. I was soaked for him already, and a needy moan escaped my lips.

"That's my favorite sound in the world." He smirked, nipping at my throat. "Other than hearing you scream my name when you come on my cock."

"Then fuck me already," I commanded, needing more than his fingers inside me.

CHAPTER SIXTEEN

Phenex

There was not a single fucking thing on this planet that could keep me from obeying my queen's command. Her body was a canvas I needed to paint with my seed, my scent, my everything. Feeling her in my arms, I knew in my soul we could get our mate bond back. Even then, I felt the quietest stir of something within me. It was there, broken and lost, but not gone.

Seraphina wrapped her legs around my waist, and I hoisted her up higher against the tree with one arm and quickly dropped my pants with the other. My dick sprang out, eager for the feel of her. I rubbed the head against her drenched core and groaned.

"You have the softest, most decadent cunt I've ever fucked." I ground my hips against hers. "Nothing and no one will ever compare to you, *mini monstra*. And I've been inside Dev's pretty mouth."

A laughing moan escaped her lips. "Why the fuck was that so fucking hot?"

"Because"—I licked a path across her chest, circling her pert nipple with my tongue—"we belong to each other, all of us."

I sensed her pain before she spoke. "No more talking. Fuck me like it's the last night of our lives, Phen."

And I did. No more teasing, soft touches. With one possessive thrust of my hips, I was seated inside her perfect cunt. It was glorious. I set a fast pace, grinding into her, keeping her body pinned between mine and the tree at her back. She made the most delicious sounds, and I devoured them, claiming her mouth as equally as I claimed her perfect pussy.

My body was too wound up for her, and the orgasm was coming on fast. Her body tightened around me, her toned thighs squeezing my waist as her own pleasure came to a head. She screamed my name, clamping down my my cock so fucking tightly I came with her, unable to hold back any longer.

"It's not the last night, my queen," I mumbled against her bruised lips. "This is only the beginning."

CHAPTER SEVENTEEN
Seraphina

We lay on the forest floor, my body half covering Phen's, catching our breath after that fast and furious fucking. Phen propped his head up slightly on one arm, the other brushing soft strokes along my back. "Tell me what you're thinking, *mini monstra.*"

Dozens of thoughts and feelings swarmed in my brain, not the least of them being my guilt for what I'd done. My shame. Even here, wrapped in his muscular arms, I couldn't feel him like before. Our connection was never as solid as it was with the others, but I still knew he was mine. Now the uncertainty of us festered in my soul like an infectious disease.

"You first," I countered. "Tell me something real. About you. About your home."

Phenex sighed, brushing his thumb across my bottom lip. His silver eyes glowed slightly, his power so much closer to the surface here. "Well, the castle was never my home. At least, it never felt like a home. Being the youngest, not long after I was born, and our mother was dead, father turned cruel and Belial was his constant, deadly shadow. Mor and I were constantly running away into the woods. We would often be away for days, staying in the witches' city further north."

Every detail he shared with me filled my insides with warmth. He spoke with such vivid detail of his life. It was as if I was there with him, sneaking into pubs and causing chaos, Morax always there to clean up the messes, lovingly, of course.

Phen's arm snaked down my side, tickling my ribs, and I swatted him away playfully. "I wasn't your typical playboy. Obviously, I have the face of a god, but it wasn't sex I craved."

His eyes searched mine, seeking something from me. But with our mate bond broken, I wasn't certain what that was. He looked away from me before speaking, suddenly shy. "I never had a mother or any close females in my life. Never experienced the love of a woman in any true sense. I didn't know how to love someone like that. Deeply and fully. But I wished for it. When I heard I had a mate, a fire lit in my soul that finally I would have someone who was all mine."

His soft words crushed what was left of my shattered heart. I broke the bond he so desperately wished for.

"It wasn't entirely altruistic." He smirked. "I selfishly needed the bond, because I knew it meant my mate could never escape me, never leave me. Bonds like that were for life."

Tears pricked at my eyes, and shame colored my cheeks.

His eyes searched my face in confusion. "What's wrong, Seraphina? Have I upset you? You must know I can't get in your head any longer."

My body flinched at his words, and I desperately wanted to run from them, but he wouldn't let me. "A lot of things. Who was that female? Mihra?"

He chuckled, pinching my side and rolling his eyes. "I met her years ago. She had a crush on me, but I had already discovered I had a mate waiting for me. We became friends. She was a link to the truxen daemons hidden away in the mountains."

"My father's people," I added, and he nodded. At least he was letting me avoid his earlier question for now.

"Mhhm. They were not, and still aren't, the friendliest." Phen sighed. "Don't blame them. Their powers are different from ours, and for that, they were hunted. My father stole away one of their princesses. Did…bad things. She didn't survive."

Rage simmered in my veins, and I closed my eyes, brushing my fingers against his jawline, hearing what he wasn't saying out loud. Even without the bond allowing us to share our thoughts. "You are not your father, Phen."

His arm tightened around my waist, and he stared down at me, his silver eyes shining. "And you are not what was done to you. Whatever happened, you did what you had to do, Seraphina."

Tears burned the backs of my eyes. "I broke us."

Phen sat up, pulling me into his lap and cupping my cheeks. "You escaped. You survived so that we could find you again. Belial and those cult fuckers broke us. And we will be whole again. I swear it."

A small, hopeful smile played against my lips. "I swear it, too. Whatever it takes."

Phen kissed me softly. "That's our girl."

Out of the corner of my eye, the dagger resting in the grass beside us pulsed with magic. I reached over and picked it up, examining the stone. A whisper of power teased my senses. It was so familiar. "What is this?"

Phen grinned. "Devon. Say hi, Dev!" He poked the deep-red stone, and my eyebrows shot up into my hairline. "It's a strange story. Basically, Nuriella killed Dev—"

"WHAT?!" I jumped out of his arms, cradling the dagger to my naked body.

Phen rolled his eyes and stood, his half-hard cock bobbing at me, and I licked my lips, unable to help myself. "He's just doing some soul traveling. As long as your sister's new power brings the gang here in time, his sweet soul will go right back into his body, good as new."

White-hot anger flooded my system. I was going to murder that fucking lumen, gods be damned if she was my sister's mate. "What the actual fuck? Explain. Everything."

My daemon prince pulled me into his arms, cupping my ass. "I will, my queen. But first, let's get you some clothing. I find it impossible not to be inside you when you're naked."

Since I was still a newbie with my power, Phen conjured up some clothing for me. It was incredible the things we could do with elemental magic. He whispered a few words, and leaves and flowers floated around in the air, morphing and forming into a simple linen dress.

We walked together, hands linked since he refused to let me go, making our way through the forest to my father's people. Sure, we could have flown, but I wanted to hear every single thing that happened since I made that stupid blood oath. Phen didn't hesitate to give me all the details. Absorbing all that went down, particularly the bit about Michaela now being a Seer, was proving almost too much for my brain.

I was a little less angry at Nuri, knowing Lailah left a message for her mate. They were parted forever, my elder sister and her mate. Lailah gave up everything, including the love of her life, to that ritual. The ritual that saved us from the Obscuritas and the daemon king, Corson, all at once. Because of the sacrifice Lailah and my mother made a decade ago, we were here now, fighting together. There were still so many holes in our plans, but there was hope. A teeny, tiny flame, but it was there.

When the forest began to thin and the mountains loomed ahead of us, Phen said it was time to fly. We shot into the air. Even from the sky, the valley between the two largest mountains looked empty, beautiful, but uninhabited.

"Get ready for it," Phen called out to me with a smirk on his sexy face.

Before I could ask what he meant, we flew through a cloud, and I gasped. The air thickened around us, and I sensed the magic in the barrier. It slithered over our bodies, looking for what, I wasn't sure, but finally, we were through.

"If we were enemies, that barrier would have incinerated us," Phen shouted happily.

I smacked his arm. "You ass. Thanks for the heads-up."

Instead of responding, he flew at a downward angle, and I followed, gasping in awe at the scene before us. Before, the valley was empty, now, it was teaming with life. City lights glimmered below us. I didn't know what I expected, but it wasn't this. The city below was bigger than a small town, with a handful of tall buildings rivaling smaller skyscrapers. The buildings had a vintage vibe, mainly made of brick and stone and wood. The streets were paved, but there were no cars. Daemons walked, flew, or used their considerable powers to travel through the city. Animals that were most definitely shifted truxen daemons meandered among them.

I followed Phenex, gliding over the city toward an imposing mansion separated from the main grouping of buildings. It reminded me of Vespertine Hall in some ways, but larger and happier. The entire city had a familiarity to it.

"Have I ever been here?" I asked aloud, not really looking for an answer.

Phen took my hand as soon as we landed at the gates of the mansion. "No, I don't think you have. By the time you were born, the Valdis royal family was more secluded in their palace. But many things in your world came from ours."

I cocked my head at him, a question on my face, and he continued, leading me through the gates. "Daemons, lumens, and witches from this world have been visiting yours for centuries. And not only yours, there are other worlds with creatures from your fairytales, and your nightmares. Humans have been influenced by otherworldly beings since their beginning."

"Well, that's insane," I stuttered, absorbing his words. "And I'm going to need to know more about these other worlds and different creatures."

Phen smiled, his fangs on display. "All in good time, my queen. Let's get you some proper clothing and ready to meet your family. More storytime later."

CHAPTER EIGHTEEN

Seraphina

There were very few people around when we entered the grounds. The entire compound was breathtaking. The manor was built with stone and wood, and sat at the base of the mountain range, colored to match the terrain. It was as if the buildings rose from the earth and into existence. There were windows everywhere to let in natural light and massive stone fireplaces with roaring fires in every room we passed. It was impossible not to peek inside each room.

The young man who pointed a bow and arrow at me earlier was our guide. He didn't speak to me but kept a side-eye on us, as if I might shift into the beast again. His distrust wasn't entirely unfounded. Now that I had shifted once, I could feel the wild cat lounging just beneath the surface of my skin. There were so many things about this world and what I was that I was no longer surprised when something new happened.

When I began my quest against the Obscuritas ages ago, I knew there was something more to the world than what the average human believed. The memory of that night, when Lailah and my mother sacrificed themselves in that ritual to save Michaela and I, flashed through my mind. There was magic in the air. It fizzled against my skin, awakening something inside me I was too young to understand. But I knew, even then, I was woefully misguided, and knowledge was power I craved.

My ability to heal inhumanly fast was the first thing I discovered after being on my own. I cut myself on a blade, and within minutes, it was completely healed. That night, I dreamt of running through a palace and tripping, skinning my knee. Even as I wailed in my mother's arms, as young as I was, the cut healed instantly. The dream felt like a memory, unlocked because of the injury. Every time I experienced something otherworldly, strange dreams followed. Michaela and I knew our mother had messed with our memories. It hurt that she would take things from us, but having them was likely more dangerous.

Michaela was at least with her father, but I was alone. It bothered me still, that he left me in that church. Even with the knowledge I now had, knowing what our parents went through for us to be here now, it still hurt.

Was I doing everything right? Did my mother know I would bind myself to Laszlo and break my mate bonds? If that was part of her master plan to save us, it fucking sucked.

The young man finally stopped halfway down a hall and several staircases later, at a set of double doors. They opened at a flick of his hand, and an elegant bedroom came into view.

"You can get cleaned up here." He finally spoke. "Your formal introduction will be in two hours."

Phen squeezed my hand. "Go. Take a nice long bath, and I'll return in two hours."

I arched a brow at him. "And where are you going?"

He planted a messy kiss on my cheek and pulled the dagger from its sheath around his thigh. "Just going to have a word with a witch and make sure our baby boy is doing okay."

Worry crossed his features, and I was ready to tell Phen I was coming with him, but he pushed me into the bedroom. "I promise, I will keep Dev's soul safe. Go pamper. If I stay, I'll be between your legs for the next two hours and we'll be late to your party."

His words had me grinning, and I watched his sexy-as-hell ass swaying as he walked away. A flicker of power pulsed within me. With all the magic of this place and swirling power in my veins, maybe there was someone here who could help us with the mate bonds. I refused to have hope, because if I did, and there was nothing that could be done, the fragmented pieces of my heart would crumble to nothing. *But it couldn't hurt to at least ask someone about it, right?*

CHAPTER NINETEEN

Phenex

Leaving Seraphina was near impossible. Even in that dull linen dress I conjured up, her toned body and perfect curves were the most enticing things I'd ever seen. Having her all to myself, even for just a few hours, was pure bliss. My soul was glowing with hope and possibilities. When I opened up to her in the forest, the tiniest spark of light hummed in my soul. And I knew with every fiber of my being it was our bond straining to come back. Of course, it was unheard of for a mate bond to return after being broken, but just because it had never been done before, didn't mean it couldn't be.

I wasn't lying about checking on Dev, either. His soul glowed within the gemstone, so I knew he was still in there, thriving and probably jealous of my time with our girl.

"Don't worry, baby," I cooed at the dagger. "You'll be out soon, and I promise you can fuck our girl as soon as you are."

The gem pulsed and heat radiated from it, as if he heard me.

I tapped the red stone. "Oh, you want me in your ass? Of course, Dev. You know I want to fuck all your sexy holes."

The young man choked, a sudden coughing fit coming on, and I grinned. "You know I can hear you, right?"

Apparently, I was not allowed to wander on my own, so bow-and-arrow boy was still here. I nearly forgot. "If your innocent ears can't handle what they hear, perhaps you should scamper back to your mother's skirts."

The male's face flushed angrily, but he said nothing. He was a soldier, a worker bee who followed orders and understood the hierarchy. I was a prince, although not to the truxens. But Seraphina was royalty, and I was hers, therefore, this soldier would not talk back.

"What's your name?" I asked, casually flipping the dagger into the air and catching it with ease.

"Elgo," he murmured.

I patted his shoulder, maybe a little too heavily, because he stumbled. "You're a good soldier, Elgo. And while I could still kill you for pointing a weapon at my mate, I appreciate your loyalty to the safety of your people."

Elgo's shoulders relaxed, and he wasn't quite so tense as we made our way to the main level of the manor.

The female we were seeing was a hybrid, half witch and half truxen. She was several hundred years older than me, with considerable power. She was a Scribe, a keeper of stories and histories of our people. Scribes retained the knowledge of all creatures, not just their own. And Scribe Lahabiel I'd heard of decades ago. My father was interested in her knowledge of the prophecies after hearing the one relating to his demise.

Scribe Lahabiel lived in a smaller home separate from the manor, close to the edge of the forest. The door to her cottage was open, the smell of some delicious stew wafting through the air. Her living quarters were simplistic and reminiscent of the medieval days. Our more primitive years ended thousands of years before the humans' Industrial Revolution on Earth.

But some of our elders, like Lahabiel, still chose to live without most modern technology. Elgo hesitated at the doorway, but I had little patience and even less time, so I pushed past him.

A deep chuckle caught my attention, and I turned to the rocking chair facing the fireplace. While it was summer in Liboteria, being as far north as we were, the air kept its chill.

"I've been waiting for you, young prince," the Scribe spoke, her voice low and slow. "Make yourself a cup of soup and come sit. Tell Elgo he can go. I've got my eye on you."

I grinned. Old crones were my favorite, so feisty. Elgo bowed to her from the doorway and took off. Because I wasn't a complete ass, and because I couldn't remember when my last meal was, I followed her instructions and poured myself some soup.

Taking a seat on a large cushion near the fire, I scarfed down the meat and vegetable stew while she watched me. Daemons and lumens kept their youthful bodies for centuries, and witches lived not quite as long, but a few hundred years longer than non-magical beings like humans.

She eyed the dagger at my hip and held out her hand. I passed it to her, trusting she understood the magic connected to it.

"Who did this?" she asked, brushing her slightly gnarled fingers over the ruby stone.

"Delphine Bellinor." I spoke between bites of stew. "He's still okay in there?"

She smirked. "Yes, for now. Delphine. It's been many years since I heard her name."

"She's coming here with the others. Any day now." My bowl empty, I did the polite thing and placed the dish in her sink before returning to my seat.

Scribe Lahabiel nodded. "It will be good for her to return home. Her magic is very strong and the spell is sound."

She handed the dagger back to me, and I sighed with relief. Delphine seemed powerful, but it was good to have the extra reassurance. I hesitated with my next question, and the Scribe watched me with all-to-clever eyes.

"You look lost, young prince." She spoke softly, as if she knew all the things I wanted to say.

A sigh escaped my lips. "I need to know something. Can a mate bond be restored after it has been broken?"

The elder watched me for several minutes, her chocolate brown eyes glowing slightly. The anticipation of her answer was going to fucking kill me.

"It has never been done." The Scribe's voice pitched, a cadence of power lifting the sound into something more. "And yet, there is a story. A tale of one who will come to unite the worlds, and this creature would share her heart with five true mates. The creature would face unimaginable hardships and lose her mates in the process."

My heart broke at her words, but I let her continue.

She rocked slowly in her chair. "The tale goes, this creature and her chosen mates would seek help from Aleya Danai Kel.

That beneath the mountain, they would find the answers they sought."

Hope lit a fiery path within my veins. "And their bonds would be restored?"

The Scribe shrugged. "The tale is thousands of years old. The ending has been lost to us. Even I cannot say what could happen."

I nodded, still feeling like this was the answer I needed. "Has anyone gone under the mountain and tried to restore a broken bond? All the stories I know of the goddess beneath the mountain talk of death. No one comes out."

She grinned. "Yes, the dark tales are mostly true. Only once did a creature return from the mountain."

This was news to me. I leaned forward, eager for the answer. "Who?"

Scribe Lahabiel leaned forward, her dark eyes twinkling with mischief that rivaled my own. "Belfegor."

CHAPTER TWENTY
Seraphina

The bath was practically life-changing. My sore limbs and battered body felt newly restored. The heaviness weighing down my soul remained, but finally being cleaned of Laszlo's horrible touch lifted my mood somewhat. I would be lying if I said I was over it. No one moves past abuse like that in a matter of days. And while I prided myself on being a bad bitch, that fucker nearly broke me. In some ways, I suppose he did. He stole them from me, my mates. And before this final battle ended, I would ruin him for it. There was no world he could run to that I would not find him.

The mirror fogged from the heat of my bath, and I swiped the water from it, revealing the stranger staring back at me. The fiery red hair was so foreign to me. Did they have hair dye here? My aquamarine eyes stood out against the natural red of my hair. But it was the haunted look in them that captured my attention. This female was plagued with memories, guilt, and insecurities.

They say time heals all wounds, but does it truly?

"Knock, knock," a somewhat familiar voice called from the bedroom.

I wrapped a towel around my body and walked out to see Mihra leaning against the far wall. Crossing my arms over my chest, I stared at her, waiting.

She spoke first. "Brought you a couple dresses. You seem more of the leather pants type to me, but this event is more formal."

I eyed the dresses laid out on the bed. One was a deep red with black beading. The next was midnight black with silver stones sparkling on it like stars. And the final dress was a deep shade of indigo. It was made of silk and lace, with multiple cutouts to show off my curves. Walking slowly to the bed, I picked up the indigo dress.

"That one was my bet." She smirked.

It was beautiful, and I would look hot as hell in it. "Well, at least you have good taste."

She laughed. "You know I do. Considering who I was crushing on."

The reminder of her desire for Phen had my eyes narrowing. "He. Is. Mine. And I'm not afraid to cut a bitch."

Mihra shoved off the wall, and I held my ground, trying and failing to look tough in my fucking towel and wet hair. She was taller than me by a couple inches, but I was trained and would unleash the beast within if she pushed me.

And then she dropped to her knees before me, bowing. "He is yours. And so am I. If you'll have me."

Well this was a turn I did not see coming. "Have you in what way, exactly?"

Her gaze snapped up to mine then lowered, taking in my curves. "In whatever way you want, my queen."

Fuck. Heat pooled in my belly, and I resisted the urge to squirm. Of course I was loyal to my mates, but fuck if it wasn't hot as hell having this sexy daemon female offering herself to me.

Reaching down, I placed my hand under her chin and pulled her to her feet with my gentle touch. My claws extended slightly, and I traced them down her pretty throat. She swallowed, her eyes glowing with power and lust.

"I'll keep that in mind," I purred. "For now, I need your help with something."

She smirked. "Anything."

"Is there hair dye on this planet?" I asked, tugging my wet locks. "I miss my blue hair and the red just doesn't feel right."

Mihra laughed. "No hair dye, but your considerable power can easily manage a glamour. You can change it to any color you like."

I grinned. Finally, some good news. "Excellent. Then you can teach me how to do it, and let's get ready for the main event."

She tipped her head down. "As you wish, my queen."

Her words sent a shiver down my spine. I could get used to being called a queen. And fuck, I needed my princes, because Mina was on the prowl.

Phenex arrived exactly two hours later, just as he said he would. And his reaction when Mihra opened the door to let him in was everything I needed.

His horns spiraled out of his hair, and his fangs snapped out. His silver-gray eyes glimmered with power. He growled low and stalked toward me like the monster he was. My thighs clamped together, and his gaze caught the movement. He grinned, his fangs looking hot as hell on his stupid sexy face.

"*Mini monstra*, you're breathtaking. I could eat you up," he purred, his claws teasing along my exposed cleavage.

I swatted his hand away, and he snarled possessively. "Do not rip my pretty dress. Behave and I'll allow you to see me out of it later."

He chuckled, his smirk deadly. "I will hold you to that." Phen tugged a loose curl of my hair with a smirk. "I see you've returned to your icy tresses. My mate of fire and ice."

His comment melted my insides. While part of me loved my natural red, the icy blue suited my general mood. "Fire and ice. I like that."

We stared at each other with emotions swirling between us, not even realizing Mihra was still in the room. The broken bonds connecting my soul to his flickered, and for a single moment, I could feel his desire. His eyes widened, and I knew he felt it, too.

"I learned something today." He spoke softly, wrapping one hand around my waist lightly so as not to wrinkle my dress. "When we are all together again, I'll share."

My eyes dropped to the dagger with Dev's soul inside strapped to his hip. Phen was dressed impeccably in a black suit with a dark-gray shirt to match his eyes. His black hair was loose and wavy brushing against his broad shoulders. I wanted to rip his clothes away and lick every beautiful, colorful tattoo on his body. It was the note of something in his voice that held me back, kept me grounded.

And it was hope.

CHAPTER TWENTY-ONE
Michaela

A mini tornado spun furiously in my outstretched palm. My command over air was significantly better than the other elements. My connection to water was almost as strong. The other two elements were more difficult. Lumens tended to lean into the former and daemons the latter. Luckily for me, I had a daemon mate, and through our bond, more access to those elements. It was a challenge, but in those moments when our souls connected and our thoughts merged as one, the power was insane. The rush of it through my body was almost as delicious as Mor's mouth on my—

"Your aura is wild right now," Nuri snarked, sneaking up on me.

The mini tornado spun away, tearing a path through the grass before dissipating. My cheeks flushed at the dirty thoughts I was leaning into when she showed up. Flashes of memories that weren't my own appeared in my mind.

"Lailah was jealous of your natural ability to read auras. She was always trying to gauge yours." The words slipped from my lips without thought.

Nuri's silence was heavy with emotion before she spoke. "I miss her." Clouds appeared overhead, and a flash of lightning charged the air around us. "We will be together again, someday. I know it."

Another vision chased the stolen memories, this one of the future. I sucked in a sharp breath, and Nuri eyed me curiously. But I couldn't tell her what I saw. Delphine warned that visions of the future were not set in stone. They changed just as the actions of those around us changed. If I told everyone what would happen, it wouldn't come to be. There was something I could say, though, a hint to follow the right path.

"The Kings and Belial hold a piece of her. There will be a moment, and I can't say when or how, but you'll find it." I slumped forward, exhausted. The visions took so much from me still.

Nuri wrapped an arm around my waist to keep me sitting upright. "I will find it and kill everyone who stands in my way."

I sighed. She would, but what it would cost her a price I didn't know if she would be willing to pay. The earth shook when my mate dropped from the sky in front of us. He knelt before me, brushing his rough hand on my cheek.

"Are you unwell, little lumen?" His voice was laden with concern. "I felt your power wane."

Nuri released me into my mate's care, and I nuzzled into him. "Just the visions tiring me out. I don't know how I'm going to be useful when this Seer power wears me out so quickly."

"Your mother told Lailah she had to fully embrace it. When she fought against the power, it fought back." Nuri spoke quietly, her eyes gazing into the stormy skies.

An irritated huff escaped my lips. "I'm not trying to fight it. It's just...a lot."

Morax threaded his fingers with mine, dwarfing my hand in his. "You are strong enough to master this new magic, Michaela. What is it that stops you from doing so?"

Having a mate who could literally read every emotion flowing through you was sometimes a nuisance. But he was right. I needed to face this.

"I'm afraid of it. Whenever the visions of the future come, I force them back. I don't know if I can survive visions of the people I love dying."

Morax tugged my body close to his, sitting along the stone wall near the cemetery of the ones we'd already lost. He turned my chin up and forced me to look into his eyes. "My love. You are stronger because of your love for others. Use that strength, that love, to guide you through the visions."

"He's not wrong," Nuri added, her face a mask. "Once Lailah accepted it fully, it was like pure power buzzing in her veins. She looked like a goddess, unleashing her true power on those assholes."

I closed my eyes, memories appearing at her words of their night under the stars, and then Lailah's final moments during the ritual. The power Lailah and our mother harnessed in that moment was astounding. And it saved us all.

"If she hadn't done what she did"—I reached for Nuri—"none of us would be here now, and the Kings would be ruling at Belial's side."

Nuri nodded. "I know."

Morax squeezed my hand gently in his. "And we will honor her sacrifice now, doing what we can to bring an end to that ridiculous cult. And my brother."

"And your father?" Nuri arched a brow at him. "He's just as terrible."

I watched his face, seeing the uncertainty in his eyes. "You don't agree?"

Mor sighed, his golden eyes glimmering in the light of the setting sun. "Sometimes I have these memories of him being caring and fatherly. But they seem more like fever dreams. And in the days before you summoned me, he disappeared. Belial claimed father was in seclusion, gathering power. But something about it didn't sit well with me."

Nuri stood suddenly. "Well, we'll find out soon enough. And if he sucks, I'll kill him for his part in my mate's death."

Morax nodded curtly but said nothing more about it. It was a difficult thing to comprehend, that someone as good as Mor or even Phen could come from someone so cruel. I tried to see King Corson with my new power, but the visions were blurred and confusing. Something was definitely off about it.

Several sets of footsteps approached, and we stood beside Nuri as Delphine, Grem, and Tibby walked toward us. The Princes mated to my sister were not far behind. Well, they were her mates, but the bonds were all mangled. I hoped to see a way around the broken bonds, but so far, this Seer power only gifted me with visions of random scenes. The ability to force a theme hadn't worked for me just yet.

Delphine stopped, hands on her hips and an air of authority about her. "It's time. The masses are gathering. When the moon is at its highest point, we will all return to Stella Terra."

The energy buzzing through our group was palpable. I'd always dreamed of returning to my mother's home. Seeing where Lailah played in the ocean, where Morax grew into the man I fell in love with. There was so much of this new world in me, and I was ready to experience it firsthand.

CHAPTER TWENTY-TWO
Typhon

The thought of having Seraphina back in my arms was driving me mad. I missed her so fucking viscerally it hurt. The pain of her being stolen away by Laszlo and Samuel was nothing compared to the terror we felt when our bonds broke. I'd never experienced heartbreak like that. It was more than a broken heart, it was as if someone carved out a piece of my soul and took it away. My own pain was mirrored on the faces of my brothers, and I knew it was happening to all of us. The mate bonds tying us to Seraphina were ripped to shreds.

Andras turned to Delphine for answers, but she had none. Her own ability to see glimpses of the future was minimal. No one, not even Morax, had heard of a way to restore a broken mate bond. But I refused to give up. Whether we were bonded or not, Seraphina was mine. Andras, Dev, Levi, and even Phenex, belonged to me. We belonged to each other. We would get our girl back, one fucking way or another.

"You're louder than a damn bull in a china shop out here, Ty." Levi chuckled, leaning against a tree.

I'd wandered into the woods after Delphine's little speech, needing some space. But my sweet brother could never give me that.

"You're so clingy, brother," I teased. "Find your way back to the others and let me brood."

"What's that, Dev?" Levi cocked his head in mock confusion. "Oh sorry, I got you confused with our moody prince. But he's soul searching."

I rolled my eyes at his terrible joke and crossed my arms, leaning against a wide oak tree. There was just enough sunlight to see Levi's navy eyes dragging down my form. His sandy brown hair caught a breeze and drifted across his face. I had the urge to reach out and brush it away but remained still. He was all swagger as he walked toward me. His biceps rivaled mine, nearly. Levi was a firefighter, after all, and spent almost as much time in the gym as I did.

"You're hot as hell when you get all broody like this," Levi taunted. "Seraphina would be dripping for you, if she could see you now."

My dick hardened at his words. I missed her perfect pussy so gods damned much. Levi stepped closer, and I snatched my hand out, tugging him against my chest by the belt loops of his jeans. "Would she now?"

Levi licked his lips, and I tracked the movement hungrily. "Mhm." His hands brushed over my abs.

I reached out with my other hand and wrapped it around his thick throat. "And are you dripping for me too, Leviathan?" My voice was the deadly purr of a predator aiming to trap its prey.

His eyes dilated at my words. "Always."

A satisfied growl built in my throat at his response. Levi was too fucking sexy for his own good, and my cock was in desperate need of attention. Would Seraphina want this? She seemed eager as fuck for us to pleasure each other when we had the most epic gangbang of the century. But did she want us to enjoy each other even when she wasn't around? Seraphina was the love of my fucking soul, but so were my brothers. It was all or none. And right now, I needed Levi.

As if he could read my thoughts still, Levi dropped to his knees and slowly unzipped my jeans. He tugged my dick out roughly, and I grunted at the treatment. I liked it rough, and Levi knew me so fucking well.

"If she could see us now, our mate would be fucking begging me to suck your cock." Levi did not fucking stutter, nor did he wait for a reply.

His lush lips wrapped around the swollen head of my cock, and he leaned forward until it hit the back of his throat. I groaned, reaching down and tangling my fingers in his soft hair. He bobbed gently, teasing. But I needed more. Tugging at the base of his neck, I held his head in place and slammed my hips forward, fucking his beautiful mouth. He moaned around my dick as I used him for my own pleasure.

"Fuck, Levi. You look so fucking good on your knees for me." The words ground out of me, and I was relentless.

His hands wrapped around my thighs and squeezed. Levi's dark-blue eyes glistened with tears as I stole his ability to breathe. But his mouth wasn't enough.

"I need to fuck you, baby boy," I snarled, pulling back and releasing my hold on him.

Levi licked his lips and grinned. "Fuck yes. Call me your baby boy and you can have me any way you like, monster man."

My heart swelled when he spoke the nickname Seraphina had given me. I loved this fucker so much and needed him to know it.

Levi undressed quickly, his thick cock springing from his briefs and dripping with pre-cum. I curled my finger, beckoning him forward. He obeyed, which elicited a satisfied rumble in my chest. Gripping the back of his neck, I shoved him into the massive oak tree face-first. Using a bit of power, I pulled water from the dewy grass and wet my dick with it. That was all the warning Levi got before I pressed the head of my dick to his tight ass and thrust forward. His loud groan of pleasure was music to my fucking ears.

"Fuck, Ty. Fuck. Fuck." He moaned, cursing over and over.

"Yeah? You're taking me so well, Levi," I groaned in pure ecstasy. "So fucking tight. Just like our girl."

Levi mumbled incoherently as I fucked him harder, slamming into his sweet ass over and over again. He started to reach for his dick, and I snatched his wrist, pulling his arm behind his back and locking him down.

"No, baby boy." I nipped at his neck. "You don't touch. Only my cock and my touch get to make you come."

Levi groaned. "Yes, fuck. I need to come."

His quick compliance made my damn dick throb with pleasure. I reached around with my free hand and fisted his cock. His moans grew louder as I stroked him, brushing my thumb over his slit and smearing his dick with pre-cum. Levi's ass puckered, and I groaned, returning to the punishing pace, bringing us closer to release. Seraphina's aquamarine eyes and ruby lips appeared in my mind. She smirked at me, edging me on and praising Levi.

The broken bond shimmered within me. I gasped, and Levi jerked forward, crying out as he came for me. I pounded into him until I found my own release, the glimmering of our broken bond sending me over the edge. As I pulled out slowly, a satisfied growl built in my chest at the sight of my seed dripping down his leg.

"Did you feel it? The bond?" Levi's breathing was shallow from exertion.

"Yes." I nodded as we dressed quickly. "It came alive for a moment. I saw her in my mind and for a split second, we were connected."

"I saw her, too." Levi's blue eyes widened, and he grinned. "She was totally into us fucking,"

By the time Levi and I returned from the woods, the clearing next to Vespertine Hall was packed with creatures. We walked through the crowd, our power at the ready if needed, but these were not enemies. My chest swelled at the thought of so many creatures coming to war with us. I spotted a familiar face and pushed through several males to get to him.

"Ty!" James smiled, and I embraced him. "Good to see you, brother."

"You, too." I smirked. "See you've been gathering the troops."

He nodded, shoulders straightening with pride. "The Umbra Noctis are ready for battle."

Hope bloomed within me at his words. This war was going to be unlike anything we'd ever fought, considering the creatures we'd be facing. But our side wasn't weak, either. Levi clasped hands with James in greeting. A tiny flare of possessiveness buzzed through me, and I pinched Levi's forearm to rein him in. He grinned and winked at me like a jackass. My eyes narrowed to let him know he'd be punished for that soon.

I'd line his ass up right next to Seraphina's. Ten slaps to hers for thinking she could break our bonds and leave us again. And ten for Levi for thinking he could embrace another man besides me and his brothers. Fuck, I was half hard again. This little plan to get us to Stella Terra better work, because I was desperate for my girl.

CHAPTER TWENTY-THREE

Andras

My usual calm and collected demeanor was close to shattering. It was finally time for us to go to Stella Terra. I'd be lying if I said I wasn't intrigued. Our fathers spoke of this world often, as it was always their goal to get there. To meet the daemon king, Corson Ormaenus, and be granted true power for their loyalty to his crown. Of course, my father would never bow for another king, and I knew he had more deviant plans.

After all these years, all the abuse and manipulation, the devastation our fathers forced upon was coming to an end. I closed my eyes, searching for the bond connecting me to the only woman I'd ever fallen for, but whatever power connected us was silent. Fury coursed through my veins. I knew my father was part of this. Seraphina was the strongest creature I'd ever met, but even she could break under the right amount of pressure. *It was our fucking fault.*

"Yes, brother, it is." Typhon's deep voice rumbled as he approached. "We will make it right."

Levi appeared at Typhon's side. "This is not our fault, you melancholy man babies."

I arched an eyebrow at Levi just as Typhon wrapped a muscular arm around his throat. Levi was hardly intimated by the brute, letting the heavily tattooed brother of ours manhandle him.

"Are you looking for more punishments?" Typhon snarled.

Levi grinned. "If you mean funishments, then yes." He shoved out of Typhon's grasp and danced out of the way of the monster's swinging fists. "And I'm serious. This is not our fault. Nor is it hers. The amount of physical and mental torture our girl must have endured to get to that point has me seeing red."

That fury threatened to boil over at his words. I'd barely slept since she was taken. Images of what they were doing to her flooded my mind every time I closed my eyes.

Levi clasped my shoulder, forcing the images away. "But if anyone can turn pain into power, it's Seraphina fucking Valdis. And whether or not we are bonded by some crazy magic, she is ours. Now and always."

I reached out and tousled Levi's wavy brown locks. "Since when did you become so well-spoken?"

Levi smirked, his navy-blue eyes lighting at my praise. "Someone has to be the clever one in this gloom. And now that it's just myself and grumpy and grumpier, I gotta do something to keep morale up."

Typhon punched Levi's bicep, but with less strength than before and a deadly smirk on his face. "We'll get her back. Even if only one tiny scrap of her soul remains intact, we'll get her back and make it right."

The words of my brothers lit a fire fueled by determination and hope. And as the moon rose into the night sky, I knew their words rang true.

We stood shoulder-to-shoulder, nearly five hundred strong. It was almost dizzying, the number of humans and creatures gathered here, ready and willing to go to war.

The Umbra Noctis made up about two-thirds of those gathered. We'd trained them to fight. Ensured they studied daemons and lumens and witches to know their powers, strengths, and weaknesses.

The others were brought in by Delphine and Nuriela. Both had spent years gathering any who wished to fight against Belial and King Corson. Many had lost loved ones to the Daemon King and his vile son. When Aurora closed all avenues for beings to travel between worlds, families were eternally separated. Delphine and Nuriela ensured those detained on Earth understood why the lumen queen did what she did. With her sacrifice, and Lailah's, Belial and Corson were forced to regroup, and we were given time to grow our armies.

"It is time." Delphine spoke, her voice level and carrying across the silent field. "When we arrive, we should be within a few miles of Liboteria. The truxens will know instantly. Do not use magic, draw weapons, or anything else that seems remotely threatening. The truxens are our allies, but they trust no one. Let's not give them a reason to distrust us."

"Will Seraphina be there?" Michaela asked, her voice steady. The determined look on her face was so much like her sister's. "I saw her in a jungle."

I may have doubted her strength at first, but seeing the work she put into honing her power and training with the new Seer magic was commendable.

Delphine nodded. "I've seen bits of her in the jungle and the city. I'm confident Phenex found her and brought her to the city. And I think if she was…gone, we would know."

"She lives," Typhon growled, power radiating from him in waves.

Gremory snarled back at him in defense of his mate. "Watch it, young blood."

Typhon grinned, the sight anything but comforting, and I sighed, stepping closer to my unruly brother. "With or without the mate bond, we would know if she were gone. And our connection to Phenex and Dev still pulses with life."

Delphine nodded. "I agree, she lives. Our fates would have changed drastically if she didn't. Michaela would see it as well." She turned away from us and stepped closer to Michaela. "With our blood combined and the words I've taught you, we will begin."

Morax pressed in close behind his mate, his hands resting on her slim waist. Delphine produced a dagger, and Michaela presented her palm without hesitation. The youngest daughter of Aurora began chanting, and Delphine mirrored her, their blended voices rising like the crescendo of a song. The air around us vibrated with power, growing so thick that I could taste the magic on my tongue. A weightlessness took over my body, and the world around us began to fade.

Power hummed in my veins, and suddenly we were surrounded by an endless night sky. The stars twinkled as we passed through the plane of our world and into a new one. It was over in seconds, and suddenly my feet slammed into solid earth. Typhon caught my forearm, steadying me.

"Oh, Toto—" Levi started, but I slammed my hand over his mouth.

"Leviathan. I will punch you in the mouth if you quote *Wizard of Oz* right now," I huffed, rolling my eyes. The man was a cinephile, and it was one of his favorites.

Levi's tongue pressed into my fingers, and I snatched my hand away, wiping his saliva on Ty's short sleeve T-shirt.

"When this is over, movie night at the Towne House." Levi smiled.

A ghost of a smile touched my lips, and even Typhon joined. The idea of a movie night at our home with Seraphina wrapped in our arms sounded like pure heaven.

"Bow before the future king and consort of Belfegor's heir!" a voice boomed over us, and my heart leapt with relief. Even if he was an asshole for announcing himself like that.

CHAPTER TWENTY-FOUR

Leviathan

Before I could stop myself, or Ty could hold me back, I leapt into the air. My wings snapped out, and I dove for the daemon prince. A dozen truxen daemons produced weapons and prepared to take me out, but they weren't fast enough.

My arms wrapped around Phen's waist, and we tumbled to the earth. He grunted, taking the brunt of our combined weight as we fell.

"You fucking bastard," I purred, pressing my nose into his neck and drinking in his scent. "Didn't realize how much I would miss you. It's been dreadfully dull with the grumpy twins."

Phen's hands circled my waist, pinching and teasing enough to make my dick half hard. He chuckled. "Hmm, I can feel how much you missed me, brother. But perhaps we save that sort of play for later."

Strong hands ripped me off Phen from behind, and I knew it was Ty. "Keep it in your pants, baby boy," he murmured in my ear, a possessive edge to his tone that did nothing to lessen my hard-on.

Andras helped Phen to his feet just as Michaela ran to us. "Where's my sister?" Morax was a step behind her, as always.

Phen grinned, and happiness flooded my veins. "She's in the palace, getting ready for tonight. There's a big welcome party for her. And for all of you." He gestured to the masses.

Andras arched a brow and slid his hands into the pockets of his suit pants. "You knew we'd be here?"

Phen laughed. "Of course. These truxens are a tricky bunch. All kinds of nifty magic." He pointed toward the road to the east. "There's a camp ready for the army that way. Don't worry, it's not like how the mortals on Earth camp. It's fancy as hell."

Several of the daemons behind Phen peeled off to greet our people and guide them to the camp. We stayed behind, along with Michaela and Mor, Delphine and her mates, and Nuri and Lo.

Morax stepped in front of us to greet his brother. They clasped forearms and nodded, communicating without spoken words until Mor broke the silence. "My mate needs to rest and recoup. Do we have rooms?"

Phen smiled and nodded, shoving Morax aside and embracing Michaela. "Thank you for bringing the army and my brother here. Even though I know his eyes are filled with growly fury right now."

Michaela laughed, patting Phen's arm lightly and pulling away until her back was pressed to her mate's chest. I didn't realize how exhausted she looked until he mentioned it.

"Yes, Michaela and Delphine"—I nodded to the witch— "you females are bad ass as hell. There's no way we won't kick ass on the battlefield with powerful babes like you out there."

Phen chuckled, watching his brother seeth at my crass words. But Grem smirked, wrapping an arm around Delphine's curvy hips. "Powerful babes, indeed."

CHAPTER TWENTY-FIVE

Michaela

The exhaustion didn't reach me until we finally left the others. Morax supported my weight with ease, and I leaned into his side while we walked.

The palace was beautiful, with old world charm. I didn't travel around the world much, but I'd seen photos of Edinburgh, and the cobblestone streets and stonework reminded me of those pictures. It was beautiful.

Our rooms were located in a tower several stories high. The room was filled with beautiful tapestries and dozens of candles. A low-lit chandelier hung from the ceiling. I heard the water turn on as I gazed out the massive, curved window looking out over the city below. My mate's arms wrapped around me from behind, and I sighed, leaning into his comforting touch.

"You were brilliant back there, little lumen." His voice was filled with pride. Mor nipped at my neck. "Brilliant, sexy, powerful. I think I fell in love with you all over again."

His words seeped into my veins, and I could feel the truth of them in our bond. I could barely contain the smile on my face. Turning in his arms, I brought my own up and twined my fingers at the base of his neck. My toes barely touched the floor as I tried to reach him. Morax purred deep in his chest as he lifted me and wrapped my legs around his waist. His rough hands held my thighs, and my core lit with need for this daemon of mine.

He leaned down, and our lips met with fire and passion. My body melted into him, and my tongue sought his, needing the taste of him. A moan escaped my lips as he nipped my lips playfully. Arousal coated my skin, and my power hummed just below the surface. It was different here.

"Morax," I panted, pulling away. "My power, it's stronger here. It feels all tingly and barely controlled within me."

Mor leaned back, and his eyes went wide. "I can see that, little lumen. Your eyes are lit up with it."

My eyes widened, and I could almost feel the power radiating from them. "What does it look like?"

He brought one hand to my cheek, caressing softly. "It's like looking directly into the sun just as it rises over the horizon. The beauty and power within these eyes could bring the world to its knees."

Gods damn, this male had a way with words. I whimpered, the need for him bursting like a damn within me. "Mor. I need you."

My mate growled with desire and walked us toward the window until my back pressed against the glass. His mouth was on me instantly, licking, sucking, and biting every bit of exposed flesh he could find. The dress I wore was torn clean off my body, leaving me in a lacy blue bra and matching cheeky panties. Mor's claws trailed down my stomach, and I shivered. But he wasn't the only one who could tease.

Using my connection to his earth power, I turned his clothes to sand and grinned against his mouth when his flesh pressed into mine.

"Naughty little thing," Mor murmured against my lips. "Are you in a hurry?" His claws traced up my thighs, and his massive cock bobbed against my ass.

I wiggled in his arms and attempted to grab for him, but Mor was faster. He grabbed my arms and held my wrists with one hand above my head, securing me against the window. It was thrilling. Mor did not like others to watch, and the idea that someone could look up and see us was making my insides buzz with renewed arousal.

Another whimper escaped my lips when his clawed hand teased so close to my slick core before moving up my stomach. "You're a tease."

He chuckled. "You're the one wearing this edible lace. Is this for me? A gift to unwrap?"

I rolled my hips, shamelessly attempting to find friction for my aching center. "Sure. Yes. A present. Now rip into it and fuck me, mate."

Mor's eyes lit up like molten gold, and I grinned triumphantly. His claws tore through the lingerie with ease, leaving the pretty lace in pieces on the floor. He brushed his knuckle over my soaked core and growled possessively.

He pressed in closer, widening my legs and leaving me exposed. His hips rolled, dragging the head of his cock between my legs, teasing me once more. I moaned, humping his cock shamelessly.

"Tell me what you need, little doe," Mor purred, probing just enough to make me beg.

"You, Mor. I need every inch of you inside me," I panted, because it was true, and if he didn't take me in the next second, I might die.

His golden eyes twinkled with satisfaction, and his grip on my wrists tightened. Mor used his other hand to position his cock at my entrance and then slowly eased inside me. My head dropped back to the glass with a thud.

I moaned his name over and over as he thrust inside me, in and out, so achingly slow.

"Fuck, little doe," he groaned. "You're so fucking perfect. This tight cunt was made for me and only me. Look how well you take me."

My eyes opened at his command, and I looked where our bodies joined. He was so damn huge. I clamped down at the sight, and his answering sounds of bliss were almost enough to send me over the edge.

"I was made for you, and you for me." My words were soft and sweet, but I wasn't done. I needed him rabid. I leaned in and bit down on his chest, hard. He snarled, his dick throbbing inside me. When I pulled away, my teeth marks remained over his heart. I looked up at him, this monster of mine. "Now fuck me like you own me, mate."

The deadly sounds that bubbled out of his throat were intoxicating. A yelp escaped my lips when he suddenly pulled out and dropped me to my feet. In a matter of seconds, he pulled me away from the window and pressed my front into the exposed brick wall. My arms were still locked in his iron grip on my wrists. With his free arm, Mor lifted my hips and plunged his cock inside me. I screamed his name as he fucked me into oblivion. My bare chest scraped against the brick, and the hint of pain mixed with the pleasure of his cock hitting that perfect spot over and over was too much.

"Fuck. I'm coming. Fuck. Fuck," I moaned, my body shaking as the orgasm shuddered through me.

"You've got a filthy mouth tonight, little doe," Mor's deep voice teased, but his relentless pace continued. "I'm going to fuck the filth out of you after the party. So when you're being sweet and demure to all those strangers later, you'll be thinking about how I'm going to have you on your knees, taking my cock."

His hand slid between my thighs, and before I could protest, Mor pressed a finger inside me, alongside his cock, filling me further. His thumb went to my clit, rubbing circles slowly in contrast to his fast pace. This mate of mine was going to kill me with pleasure. And I'd die happy.

"Morax," I gasped between thrusts. "I fucking love you."

My mate leaned in and nipped at my ear. "I love you, too, mate. Now come for me. Squeeze my cock like a good little lumen while I fill you up."

The combination of his words, his hands, and his perfect cock brought me to the brink once more. I shouted his name over and over as I came. My pussy clamped down around him. His pacing finally slowed as he pumped his seed inside me. My body gave out almost instantly, and Mor carried me to the bath.

We sat in the tub, nestled in each other's arms, until my fingers started to prune and he forced us to get out. I was more than willing to skip the party and spend the evening in his arms. But he reminded me Seraphina would be there, and the lust-filled thoughts dissipated. Seeing her was the next best thing.

Once more, we were being reunited after one of us being held captive by the damn Obscuritas Kings. But Sera was the strongest person I knew. She was a survivor through and through. And it was time we took those assholes down for good.

CHAPTER TWENTY-SIX

Seraphina

Phenex disappeared for almost an hour after walking me into the party. And while I was enjoying meeting lost relatives and the many creatures my father spent time with, I was getting restless. Small talk and parties weren't really my thing. If I hadn't destroyed our bonds, I'd be cussing him out right now for leaving me here. So until then, I'd cuss him out in my head and tell him about it later.

Nervous energy buzzed through my veins, and I flinched when someone's arm brushed against mine.

This event was a little too similar to the one I attended recently, locked in a cage. Just the thought of it brought other memories to the front of my mind, and my skin flushed with rage and shame. The air around me grew heavy and cloying. It was too much. I walked as quickly as I could, without drawing curious eyes my way, to the nearest exit. Cool night air caressed my heated flesh as I sucked in several long breaths, but it wasn't enough. Belial's voice whispered in the corners of my mind, and Laszlo's touch lingered on my body.

In all my years plotting and planning my revenge, I knew there was a possibility of sexual assault. Going up against some of the most vile and dangerous monsters like the Obscuritas

Kings naturally put me in harm's way. I honed my body and my mind, preparing for any situation. Except for this one. The one where those fuckers and the daemon were able to shatter me so thoroughly I consented to my own destruction. It was my words that gave them the ability to break the bonds. It was the fight in my eyes that provoked Laszlo to finally force himself on me.

In the end, the rift, no, the fucking chasm between my soul and those of the men I cared for more than anything was my fault. Salty tears burned the backs of my eyes, and I looked to the stars, begging for the forgiveness I didn't deserve.

A vibration in the air was all the warning I had before muscular arms wrapped around my middle from behind. Rough hands clamped down on my mouth before I could scream.

"As much as I love to hear you scream, Seraphina," Ty purred into my ear, his lips brushing against my exposed neck, "let's save that bit of fun for later."

Purest happiness filled my soul at the sound of his voice. I elbowed him in the stomach, and as soon as his grip loosened, I whipped around and slammed him to the ground, my knife at his throat. Leaning down, I pressed my lips to his, kissing slowly before biting hard enough to make him bleed. "You found me."

Ty threaded his calloused hands into my silvery blue hair, tugging hard. "I'll always find you, mate bonds or not. I told you that, pet. If I have to chase you across all the worlds to bring you back to us, so be it."

My gaze slipped from his at the mention of the bonds and the rift I created.

He gripped my hair harder, forcing me to look at him. "You listen to me, Seraphina Valdis. We know you did whatever you had to do to survive, and none of us hold it against you."

Shame burned my cheeks, and I shook my head, the tears already in my eyes falling on his perfectly ferocious face. "But I didn't. I wasn't strong enough to keep them out of my mind. My body."

"*Belle femme*," Andras whispered, his voice filled with more emotion than he normally allowed. He pulled me from Ty's arms, and I let the dagger clatter to the stone balcony. His dark eyes sparkled with relief as his hands roamed my body, as if needing to feel me to know I was really there.

The memory of his father's hands on me slammed into my head, and I choked back a sob. Apparently, we were all getting emotional at this reunion.

Andras caressed my cheek. "When you're ready, I want to know what he did to you. Every single detail of my father's abuse against your mind and body. Give me your hurt, angel. Let me carry the burden. And when we see him again, we will cut him to pieces together."

His words were laced with fury and pain.

I shook my head. "It was my fault. I—"

"Don't you fucking dare, Sera." Levi cut me off, coming to stand at Andras's left shoulder. "I know what it's like to have memories planted and your mind invaded. You're the strongest creature I've ever known, but no one can be that strong all the time."

Phen walked out of the shadows and joined us. My men surrounded me as one, creating a cocoon of love and safety.

"I know how strong my father's ability to manipulate minds was," Levi continued. He spoke softly, a dangerous edge to his voice. "And you were surrounded by monsters with abilities even more powerful than his."

Phen nodded. "That you are as fierce and fiery as always only shows that they did not break you. Cracked your armor, perhaps, but you are not broken, my queen."

I sighed, absorbing their words. "I can still hear Belial in my head. Still feel Laszlo's hands…"

Even without the mate bonds, the rage coming off my men in waves was impossible not to feel.

Ty spoke first. "I will cut off his fucking hands and watch him bleed out at your feet."

"You hold him down, and I'll do the cutting," I snarled.

Phen smiled, but it didn't touch his eyes. The anger in his silver gaze pierced my broken heart. "We will make it so. Now, how about some good news?"

We turned to Phen, and I remembered his words from earlier. "Oh, yes. What is the secret you were keeping earlier?"

Phen crossed his arms, muscles bulging in the short-sleeved white shirt he wore. "Well, there is a way to restore our bonds."

"Hell yeah!" Levi shouted, punching Ty in the arm, which earned him an elbow to the gut.

Phen grinned, smacking Ty on the opposite arm. "My thoughts exactly. Just one teeny tiny problem."

Andras rolled his eyes. "Of course. Out with it, daemon prince."

I slipped from Andras's arms and into Phen's, hope blossoming within me. There was a way to fix the mess I caused. Phen's arms circled my waist, and he nuzzled into my neck. He smelled of the jungle, and desire surged through me as I remembered our moment alone. And the dagger.

I shoved off him and grabbed the beautiful dagger sheathed at his waist. "Phenex. Bring Devon back, right fucking now. The rest can wait until we're *all* back together."

Pulling me back into his arms, Phen plucked the dagger from my hand and tossed it to Ty. He caught it easily, brushing his thumb over the red jewel pulsing with Dev's essence.

"Come on, then." Phen smirked. "We'll be bringing our beautiful brother back into his body with the help of your father's family."

CHAPTER TWENTY-SEVEN
Delphine

I held out the drawing to the lumen queen. She was beautiful, radiating with power. It was difficult to guess her age, considering how much longer lumens lived than witches. We had longer than average lives, but lumens could remain young and beautiful for thousands of years.

Aurora Valdis looked up from the drawing in confusion. "Who is this child?"

Even as a teen, my power to see things happening in the future was strong. And I knew it was accurate. "The child is yours."

She brushed her fingers over the portrait. "She does not look like Adriel."

I nodded. "She comes from another. Not of this world. And this one." I handed her another drawing. "She comes before the girl with mis-matched eyes. Soon."

Aurora's face dropped for a moment, but she recovered quickly, hiding her emotions away. "They do not share the same father."

It was a statement, and I only nodded.

The queen sighed, the weight of so many lives resting on her shoulders. "You are strong, young witch."

This time, it was my turn to sigh. "Not strong enough. When the final moment comes, I won't be there."

Aurora smiled sadly. "Neither will I. But if the ones we love most are safe, it will all be worth it."

I huffed in annoyance. "Can't say I'm quite that evolved yet."

The queen's eyes twinkled with mischief. "Meeting your mates will change your tune. When you find them, you will be ready to sacrifice everything."

Her words sank in as she turned and walked away. I sucked in a breath. "Wait. THEM?"

But the queen didn't respond. Only her soft laughter filled the marble halls as she left me with that dramatic bit of information.

Having a rough idea of when you were going to die wasn't exactly a fun insight. But after we met Tibby, the memory of my meeting with the lumen queen all those years ago came rushing back. Not even meeting Gremory brought that memory to the surface.

"Stars above," I whispered with a sigh. It was as if my ancestors knew when I'd met my second mate that I would need that knowledge returned. Because the queen was right. I would sacrifice everything for them.

And knowing that my death would give them a future, with love and happiness to be found, I would die not happily, but comforted. A tiny, selfish part of my heart ached to know they would live on without me. Gremory and Tabitha were my everything. Was I not theirs?

Without realizing where my feet led, I'd wandered into the gardens, away from the party. They'd need me soon, to bring Devon back into his body, but not just yet. I plucked a rose from the bush, a thorn pricking my finger. Blood trickled down the stem until a single drop fell to the dirt at my feet.

"Returning your blood to your homeland so soon, Delphine Bellinor?" A voice I hadn't heard in ages chuckled from the shadows.

I turned to the old crone, bowing before meeting her gaze. Technically, because of my royal blood and status among the Mal-Regia, I wasn't required to bow to the Scribes. But Lahabiel was someone I admired. Her story was one of resilience and deserved respect.

"My blood was always meant to return to this world, one way or another," I murmured, bending down to stick the stem into the earth. Whispering a few words, I brought it back to life, a new rose bush growing around the cut flower.

She nodded. "Yes, but that is not what troubles you now."

Lahabiel was much too discerning for her own good. I held out my arm to her, and we walked the garden at her pace. "I know that I will leave them behind, but I worry for their future. There must be something I can do to ensure their survival."

"Nothing in life is ensured, young witch." She spoke somberly.

If the subject matter wasn't so depressing, I'd enjoy her nickname. Today, I felt anything but young. "True, but that doesn't mean we can't leave something behind to help the ones we love."

Lahabiel looked up at me, the wrinkles around her eyes crinkling as she smiled. She patted my hand affectionately. "There is one thing you can do."

She pulled a pouch from her pocket, and I emptied the contents into my palm, my lips parting at the rare object in my hand. A genuine smile graced my face. "Thank you, Lahabiel."

CHAPTER TWENTY-EIGHT

Devon

The moment Nuriela cut my throat, I truly thought my life was over. And then I was certain the afterlife was claiming my soul. I hovered above the people I loved, watching them lose their shit when my body dropped to the floor. But then Delphine tossed Phenex the dagger, and suddenly I was sucked into that bright-red stone. It wasn't consciousness, but something else. Like I was made of everything and nothing. I was a soul untethered.

And yet I could feel every damn emotion radiating from Phenex. He was a conniving shit and most definitely knew it, too. When he was fucking Seraphina in the jungle, his feelings of lust and dominance pulsed through the stone and seeped into my being. I'm sure he thought to make me jealous, but whichever part of my soul that lived in the stone was simply relieved to have her back.

When the other Princes joined us and our group was finally reunited, I could feel a steady thread of joy through each of them. We were bonded on a deeper level, one not even the breaking of mate bonds could truly sever.

And now it was finally time for me to join them back in my own body. I felt Seraphina's fierce soul so full of life as she cradled the dagger to her chest. When the blood of my brothers and my girl coated the blade, shining life grabbed my essence and ripped it from the stone.

My eyes snapped open, and I sucked in a breath, relief filling my mind when I could feel my body once more. The others leaned over my splayed form on the floor. Before anyone could move, I rolled to the side and punched Phen directly in the dick.

He fell to the floor, groaning. Ty laughed as I leapt to my feet and snatched Seraphina's waist, pulling her into my arms. She jumped up, wrapping her legs around my hips, and our lips met, a mess of teeth and tongues, eager and desperate for each other. She tasted like my salvation and my darkest desires. My beautiful mate moaned, and my dick pressed against my dark jeans, begging to fuck her.

I pulled away first, staring into her stunning aquamarine eyes. "I missed you so fucking much, *mera dil.*"

She smiled at me, a tempting thing, her fingers teasing the short hairs at the back of my neck. "Not as much as I missed you, Devon Parrish. We're never doing that shit again."

I grunted in agreement. "The next time we need a soul sacrificed, it's Phen's turn."

The jackass in question wrapped his arms around us both and licked my neck with his forked tongue. A shiver rippled through me at his touch, and my need to fuck Seraphina intensified.

"Let's get out of here before Dev turns us all into exhibitionists," Andras murmured at my side, pressing a hand to my back.

A daemon I didn't yet know clapped twice to get everyone's attention. My mind had zeroed in on my girl, and only now did I realize the massive throne room was filled with strangers, and some friendly faces.

"The party will continue in the catacombs. All are welcome!" the daemon called out, and merriment carried throughout the room.

"We can join the party, but if I don't fuck you in the next ten minutes, I'm going to lose my damn mind," I growled, nipping Seraphina's perfect pale flesh. I needed my mark on her body immediately.

She moaned, a sassy smile on her lips. "Yes, please. I need my princes all to myself for a little while."

Andras stepped in front of Seraphina, towering over her like a dark god, his eyes glittering with wicked intent. "And do you think you deserve pleasure, sweetheart? I have not forgotten. Punishments first, and if you beg prettily for us, only then will we let you come."

My dick thickened at the combination of his words and the lust in Seraphina's eyes. She smirked at him, running her nimble fingers up his chest. "I'll take my punishments like a good girl. Promise."

"Fuck." I groaned at the sinful voice of our girl.

We'd retreated to a deserted hallway, far enough from prying eyes, but the tension in the air was building and I was ready to explode in more ways than one. Andras snatched Seraphina's hair and tilted her head back.

"On your knees and open your mouth," he commanded, and she obeyed without protest. Andras spat down her throat and turned to us. "Remind our girl who she belongs to, brothers."

Seraphina's moans of pleasure as the five of us each took our place before her and spat on her tongue were fucking sinful. She was just as desperate and eager as we were for her. Andras ordered her to swallow, and she did, behaving like the good girl she rarely was. He smacked her cheek, satisfied.

"When we get to the room, you're going to strip, and take ten slaps to your perfectly round ass. From each of us." Andras's words were nonnegotiable.

Seraphina nodded, her cheeks flushed and eyes dilated. "Yes, sir." She spoke the words softly, as if she were the innocent flower she pretended to be. And while seeing her play along was doing things to my body, I couldn't wait for our perfect mate to let her own beastie out to play.

The orgasm that flooded my body was earth-shattering. Literally. Seraphina screamed my name in garbled moans, her mouth filled with Andras's cock. Her body bowed beneath mine, her sweet cunt squeezing me tightly as I filled her with my cum. She was exquisite, and I wasn't even sorry I didn't last quite as long as usual.

"My turn, Dev," Ty growled, ripping me away from her with ease. He was completely naked, his pierced cock bobbing as he gripped Seraphina's thighs. "Levi, clean up Dev's messy dick, won't you? I know you need that slutty mouth of yours filled."

Ty's words and Seraphina's lusty gaze on me had me half hard already. Levi shoved me on the bed beside her and dropped between my legs, biting my thighs and licking his way toward my cock, dripping with Seraphina's arousal and my own seed.

I groaned, threading my fingers in his hair. It was insane that these were the same men I once left behind, believing my time as one of the Princes was over. But these were my brothers in arms. The ones who knew my secrets, my shame, and my hopes. My bonded brothers. Never would I have guessed we would become intimate in this way. In my most hidden dreams, maybe, but it wasn't until Seraphina brought us back together that the bonds between us became so much more.

"Fuck, Levi," Sera whimpered. "You look hot as hell between Dev's thighs."

Phen circled the bed, coming up behind Levi and palming his ass. "Seraphina, my queen. Scream my name when Ty makes you come with his monster cock, will you? And I'll make Levi moan yours."

The room reeked of sex, and the air was thick with our heightened lust. Andras gripped Sera's hair and forced her to take his thick cock to the back of her throat, his pace matching Ty's.

Levi's mouth wrapped around my dick, and a needy sound escaped my own lips. He grunted when Phen entered his ass with his own punishing pace. The six of us moaned and murmured filthy words to each other, bringing us closer to the edge of oblivion. The second orgasm washed through me like a tidal wave, and the others moaned and praised each other. We were almost completely in-sync with our pleasure.

The suite we were given held a massive bed, bigger than any I'd seen before, and easily fit all of us. We lay there, breathing heavily and soaking in the pleasure.

"So," Phen drawled. "Now we can party. And then tomorrow, we journey to the mountains, get our mate bonds restored, and try not to die in the process."

The room went completely silent at his words.

Seraphina snorted a laugh, probably one of the cutest sounds I'd ever heard from her. "Fucking hells, Phenex. Way to be a mood killer."

He sprung up from the bed, naked and glorious—it would be a lie to say he was anything but beautiful with his muscles, tattoos, and freshly fucked hair.

"If anyone can survive a trip beneath Mount Monkara, it's us." Phen crossed his arms over his chest. "With the daughter of the only other daemon who came out from the mountain alive a few decades ago, we're destined to succeed."

Andras sighed audibly to my right. "Phenex, please explain in detail exactly what the fuck you are talking about."

He rolled his eyes. "Obviously I will. Now get your party clothes on, gang. My brother has something big planned for his lady, and we don't want to miss it."

CHAPTER TWENTY-NINE

Michaela

Morax walked at my side, his big hand wrapped around my own, as we made our way to the underground party. They called the tunnels winding beneath the mountainside city The Catacombs, and Morax said they resembled Paris, but apparently the daemons gave the French humans the idea. From the way the daemons and lumens tell it, almost nothing on Earth was an original idea. Creatures from all kinds of worlds had been leaving their mark there since the beginning of human existence. It was wild to think, and way too much to wrap my mind around. Especially with so many other more pressing things coming, like my sister preparing to leave with her mates on some magical quest to restore their bonds.

"Your inner thoughts are loud, little lumen." Morax chuckled. "Is that irritation I sense?"

"No," I huffed at him. "Not exactly. Maybe. It just doesn't seem all that important to repair mate bonds when we are literally about to go into battle. We need them here."

Mor squeezed my hand, bringing us to a stop in the dark tunnel. My eyesight was three times as clear, and I could see his perfectly chiseled face, even with the low-lit sconces on the walls casting shadows.

He pressed my back to the wall, leaned down, and pressed his lips softly to my forehead. His golden eyes glowed in the shadows, and he looked every bit the daemon prince. "Do you feel the connection between us? Not just the power, but the essence of your soul woven with mine?"

Of course, I could feel it. From the second our mate bond clicked into place, it was as if we were always meant to be linked. "You know I can."

Morax smirked down at me. "Now can you imagine the agony of losing that? I know if my connection to you broke, I would become a shell, an empty vessel never to be filled again."

His words brought ugly guilt to the surface. I was being insensitive to my sister and her princes. And if I was being extra honest, it wasn't just that. "You're right. I'm just scared. I'm scared of losing you and failing our friends because I'm not as strong as she is. She's a damn daemon and lumen hybrid. I'm barely a lumen."

My mate growled, his claws snapping out as he snatched my chin and forced me to look into his eyes. "You are not strong because you are half lumen, you are powerful because your soul is filled with light. You, my love, are the strongest creature because of what you endured and still came out of that darkness with love in your heart. And I will spend the rest of my days professing this until you believe it."

I smiled up at him, brushing my fingers over his sharp jawline. "You are such a sappy monster. Always saying such pretty things to me."

He growled, revealing sharp canines, and pinched my side with his other hand. "I'll whisper filthy things to you later, little doe."

Desire raced through my veins, and our bond pulsed with need. I bit my lip, and he ripped it from my teeth, capturing my mouth with his own. His massive body pressed into mine, blocking anyone from seeing me. My possessive and protective mate. I loved him so damn much.

Mor pulled away first, and a whine slipped from my lips. He chuckled. "Let's go to the party and enjoy our friends' company for an hour or two. Then I'm stealing you away for the night."

I smiled brightly up at him. "Deal."

The party was wilder than any rave I'd ever attended, and I'd been to my fair share of underground events. The iridescent bodycon dress I wore shimmered in the lights blinking in time to the beat of the song. My sister and I danced until my feet went numb and the worries of our tomorrows faded into the background. We were surrounded by friends who were becoming family, and hundreds of others loyal to our cause. The energy was infectious, building to a crescendo of epic proportions.

Muscular arms curled around my middle, pulling me close until I could feel the outline of my mate's hard cock against my backside. "Do you know how difficult it is to watch your body move like that and not bend you over and fill you up right now? The need to claim you in front of everyone is eating me alive."

I whipped around in his arms and reached up on my tiptoes to kiss him. "Everyone here knows exactly who owns my heart, my body, and my soul."

The music around us suddenly faded to the background, and I realized Morax created a bubble for us to hear each other. His expression changed, and his eyes stared into mine, ripping away any barriers I might have had left between myself and this creature of mine. Endless love filled my soul.

Morax slowly dropped to his knees, as if he were begging me for something. He was so much taller than me; even on his knees we were at eye level.

"I was lost in my own darkness before you summoned me. I wished for something to pull me back to the light. In the deepest corners of my soul, I wished for you." The world faded away as Morax spoke, until it was only him and I left in the room. A tear trickled down my cheek, and he brushed it away. "Our souls are entwined for eternity, but I'd tie my flesh to yours in every way as well. Michaela Valdis. Until we join the stars, will you be my wife?"

Tears fell from my eyes, and emotions welled within me at his beautiful words. I nodded, unable to speak, and wrapped my arms around his neck, pulling him in for a searing kiss. He kissed me back with every fiber of his soul. I mumbled I love you's between each kiss.

A shock of raw energy thudded against the cocoon Morax had created for us, and I sensed my sister's power on the other side.

I grinned like a kid on Christmas morning, pulling away from my betrothed. Mor barked a laugh when he noticed Phen licking the invisible barrier around us while my sister punched at it with her fist coated in ice.

"Okay, gods!" I shouted just as Morax dropped our barrier, and she ran at me, pulling me into a full body hug.

"Kaela, oh my fucking god, did you just get engaged?" She squealed and squeezed me until I nearly choked.

"Stop throttling my future wife, Seraphina," Mor grumbled but didn't pull her off.

The Princes surrounded us, clapping Morax on the back and offering congratulations. The word spread quickly through the crowd, and soon dozens were coming to congratulate us. And through it all, my future husband held my hand, refusing to let me go.

Chapter Thirty

Seraphina

My baby sister's engagement turned the rave into a wild celebration in seconds. I was so fucking happy for her, I thought my heart might burst. We needed something like this. The energy running through the crowd tasted like hope and happiness. It was so strong that I almost missed the dark mind slithering through the throngs of people.

It was strange, I'd never had the ability to sense minds outside of my mates, but something about this one stuck out, like I met this particular beast before. Scanning the masses, I stepped away from my sister and the line of people forming in front of her and Morax.

"What is it, Sera?" Dev asked, pressing his hand to my back.

My brows furrowed, and I shook my head. "I'm not sure. It's like I can sense something or someone in the crowd. And they feel…vile."

Dev frowned, craning his head around to get the attention of the other Princes. Within seconds, all five of them were at my back.

You can't trust them. They'll never take you back.

"Something isn't right. This creature is not one of ours," I murmured, knowing the superior hearing of the Princes would pick up my shaky tone.

Someone else crept through the throng of people, but Ty stopped her before she could get close to me. I grabbed his arm, tugging it away from the female. Partly because I trusted her, and partly because it irked me when any of my men touched another woman. "She's not the one I'm sensing, Ty."

Deccaria frowned, her gold dress shimmering in the lights as she moved to my side. "What are you sensing?"

I shrugged. "I'm not sure. It feels…familiar." There was a tiny voice in my head that screamed at me for not telling them everything.

Andras arched a brow and reached for me, but I stepped back. His eyes widened slightly, but otherwise, he kept his emotions hidden. The others didn't notice while they scanned the crowd for an enemy, but Deccaria saw the interaction. Her eyes darted between me and my dark prince.

Only the true leader of the daemons can give you what you seek.

"Fuck this," I snarled, closing my eyes and grounding my power within. *Whoever the fuck you are, I'm coming for you.*

As if you could fight me. I felt your lust for power. The voice was laced with desire, but I shoved the feeling away. It wasn't my own. Someone's fingers brushed across my back, and I shivered, bile rising in my throat. I recognized that touch.

Two razor sharp daggers appeared in my hands, and I whipped around, using air to aid me, spur me on. He was several steps away, but not far enough. And my wrath was stronger than his. He screamed the second I slammed my daggers into his back as I leapt on him. We fell to the floor. My uncle tried to form a block of ice as a shield, but my fury burned hotter.

Using my rage, I set fire to the daggers and stabbed again, and again, and again.

Strong arms snatched my waist, and I turned, ready to stab them too. My blade cut into Ty's hand, and a strangled sound escaped my body when I realized what I'd done.

But he didn't let go of me. With blood running down his arm, Ty held my waist firmly and cupped my cheek with the ruined flesh. "Seraphina. It's all right. Come back to me."

The others were there now, surrounding the mutilated lumen at our feet. He wasn't dead. My blades weren't made of stellatium, the only metal that could truly harm a daemon or lumen. And his wounds were already healing.

Soldiers were rushing in, wrapping the aforementioned metal around his wrists in the form of cuffs.

I barely registered any of it as Ty held me in his grasp. "Seraphina?"

He swiped his thumb across my cheek, and only then did I realize I was crying. "I'm fine."

"Who the fuck is he?" Levi growled, his body glowing with rage.

Phen was at his side, looking equally murderous, but it was Nuriela who spoke first, having arrived without anyone noticing.

"His name is Halphas." Her voice was soft, but the room was once more silent, the music cut off. "He is the brother of Adriel, Lailah's father. I never liked him. Seems he defected to the enemy."

"He was with Belial," I murmured. "He…pretended to be an ally."

Nuri sent a shard of ice into the groaning lumen's arm, and he shouted in pain. She was cold and calculating, standing over him. "You had a hand in my mate's demise. I'm going to destroy you."

The lumen's eyes widened. He attempted to reach up and touch Nuri, but she was faster. A second shard of ice slammed into his other arm, securing him to the floor. "Don't let him touch you. He has a strange power and can manipulate your feelings once he's laid hands on you."

Ty's hand on my cheek brushed away another tear, and he lowered his head, hazel eyes filled with understanding. "He convinced you to break your bonds."

Guilt burned through my insides.

"I wasn't strong enough to keep him out. I should have known." The energy rushed from my body at the admission and fatigue took over. I slumped into Ty's arms, and he scooped me up effortlessly.

"Please. Let me take her," Phen whispered, his voice needy.

Ty nodded and passed me into his arms.

Morax stood nearby with my sister tucked behind him, shielding her. He turned to the crowd. "This incident is a reminder that even here, we are not safe. If Halphas could find us here, others will already know. Belial will come with his army and destroy this place. We are out of time."

Murmurs rumbled through the crowd, and the energy in The Catacombs turned from joyous to dread. Morax wasn't finished.

He pulled Michaela to his side. "Tonight's events have shown us we must celebrate when we can, and prepare for the inevitability of war. At moonrise tomorrow, I will marry my mate. And then…let the revolution begin."

Shouts of hoorahs and a sense of unity washed through the room. I wanted to feel the happiness and determination of the others, but all I could feel now was my guilt. He came here for me; I led the enemy to my father's people.

I continued to fail those I cared for most over and over. Should I have stayed in the castle? Would they have been safe here if I remained Laszlo's prisoner? If I had the power Belial promised, maybe I would be strong enough to stop this war before it even began.

Andras threaded his hand in my hair and tugged my head back to look at him. I relished the pain of his hard grip, deserved it.

"Seraphina, your guilt is written all over your face, and I won't fucking have it." My dark prince raged. "It's time we got our bonds back. We're going under that mountain. As soon as your sister is wed, we're leaving."

Dev nodded in agreement. "Let's get those fuckers out of your head for good."

"What did I say about your tears, Seraphina?" Ty purred, squeezing my calf with his massive hand. "Only I get your tears. Every one that falls from your pretty eyes because of another, I will mark their death. Starting with this one."

Ty turned just enough to see Halphas and sent a blast of fire at him, starting at his feet. The piece of shit screamed in pain. No one moved, no one helped him. Ty wouldn't kill him yet, not when he could provide valuable information about the enemy. But his screams made me feel marginally better.

CHAPTER THIRTY-ONE
Phenex

The only thing keeping me from flying to Zamina Castle and strangling my brother with my bare hands was my mate in my arms. Her head lay gently against my chest, her body weighing no more than a feather in my arms. It was similar to that first night when she brought me to Earth through the ritual. When I felt her power, her beautiful dark soul calling to mine, I knew then she was meant for me. Even at her worst, she was defiant, sassy, and strong.

But not now. No, not this time. This was worse, her silence, her defeated face. That bastard fucked with her head, forced her to break her mate bonds, and somehow convinced her she wanted all of it. And that was not acceptable in the slightest.

We walked in silence to our rooms, the six of us. The night started with a celebration and ended with fury. Morax gave a pretty speech. Didn't realize my stoic brother had it in him. And it worked, a little. The spirits of our people were lifted at his words, but not ours.

Until our girl was back to her fierce and confident self, we would remain her guardians. It was collectively decided: Seraphina would never be without one of us. We would be there for her, a constant reminder that despite everything that happened in that fucking place, those assholes would not break us. And whatever horrors awaited us under that mountain, I'd face them all if it brought Seraphina back to us.

Seraphina stirred in my arms, and I held her close. "Need anything, my queen?"

"A scalding hot shower," she grumbled. "And the painful deaths of all my enemies."

Levi groaned. "Can this be a group shower? I think it would be a great bonding activity."

Several chuckles followed Levi's comment, and even Seraphina offered a sly little smile in my arms. Levi always knew how to make her smile, and I loved him for it.

"Phen, please," Seraphina moaned my name as I pumped my cock inside her in slow, languid strokes. The others watched, having filled our girl and given her so much pleasure she was nearly spent.

We started in the shower, not quite big enough for all six of us, but at least three. Andras and Dev joined her first. There was tension between Andras and our girl. He was almost hesitant, giving Dev commands first to tease her perfect body until her skin was flushed with desire. Only when she reached for him did he give in and fuck her so thoroughly against the shower wall.

Then Ty plucked her from the shower and tossed her onto the bed. She flopped like a ragdoll, her perfect tits bouncing and making my very hard dick ache for attention. I may have forced Dev on his knees and filled his mouth while I watched Ty ravage her. He pinned her down, taunting her with his filthy words and praising her when she took Levi's thick cock in her mouth.

I nearly came down Dev's throat, which was quickly becoming a favorite pastime of mine. He liked it just as much, even if he was still coming to terms with that feeling.

But I held back, forced my dick to wait for the tight little cunt only my queen could provide.

"I need to come, Phen. Please," she begged, and desire zapped through me like lightning.

Seraphina knew me so well. Knew how much I needed to hear her beg for me. To know she wanted me as much as the others, even when they stole her heart first.

I pressed my chest to hers, caging her against the wall of the bedroom. "Look at me."

Seraphina opened her aqua eyes and gazed into mine. As much as I loved when she followed commands, the fire behind those eyes was dimmed. But I would get it back.

"What do you want from me?" she whispered, wrapping her arms around my neck and threading her fingers in my dark hair.

"Everything, Seraphina," I growled. "I want your submission and your fire. I want all the pieces of your soul, even the ones you're ashamed of."

She tried to turn from me, but I snatched her chin in my hand and held her in place, thrusting inside her with more force. My queen groaned in pleasure, but her eyes remained guarded.

"It doesn't have to be tonight, but I will bring you back to us," I purred, fucking her deeply, feeling her body tighten around mine. "One way or another, my queen. My mate. Mine."

I held her there, pinned to the wall and forced to face my words as I fucked her into oblivion. Her eyes rolled to the back of her head and her perfect pussy squeezed my dick when she came. Seraphina screamed my name like a prayer, a desperate, hopeful prayer, and only then did I let go too.

CHAPTER THIRTY-TWO

Morax

I paced the rooms, anxiety flooding my veins. Michaela had not been out of my sights for more than handfuls of minutes ever since Belial and the Kings stole her sister away. She was almost stolen from me that night. My heart nearly cracked in two when I realized she was being taken, but she escaped. And the idea of being parted from her for more than a moment sent my mind tumbling into a rage I couldn't control.

The only reason I wasn't going completely mad being parted from her now was the mate bond. I could sense her happiness, her elation, and I wouldn't ruin that for her. Michaela was with her sister, preparing for our upcoming wedding. And she was safe with Seraphina. The crazy one might be a little damaged at the moment, but she was still the only being I trusted to keep my mate safe besides myself. The fact that the cult princes were hovering outside the room also helped.

"It's almost time, my domesticated brother!" Phen shouted at me, bursting into the room like a bull in a china shop.

"You know we have exceptional hearing, right? There's no need for all the shouting," I grumbled, but it was not nearly enough to tame my wild brother.

He smiled broadly, clapping me on the shoulder. "Yes, but sometimes it's just fun to be loud. Happiness is loud. Love is loud. Shout to the rooftops, Mor. It's your fucking wedding day."

Phen's joy was infectious, and I let it wash away some of my anxiety. Because he was right, love should be celebrated loudly, and Michaela deserved that. She deserved a day of pure goodness, and I was determined to give that to her.

It was a strange thing. I knew she was mine, body, mind, and soul. And yet, I needed to tie her to me in this way. Perhaps it was part of my primal need to claim her. She was my everything, and tying her heart to mine in this way meant more to me than I realized. I could only hope it was just as meaningful to her.

Phen reached out to toy with my tie, and I smacked his hand away. He wore a bowtie in the same bright-blue color as my tie. I chose it because the color reminded me of my mate's stunning sky-blue eye. And my cufflinks I created in a brilliant light brown with flecks of gold to match her other eye. My mate's heterochromia was mesmerizing, and staring into her eyes would never not enthrall me.

My wings and claws were out of sight for now, but with my anxious emotions still simmering, my horns remained out.

So were Phen's, but his were never not out. He cocked his head, staring at mine. "You're like a damned teenager. Can't even control your beastly side."

I shoved my shoulder against his. "Perhaps I'm just attempting to be more like my wild brother."

Phenex laughed, and I joined him in the merriment as we exited my rooms and made our way out to begin the ceremony.

Guards trailed us on our walk. There were hundreds of soldiers between the truxen army and the diaspora brought from Earth by the Obscuritas Princes. Everyone was on high alert now, ready for an attack at any moment.

Despite my speech, I didn't think Belial would come here himself, but he would send others to destroy these people, and he had plenty of monsters to aid him. Which reminded me of another.

"Is Halphas still alive, or did you kill him?" I arched a brow at my brother.

Rage clouded his silver eyes for a moment before he regained his composure. "He's alive. The truxens have him locked down tight. And Nuriela has been down in the dungeon torturing him regularly. That one is insane."

I sighed. "She is not insane. She's heartbroken. Lailah was her mate, and it does not seem she has another."

Phen nodded. "Yes. Although, if even one of mine were killed, I think I'd go insane as well. Having multiple mates doesn't make it easier if one is lost."

Squeezing my brother's shoulder, I paused in the hallway just before heading out to the ceremony. "I know, brother. And I believe you will bring your mates back together. If anyone can pull off something unheard of, it would be you."

Phen wrapped his arms around me, and we shared a long-overdue embrace. "You stay alive until we get back, alright?"

His words were spoken casually, but I understood the implications. We were going into war without several of our most powerful players. "Don't lose your head under that mountain, alright?"

We pulled away and clasped forearms with grim smiles. There wasn't much else to be said. And it was time for me to take a wife.

Standing by the floral archway waiting for Michaela to appear was quickly bringing my anxiousness back to the surface. It was only a few moments, but it felt like a lifetime. Music began to play, soft and slow, and suddenly, time stopped altogether.

She appeared through soft clouds, an angel come to save my blackened soul. My mouth dried up, and my heart nearly stopped at the sight of her.

Michaela wore a form-fitting gown made of lace and silk. The color was the palest shade of blue, even lighter than her sky-blue eye, and paired exquisitely with her fair skin. Her long, golden hair was piled high on her head, with soft curls framing her face. She was gazing at me with a brilliant smile, and it was impossible not to smile back.

The faces of our family and friends faded away, and only Michaela remained, shining like the brightest star, sparkling only for me. The aisle between us was decidedly too long, and I took three long strides, unable to wait to have her in my arms.

"Someone's in a hurry." She laughed softly as soon as I pressed her slender frame to my side. "You look fine as hell in a suit and tie, mate."

I pinched her side, and she yelped. "Watch that filthy mouth, little lumen. Or I'll be forced to spank my wife on our wedding night."

My dick twitched as soon as her cheeks flushed at my response. Her eyes dilated, and the beast within growled softly. This ceremony better be quick.

Scribe Lahabiel stood just beyond the floral archway as we approached. She wore silver robes, and her wolf-like eyes twinkled with amusement. "Let's hurry up and finish this before this horny male mounts his mate in front of all these witnesses." She chuckled.

The guests laughed, and one particularly loud whistle from Phen soared over the others. She wasn't entirely wrong, though. The Scribe began her monologue, reciting the words of the old gods, those who created our kind and gifted us with the afterlife among the stars. Michaela listened with rapt attention, being new to this world, but I was focused completely on her.

Labahiel wrapped our clasped hands in silk ribbons, and we each repeated the words to bind our minds, bodies, and souls as one. We did not say until death, as I have seen in the mortal ceremonies, for death is not the end.

"I give you my heart and my life. Now and always," I murmured the words, brushing my thumb against her racing pulse at her wrist. "And if the stars claim my soul before yours, I will wait for you among them. Now and always."

Tears welled in my wife's eyes as she repeated the vows. The mate bond hummed with life, shining through us nearly as bright as the stars in the sky. Our vows were accepted, and Lahabiel announced us, bound as one in this life and the next.

I couldn't wait a moment longer. Snatching Michaela into my arms, I crushed my lips to hers and claimed her once more for the world to see. She was mine. This brave, beautiful creature was bound to me in every way, just as I was to her.

CHAPTER THIRTY-THREE
Michaela

Power burned through my veins as soon as I repeated my vows. It felt like starlight in my blood, and the purest love radiated down our mate bond. It was damn euphoric. Scribe Lahabiel's quip about Morax taking me right here at the archway sent pleasure buzzing south, and I could see in his golden eyes he definitely wanted to do just that.

"So, is this like a thing?" I whispered to my now husband.

He cocked his head, brushing his thumb across my bottom lip. "Is what a thing, little lumen?"

Even the familiar nickname sent shivers of pleasure down my spine. I pressed up on my toes, barefoot under my dress now that the ceremony was over. "Being really horny after that ribbon thing."

Morax barked a laugh, sharp and surprised, his eyes glittering with mischief. "Hmm. Perhaps. Or maybe it is just something we share. Tell me, wife, is your sweet cunt dripping for me?"

He might have been more eloquent than I was, and better at the dirty talk, but I knew what he wanted. What he needed. I shoved away from him, taking several slow steps back. "Come find out for yourself, husband."

I registered the surprise in his glowing eyes but didn't wait for a response. Snatching up my dress, I ran for the forest using my elevated strength to push my legs faster. I could feel Morax behind me, but this wasn't going to be easy for him. Using my power, I dropped branches in his path and urged the wind to aid me, speeding away from him.

He cursed as a tree fell at his feet, forcing him to redirect. "You cannot hide from me, little doe," Morax snarled, his beast rising to the surface. "You are mine. And I always catch my prey."

A stupid needy whimper escaped my lips at his feral declaration. His laughter rang out in the silent forest, and it only increased the desire for him to catch me. But I could at least try to make him work for it. I used the wind to shove off the ground and leapt into a tree, standing nimbly on a thick branch among the dense leaves.

Morax came crashing by, not even pausing as he passed me. A smirk teased at the corner of my lips. I waited a few more minutes, but the forest was silent. My heart raced, the rush of the chase still coursing through me. Leaning forward, I bent my legs and pushed off the branch to descend.

Oh, was I a fool. Clawed hands snatched me back, one around my throat and the other groping my breast. I nearly screamed, but Mor gripped me too tightly for sound to come out.

"Did you think you were clever, little doe, hiding up in the tree?" Morax purred, his voice sinful. "As if I couldn't sniff you out. Your tight cunt is begging for my cock, and the scent is intoxicating."

His claws tore at my dress, ripping the pretty silk to shreds so he could reach my flesh. My husband growled at what he found.

"A gift for you, mate, unwrapped and ready to be filled," I panted, teasing him.

His hand slid through my arousal, claws raking over the sensitive skin between my thighs. I pressed back into his body, grinding against his hard-as-hell dick still trapped inside his pants. Mor bit down on my neck, and I moaned when his sharp canines broke the skin.

Closing my eyes, I reached back and threaded my fingers in the hair at the nape of his neck, pulling him closer. His other hand teased my clit, rubbing steady circles over the throbbing bud.

"Morax. My love. My mate," I moaned. "My husband. Please fuck me."

Mor pulled away from my neck slowly, licking away at the wound he made. "With pleasure, wife."

The world around us suddenly faded away, reality squeezing tight as Mor used his power to transport us somewhere new. I opened my eyes to see the city below us. We were on the roof of the tower where our rooms were located. Mor didn't give me time to adjust. He slashed at my dress, further destroying the beautiful gown until it fell to pieces at my feet. He ripped his own clothing off before I could assist. His eyes were wild, feral and desperate. Another needy whimper escaped my lips, because I was just as feral for the beast before me.

He strode forward and whipped me around to face the city below. "Hold on to the ledge," Mor commanded.

I'd only just gripped the stone when he kicked my legs apart, fisted his clawed hand in my hair, and thrust his thick cock inside me. We moaned as one at the feeling of our bodies finally joined after the chase. He set a merciless pace, his other hand holding my hip in a bruising grip. I relished the pain of it, the marks he was leaving on my skin, claiming every inch of my flesh.

"Who do you belong to, Michaela Valdis?" Morax growled, fucking me harder, deeper.

My nails bit into the stone as I held on for my fucking life, his cock hitting that perfect spot inside me, sending waves of pleasure through my body. "To you, Morax. My husband. My fucking mate."

A groan of pleasure escaped his lips. "I love hearing those words on your lips, *mae domina*. My queen." He thrust again and again. "Master of my heart and soul."

Pure bliss spilled through my body at his words, and when he thrust again, I clamped down on his cock, unable to stop the orgasm rushing through me. I screamed his name over and over.

Morax didn't give me any time to relish the feeling. The world dissipated once more, and we were in our rooms, my husband rearing over me. I wrapped my legs around his waist as he leaned over my body splayed out on the bed. He was inside me again in seconds, fucking me with raw, animal need.

"Come for me again, my love," Morax murmured, brushing his lips against mine as he spoke. "I need to see your face when you come undone."

I moaned at the combination of his words and the deep, slow thrusts. "I want to mark you, too."

A sexy-as-sin grin graced his face, and he leaned down, offering his throat to me. His hand slipped between my thighs and teased my clit, waiting for me to bite him.

My own sharpened canines pressed into his skin, and I slowly bit into my mate's flesh. His blood rushed to the surface and slid down my throat. I'd never taken drugs, but if I had, this must be what it felt like. His blood raced through my body like lightning, burning me from the inside out in the most indescribable way.

"Fuck. I love you, Michaela," Mor declared between thrusts.

"I love you, too, Morax." I screamed the words, close to the edge.

He smiled down at me, the beast snarling within. "Now come for me, wife," he demanded, and I obeyed.

CHAPTER THIRTY-FOUR

Leviathan

We were hiking the trail to some entrance at the base of the mountain like peasants.

"Why can't we fly there?" I asked for the third time, because I just wasn't satisfied with the answer.

"That's too easy," Phen responded for the third time. "This is a team-building activity. No wings unless absolutely necessary."

I eyed Seraphina's luscious ass and toned thighs, wrapped around Ty's back. "Why doesn't she have to walk, then?"

"Because I'm a lady." Seraphina turned back and winked at me. "Yah, horsey, yah!" She smacked Ty's thigh.

He growled, snapping his teeth at her. "Careful, pet. This stallion has no problem dropping you to all fours and mounting your sweet ass right here."

"Oh noooo," Seraphian drawled. "What a punishment."

Ty chuckled, squeezing her thighs. "You might change your tone when my dick is balls deep in your tight ass."

I groaned. "Please, can we stop and act this out? I'm hard already."

Andras sighed audibly. "No. We have thousands of people counting on us and not enough time to return before the first battle begins. Mate bonds first, fucking later."

"Who invited the party pooper?" Sera grumbled.

Andras stopped and turned, walking calmly toward our girl. She squirmed, but Ty held her firmly against him. Andras snatched her chin between his thumb and forefinger. "If you think that for one moment of the time we've been together, I haven't craved your slutty little cunt wrapped around my cock, you are mistaken, sweetheart."

Seraphina's eyes dilated, and my half-hard dick was at full-mast. "God damn, Andras. If you're trying to steer us away from the orgy idea, it's not working."

My stoic brother smirked but said nothing before returning to the head of the line, leading us to the entrance of the magic mountain bullshit. Well, Elgo was leading, at the insistence of Scribe Lahabiel. Because almost no one made the journey, and even less survived, there weren't exactly directions other than a general idea, guarded by the truxens from outsiders. And apparently the entrance could even hide from those not deemed worthy enough to enter. I was confident we'd get in, but considering we had no idea what waited for us within, my hopes were a little more grim than normal.

Not Phen, though. He was already making plans for our grand entrance. Some kind of epic jump into the battle with fire, lightning, the works. As long as the others could hold the line until we returned. We hadn't really spent a lot of time with the truxen daemons, but they seemed capable enough. Even the young male leading us now, who was apparently older than us by a century or so, was considered a top bowman. The truxens required all their warriors, male and female, to learn skills without using their power. The elders said it was important for their people to be able to defend themselves, even if disconnected from the magic the elements provide.

It was rare, but apparently there were all kinds of powers we hadn't heard of, including the ability to snuff out another creature's power. That would be badass. When our mate bonds first locked into place, I felt something shift inside me, a power waking within, but our bonds were severed before I could fully understand it.

My brothers had similar experiences. Ty said his was more explosive, a volcano ready to erupt. Andras said his felt cold and stinging, like touching dry ice. And Dev, his was more like mine, something subtle that was too far away to grasp. I was curious to see what would come of those powers when our bonds were restored. Hopefully we'd become strong enough to defeat the bad guys.

"The air has shifted," Elgo announced, pausing at the fork in the path ahead. "We go left."

"How do you know?" Seraphina asked, cocking her head at the daemon.

He didn't look at her when he spoke. "My eldest brother made this journey some time ago." Elgo didn't offer any further information.

It was a strange reply, but none of us pressed him further. Even Phen wore an uncertain frown, as if he could sense something wasn't quite right.

CHAPTER THIRTY-FIVE

Typhon

Seraphina's teeth nipped at my ear for the hundredth time. I carried the little tease on my back like the most tempting treat. We'd hiked for several hours, but I wasn't even close to tiring. She weighed next to nothing, considering I squatted three times her weight. But if the vixen continued to torment me with teeth and tongue, I'd shove her against the nearest tree and fuck her until the entire mountainside knew the name she screamed was my own.

Even with her playfulness, I could feel her unease. The mate bonds might have been severed, but the connections I formed with this goddess and my brothers formed before those threads ever tied us together.

The mountain loomed before us, casting shadows on the forest at its feet. Stars glittered overhead, some almost too bright to look at directly. We slowed, Elgo pausing in front of a massive boulder leaning against the mountain. It didn't look like it belonged, almost as if someone placed it there. But the damn thing was likely too heavy for even me to move, at least not without using earth magic.

"This is the way," Elgo spoke, staring hard at the boulder before turning to us. His eyes were filled with anger.

I could sense his rage even before he drew his bow, pointing the deadly sharp arrow at Seraphina. A snarl built in my throat, and I attempted to keep her behind me, but of course she was too stubborn to listen.

"Elgo?" Seraphina slid off my back and took a step toward the daemon, and my brothers and I did the same, but his arrow remained pointed at my woman.

"There is only one way to get through." Elgo spoke softly in the heavy silence. "And I won't die for you."

"El, my man," Phen spoke, his tone casual, but his back was ramrod straight. "What do you mean? No one is trying to hurt you. We're on the same side."

"No," Elgo snarled, his stance unwavering. "I thought we were, but then he killed my brother. And then died anyway, they all did. So it was for nothing. I won't die for nothing. I volunteered to guide you, only to stop you."

"Who killed your brother?" Seraphina stepped within a few feet of the daemon, his arrow pointed straight at her heart. "Belfegor?"

As soon as she said the name, angry tears fell from Elgo's dark eyes. "Your father! The one who wishes to enter must spill innocent blood. He murdered my brother to get under the mountain. And for what? Nothing good came of it."

His words rang out in the silence, bouncing off the mountain and echoing down the valley. No one moved as we absorbed what he'd said. We had to kill an innocent to gain entry? Which of us would bear that burden? I sure as fuck wasn't going to let Seraphina do it.

"Elgo, I don't think—" Phen began, but Seraphina held up her hand, silencing him.

"I cannot begin to know why my father did what he did all those years ago." Seraphina's tone was quiet but strong. "But I can tell you now, I will not kill you just to get inside the mountain."

The daemon's hands wavered, his eyes darting between each of us to see if we would object, but he didn't know us well enough. Not one of us would go against her words. If she was declaring this mission a fail, then we would find another way.

"What do I have to do, besides spill innocent blood?" Seraphina asked, eyeing the massive boulder.

Phen spoke first. "Lahabiel neglected to mention the innocent blood bit. But she did say it would take a drop of blood from Belfegor's heir."

"It doesn't matter, though, does it?" Dev spoke up. "We aren't killing Elgo."

Seraphina walked around Elgo, his bow and arrow now at his side. She placed her hand on the stone. "We don't need to kill him. I've already spilled innocent blood."

My brows scrunched together as I tried to understand what she was saying. And then I remembered.

Serapina turned back to us, regret coloring her face. "Does it matter when the innocent died, or only that I have spilled innocent blood at some time?"

Elgo shrugged. "I don't know. Who did you murder?"

My girl's shoulders dropped at his words, and I was at her side in seconds. "She didn't murder anyone. It was an accident. A fire meant for a fiend."

"But a young girl died at my hand, so it doesn't really matter. She was pure, innocent, and I took her life." Seraphina produced a dagger and cut into her palm without hesitation. "Here goes nothin'."

We watched in silence as she placed her bloody palm on the stone. For a few seconds, nothing happened. Until the mountain rumbled. The boulder began to disintegrate, crumbling to pieces before us and revealing a pitch-black tunnel.

"Time for you to return to the others. Let them know we've gone under." Phen slung his arm around Elgo's shoulders. "That's twice now you've aimed an arrow at my mate. Innocent or not, there won't be a third."

Elgo winced at the considerable pressure I assumed Phen was putting on the daemon's arm. Couldn't say I disagreed.

"Understood." Elgo bowed his head and left without another word.

"That little shit pointed an arrow at Seraphina more than once?" Levi scoffed. "I'm about to bring him back and beat his ass. Sounds like his blood is not so innocent."

"In his defense, I was a snarling jaguar at the time," Seraphina quipped, walking into the dark tunnel.

We followed her, Phen and I both using our power to brighten the pitch black with fire. I pushed the little ball of fire into the air above our heads and let it hover there, lighting the way.

"I really hope there's a dragon." Levi's voice was teasing. "How cool would it be to show up on the battlefield riding a fucking dragon?"

"Let's just hope there is a battlefield left for us to join," Andras murmured.

He voiced what we were all thinking. The hours were dwindling, and whatever waited for us within, it better fucking happen fast.

CHAPTER THIRTY-SIX
Gremory

My little sprite was becoming almost as obstinate as Delphine. Tabitha insisted she join us on the battlefield. I was vehemently against this, but Delphine was giving in to our new mate. If only Tabitha had found us sooner; who knew my alpha could be so agreeable?

Watch it, boy.

A smirk played on my lips. My thoughts were loud, and Delphine was always listening. But I preferred it that way. There were no secrets between us, until recently. Well, it wasn't a secret, but there was information Delphine was keeping to herself. I trusted her with my heart and soul, and if she wasn't ready to share whatever it was with me yet, I knew there was a good reason.

My mate brushed her ruby-red nails against my arm affectionately. "Tabitha needs to be there. I've seen it."

I scowled. "She is powerless, Delphine. I cannot command the army and keep her safe." As the commander of the daemon army for decades, I was now the commanding officer of the army assembled to stand against Belial.

There were several military-minded daemons, lumens, and humans whom I spoke with for many hours, drawing up plans and preparing to lead our people into battle. Even with the little time that we had back in Stella Terra, I was confident in our plans. Delphine and Michaela both said there was something coming that we couldn't fully understand. Whatever trick Belial had, I was certain it would be terrible.

When we were younger, Belial was a conniving shit. He was too clever even in childhood, manipulating those around him. The eldest daemon prince carried himself with such aura, even elders were wary of him. King Corson was strict, and never particularly pleasant, and when he took a more sinister turn, Belial was right there with him.

The King was a monster of a daemon. Typhon might have been the closest in size to him. The fact that Seraphina didn't see King Corson when she was held captive in the castle was concerning. Wouldn't he want to see the prize Belial brought to him?

Seraphina recounted her time there in as much detail as she could remember. Her memory wasn't entirely credible, considering her conniving uncle and Samuel, the Obscuritas King, were doing their damnedest to influence her thoughts.

"I want to take a trip to see our prisoner." I stood from the table. We were eating a meal, the last before our journey to the barren lands.

Delphine arched her brow at me, hazel eyes filled with curiosity. "What for?"

I leaned down and planted a kiss on her lush lips. "I'd like to ask him a question we haven't tried yet. And his reaction to it will be quite telling."

My mate nodded, trusting my judgment, and followed me to the dungeons. There were several guards and even more magical barriers to keep the lumen royal locked up. Lumens could survive on very little food and water, using their power to restore energy to their bodies. But with the stellatium dampening his power, Halphas was too weak to be a danger to anyone.

"Hello, traitor," I purred, sauntering up to the bars of his cage. Halphas barely acknowledged me. "I'm looking forward to meeting your master on the battlefield."

"Belial will destroy you all," the broken lumen grumbled, his chains rattling.

I crossed my arms, watching him intently. "Don't you mean King Corson? He is the true mastermind behind this plot, is he not?"

Halphas's shoulders tensed, and his eyes darted away. He recovered quickly, but it was enough. I dropped down, balancing on the balls of my feet and using a bit of air magic to force the lumen scum to look at me, unable to turn away.

"How is Belial controlling the king?" I demanded.

His body was rigid, trying desperately to fight against my hold. "I don't know what you mean."

"Sure you do," I drawled, taking a sharp vine and cracking it across his cheek, drawing blood. "Because it's not King Corson's orders you follow. It's Belial's. What has he done to my people?"

Halphas spat at me. "Belial is not like you or your people. Beasts and imbeciles. Ruled by soft emotions and small minds." He heaved a breath mid-rant. "That's why they were so easily manipulated. Even that idiot king. He never deserved the crown. When Belial wins, I'll be at his side."

Curious.

A smile crept across my face. "Sounds like you're feeling some of those baser emotions. Does Belial know you're in love with him?"

"Fuck you," the lumen snarled, but his threat fell away and I turned my back on him.

Delphine's eyes were glazed over, a look she often got before sketching something only she could see. I wrapped my arm around her waist and guided her out of the dungeons. We walked back to our rooms, whereTabitha was resting. It brought me immense joy that she could sleep on her own. Of course, I loved having her in my arms, but the fact that she was now able to sleep alone was just another sign of her resilience, her overcoming of the horrors she suffered under the thumb of Laszlo Blackbyrn.

The mate in my arms stopped several paces from the door to our room. "That's what it is. Belial is controlling them. He's somehow managed to force his will on the army. Corson is still out of my reach, but some of the others are coming through. I need to see Michaela."

CHAPTER THIRTY-SEVEN
Morax

My fingers grazed the pale flesh of my mate's perfect thighs wrapped around my own. Her eyes were closed, her head resting against my chest. Since our wedding, I was damn near insatiable, and she met my passion with equal measure.

Michaela was determined to prepare for the coming battle, absorbing knowledge, learning new ways to fight, and practicing with her new Seer gifts. And between all her preparations, we found time for ourselves. It was imperative that I brought pleasure to my mate, fed her soul with hope and love.

The moment her sister left, Michaela's anxious thoughts and feelings were a constant companion. I was unsettled as well, knowing where my brother headed with his mates. The stories we heard as children about the cursed mountain were not pleasant. No one survived. But it was more than that. Whatever monster lurked in the dark not only destroyed the body, it was said the souls of the daemons and lumens who attempted the venture there lost their souls, never to join our ancestors in the stars.

My wife stirred in my arms. "Knock knock," she mumbled, and seconds later, someone pounded on our door.

I left the comfort of our bed and found clothes for us both. Even if the voice calling out on the other side of the door was the witch, no one was allowed to see my mate's beautiful nakedness.

Michaela quickly slipped into the pale-pink dress I handed her and opened the door. Her eyes were bright with some new knowledge. "Zombies!" She shouted the word, and Delphine's eyes widened.

Gremory and Tabitha were also with her. The witch chuckled. "Something like that."

Gripping the back of Michaela's neck only a little possessively and smirking down at her, I spoke first. "I don't believe we have zombies."

"And yet"—Michaela rolled her eyes—"you do. Belial basically turned all the daemons, and the prisoners, into zombies. He's controlling them."

I shook my head, unable to grasp what this meant. "How on earth could Belial do this?"

Michaela shrugged, but it was Gremory who responded. "I think he is using the king. When I questioned Halphas, he alluded to it."

Keeping one hand caressing the nape of Michaela's neck, I contemplated his words. "Belial was always testing old magics and new ways to grow in power when we were younger. I suppose he could have found something. But I cannot imagine my father would give up control to him."

Michaela glanced up at me. "Maybe he didn't. Maybe your father is zombified, too."

Tabitha's tinkling laugh caught our attention. "Sorry. That was funny. But that might be right. When I was…with the Obscuritas Kings, they only dealt with Belial. Darren called Corson a lovesick fool once."

A sharp laugh escaped my lips. "You must be mistaken. My father never showed any gentle emotions like love."

My wife wrapped her arms around my waist, looking up at me with her beautiful, mismatched eyes. "Are you certain? Never?"

Her question made me pause. "Hmm. Maybe. But I was barely a teen. It feels more like a dream than a memory. I do recall the day he became vicious. As if a switch flipped and the blackness in his soul finally broke free."

"Unless it's Belial's will," Gremory added.

I nodded. "If it is, then perhaps we have a chance. Find a way to sever the connection my brother has to him and his zombies, as you call them."

Michaela smiled. "We're going to war with zombies. This should be fun."

Our army of rebels moved south from Liboteria to Terrae Mortu. Terrae Mortu was once a thriving city with a marketplace where all creatures intermingled. Thousands of years ago, before the Ormaenus line held the royal titles, before even the distinguished Valdis family thrived, Stella Terra was a peaceful country. We shared knowledge, traveled to other worlds, and mingled with creatures far and wide. There are very few stories of this time in our history; most of the books were destroyed.

There would always be villainy in the world, because greed always finds a way into the souls of devils.

"You're very serious, husband." Michaela twined her fingers with mine, my hand engulfing hers. "I caught a glimpse of that world."

I arched a brow at her. "What world?"

"The one you were thinking of just now." She gazed into the distance. "Your thoughts were enough direction for me to point The Sight that way. It was wonderful."

Our bond pulsed with vitality, and I saw through her gift and our connection flashes of the city teaming with life. Bringing her hand up to my lips, I pressed a soft kiss to her fair skin. "Perhaps we can bring it back?"

My mate smiled broadly up at me. "You can count on it. I want to make a life here, in this world, with you."

Her words filled my soul with so much joy. If someone had told me I'd be completely head over heels in love with a lumen princess, I'd have told them they were insane. How could I, the son of a devil and brother to a demented daemon, be gifted with a mate who radiated so much light and goodness?

I pulled Michaela into my arms, lifting her off the ground. She wrapped her legs around me instantly. Instead of her usual dresses, Michaela was dressed for travel in buttery soft pants and a fitted sweater. Her golden hair was braided down her back, and I itched to get my hands in it. I captured her lips with my own, and as if she could read my every need, she opened herself to me. My tongue dominated hers, and her slender body melted into mine. I relished the submission.

She giggled when several wolf whistles filled the air, but I didn't care. They could all watch me claim my mate, watch me worship the queen she had become.

When our lips parted, her eyes glowed with power. "What was all that for?" She breathed heavily, nipping at my lips.

"I vow here and now, on all the stars above. On my soul, I will make sure we survive this," I promised her. "You will have a life here, one filled with love and peace unlike anyone has ever seen. I swear it. And I will be by your side through it all."

Tears welled in her eyes at my declaration, and I knew she could feel the truth of my words through our bond.

"I swear it, too, Morax. You and me. And maybe a kid or two."

A groan escaped my lips at her words, and the beast within reared his head. My cock ached, pressing against my pants with the need to breed her right fucking now. "Little doe, do not say another word about children. I may drop you to all fours and breed you right fucking here."

Michaela laughed, the sound filled with mirth. "Good to know." She leaned in, her pink lips brushing against my ear. "Perhaps we can find time for a walk in the woods later, and you can fill my pussy with your seed."

My wings snapped out in seconds, and I leapt into the air. As if I would just let her speak such filth and get away with it. Her laughter carried on the wind, and her capricious grin told me she knew exactly what she was doing to me. I flew us away from the others, zipping over the trees and moving deeper into the forest and closer to Terrae Mortu.

Her hands teased me without mercy, rubbing my hard cock through my pants near enough to cause me pain. I dropped out of the sky, pulling her sweater over her head and tossing it to the forest floor. Her pants were next. The last of my restraint disappeared the instant I saw her lacy red lingerie.

"You little minx," I growled, slashing my claws through the flimsy fabric until she was completely nude before me. "On your knees, wife."

She obeyed, and fucking hells did that do things to me. Michaela had my dick down her throat before I could issue another command. Every single inch of her body and soul was perfect. My hand instantly went to her head, threading my claws in her braid and tugging her long hair free. I fucked her mouth mercilessly, and she took it all.

"Such a good fucking girl," I moaned. "You know you deserved to be on your knees after whispering those filthy words to me."

Leaning over her head, I smacked her ass in three rapid strikes. Michaela moaned, her spit dribbling out of her mouth stuffed with my cock.

"You like that, don't you, my dirty little lumen."

She felt like heaven, but I needed more. Using the hand wrapped in her hair, I pulled her away and forced her up. The dirt on her legs only encouraged the primal beast within me. Michaela grinned when I dragged her to the nearest tree and lifted her in my arms. I didn't give her time to adjust, just slammed her back into the tree and filled her with my cock,

She screamed for me, her sweet cunt taking me in so well.

"You're soaked, little lumen. I think you enjoyed that."

Michaela groaned. "You know I did, mate. Now make me come. Please. I need it."

"How could I refuse, when you beg so prettily for me?" Setting a ferocious pace, I fucked my perfect mate until she screamed my name. Until my seed filled her. Until we both fell to the earth in a heap of sweaty limbs and unimaginable bliss.

CHAPTER THIRTY-EIGHT
Leona

The closer we got to the castle, the more my insides buzzed with nervous energy. I didn't know what else to call it, this feeling. Something inside me was screaming to be let out. Maybe it was the absence of him. Since the army arrived at Terrae Mortu, the monster in my head was deadly silent, and the darkness within me was going to eat me alive without him. He was the only thing keeping me from going insane.

My mind was a mess of rage and guilt. I was angry all the time. Nuri helped me channel it, but she had her own shit to deal with. And as much as I ached to get high or drunk, it didn't help. It only made the screams of my sister louder. The only one who could dull the screams was him. The monster in my head.

Nuri was getting suspicious. Whenever the inner thoughts were too much, I sparred with her. But lately, I preferred to be alone, so I could hear him. She was too observant and already tested me with questions.

"Lo," Nuri called out, folding herself gracefully into the grass beside me.

We sat in silence, staring out at the dead lands before us. It was wild to see, the forest ended abruptly where Terrae Mortu began. Apparently, there was some crazy battle here, and the creatures who fought sucked the life right out of it.

"It is fitting that we are brought to this place." Nuri spoke softly. "This is where the sins of my people took root. Where the start of our destruction began."

"Did you see this place before it was ruined?" I asked, because I honestly did not get how these creatures aged. She could be five thousand years old for all I knew.

Nuri shoved me playfully. "No, asshole. I wasn't alive then. Not even close. There are very few of us left who were, and almost all written records of it were destroyed. They wanted to bury their sins and pretend the war was necessary."

"Do you think this one isn't?" I cocked my head in her direction.

She sighed, the sound heavy with burdens I didn't understand. "I wanted to run away. When Lailah was faced with her responsibilities to the crown, I wanted to run. Would've left everyone behind. Convinced her it was right. In the end, it was Lailah who did the right thing. She returned, she was the brave one."

I didn't respond.

Nuri's eyes stared into the bright blue sky, almost mocking in its sunny happiness. Nuri continued. "This battle, it will be the last one for me." Her voice was quiet but filled with certainty. "It will be the last one for many. Lailah believed her sisters could finally make things right. And I trust my mate."

Her declaration eased some of the buzzing energy beneath my flesh. For as long as I'd known her, Nuri was in mourning for her mate. I'd never loved anyone that way. The idea of a mate, a creature out there meant to be mine, it was unlikely. My soul was too damaged for something as pure as a mate bond.

"I spoke to Lahabiel before we left. After I killed Halphas." Nuri's words were devoid of the emotion from her previous declarations.

I knew she killed the lumen traitor. Lailah's uncle had apparently been loyal to Belial long before anyone knew of his treachery. There were several mysterious deaths in the palace that were acted out by him, some at Belial's command, and some he did for fun. Nuri claimed his death for herself. For Lailah, and for Aurora.

"Halphas told me it was he who led the rebellion that killed Belfegor," Nuri continued. "Seraphina will be sad to have missed his death, but I think I made him suffer for it. Lahabiel asked me if killing him made me feel better."

"Did it?" I knew the answer.

"Superficially, yes." Nuri shrugged. "He deserved his death, but it doesn't bring her back. It doesn't bring any of them back."

I sighed. This was not a new lecture. Nuri told me a decade ago my anger at Seraphina wouldn't bring my sister back. Obviously not, but revenge still didn't seem all that bad.

"She also told me that before the end, I would end up in the castle. And you would be with me."

Now that was new information. "Why would I be there? I thought the plan was to keep non-magical creatures away from the battle unless absolutely necessary."

Nuri shrugged. "The Scribe didn't share the why of it. Just that you would know when it was time."

"Why the fuck would I want to go in there?" My voice was a notch higher than I meant it to be, and Nuri eyed me with suspicion. "Maybe she was wrong."

My mentor and only friend laughed. "Scribe Lahabiel is never wrong. Keep whatever secret you have a little longer than, Lo. But it will come out eventually. All secrets do."

CHAPTER THIRTY-NINE
Michaela

I was really hoping the crazy orgasms would relax my husband, but no such luck. Not that I regretted taunting the beast, but damn, I really thought my plan was solid. Instead, the brute was growling and snarling anytime any single creature got too close to me.

Gremory laughed to my left, and Mor nearly ripped his head off. He was in full daemon mode. Horns, wings, claws, all of it on display. His skin glowed a deep red with the power radiating out of him.

"It's called resource guarding," Grem quipped. "You know, like what mutts do with their food?"

Morax launched a massive tree at the daemon. Tabitha yelped in fright, but Grem was ready for it. The tree burst into a billow of leaves, floating to the ground like confetti.

"Watch yourself, Grem," Deccaria teased, leaning on a tree and watching the show. "He's in full beast mode."

"Mor." I rolled my eyes. "Will you chill?"

Steam literally blew from his flared nostrils, and I laughed. This was absurd. Apparently when I taunted him with having his babies, I ignited some primal urges within him to not only breed his mate, but also keep the world away. Gods forbid I get a papercut, let alone go into battle.

I stood, shoving my hands on my hips. "Morax. You need to snap out of it. We are going to battle a million bad guys, including your brother. I need your head in the game here."

He snarled, eyes glowing bright gold with his power. "I will never let them harm you. And you will not be going on that field."

Folding my arms, I glared at him. "Are you going to force me to sit out while all my friends go to war and die for me? This is my fight, and you won't keep me from it. I've seen it."

My own power glowed within me at the conviction in my words. I had seen it. Before midday, I would be on that field. The part that terrified me was all the dead bodies I recognized at my feet.

Mor dropped to his knees before me, circling my waist with his muscular arms. He was barely below my eye level even now. I stroked his hair and caressed his strong jaw.

"I'm terrified of losing you," he murmured. "Of losing what we might have."

I pressed my forehead to his. "So am I. But if we lose, we won't even get the chance."

He sighed heavily, his wings fading away with his horns and claws. Mor was still big and scary, but at least the beast within was snoozing again.

The moment came to an abrupt end when strange horns blasted through the air. Everyone tensed, knowing it was time. We had our plans, we'd trained and prepared as much as we could. Gremory kissed Tabitha and Delphine with equal amounts of passion before leaping into the sky. He began calling out orders, amplifying his voice to ready the soldiers.

Our plan was to draw out the zombie army and surround them. I ordered our people to do everything they could to subdue, not kill. Not all of these people were in this army by choice. I'd seen it, visions of Belial and Halphas and others coaxing or threatening creatures to submit their will to Belial. That was the trick, they had to consent, one way or another.

There would be others, though. Daemons and lumens with more power and free will. Mor, Grem, Nuri, and some of our strongest would take them out. Delphine and I would stay back, for now, guarding those who couldn't fight. The visions for the day continued to change. While I was learning to control this power, there was still so much about it I didn't understand, like the potential to slow time. Maybe even rewind it. The ability was so unique, and there were very few books written about it, due to it being such a heavily guarded power.

Mor tore my attention away from my rambling thoughts with a soul-searing kiss. "Anyone lays a finger on my wife, I'll shred them to pieces with my bare hands."

"Yeah? Well, if anyone gives my husband so much as a scratch, I'll turn them to ash." I kissed him again and shoved him away. "I love you. Now go."

Morax pushed off the ground without a word and flew away, his dark wings glinting in the sunlight.

Delphine stepped up next to me, and we watched our mates lead our army into battle. "No turning back now."

"I still see Seraphina here, just not when or if it's in time to make a difference." I swallowed my fears, my throat dry. "I don't know how this ends."

"If I told you, it wouldn't come to pass." Delphine glanced at Tabitha and then back to the battlefield, the first cries of pain reaching our ears.

Leona joined us, standing on my left. "Nuri trusted Lailah. And Lailah said it would be her sisters who ended Belial."

I nodded, taking heart from her words. Nuriela told us everything she knew of Lailah and my mother's visions. Their blood flowed in my veins. Royal blood. Vengeful blood. And I would do whatever it took to bring down the monster who started the destruction of my family.

CHAPTER FORTY

Delphine

Our efforts to draw out the more powerful monsters under Belial's command weren't working. The Obscuritas Kings weren't on the battlefield, Belial was nowhere in sight, and our people were dying. It wasn't enough. Morax wasn't tempting enough to draw out his brother, but someone else was.

I jogged over to Michaela. Her blonde hair was tied back, and sweat coated her brow. She had blood on her clothes as she worked over injured daemons, lumens, and even some mortals. The trained army of humans brought to us by the Obscuritas Princes were dying too quickly.

"We need to level the playing field," I mumbled to myself, an idea beginning to form.

"Delphine!" Michaela shouted, running toward me. "I saw something. I think it will help."

A smile played on my lips. "Your gift is strengthening. And I think you're right." Without another word, I called to my fellow witches.

Those with more offensive magic were on the field, but a handful that were primarily healers and shields stayed back to tend to the wounded. But what I needed now was a damn impenetrable bubble to keep everyone I cared for safe.

"I have a plan, but not everyone is going to survive it," I began honestly, because they deserved to know what would come of this. "With the zombie army intact, we cannot draw out the real players. And if that doesn't happen before midday, we will lose."

"What do you need?" a young female witch with jet-black hair and stormy gray eyes asked, her face filled with determination.

"Those of you with the ability to syphon," I continued, gazing at each of them. "I need you to use every ounce of your magic to break the connection between Belial and his army. At least then, maybe some of them will bail and they will no longer be able to function as one. The generals will have to enter the field to restore order."

Several witches, male and female, understood what this meant and one by one, agreed to take this task. Seven in total.

"What of us, Imperia?" An older male witch spoke, his words catching me off guard.

The term Imperia was given to the highest ranking witch of the Mal-Regia. I hadn't been an active member of the court for over a decade. Hadn't been back to my home, my city, or my people. Grem and Tabitha were the only souls who knew of my nerves regarding my return. Would they accept me?

The others nodded encouragingly, whispering words of fealty to me as their leader. There were roughly thirty witches in all. Ten of them I bid return to the camp and remain healers. The other twenty I sent to the field as shields for our army. These witches could create invisible armor around each creature, protecting them from other magical attacks, and hopefully give us more opportunities to fight back.

With their orders, the witches dispersed. The syphons spread out at the edge of the battlefield and dropped to the earth, digging their hands into the soil. The shields guarded them while they chanted. Magic crackled around them, tunneling into the earth beneath the armies. The witches chanted, reaching a crescendo, the strain in their voices piercing my heart. This magic would kill them. It would suck every bit of power from their veins and their bodies, turning them to dust.

There was no doubt in my mind, Belial would feel the souls of these creatures being cast away from his source. He had to have some kind of anchor to manage all that power.

Chaos erupted across the barrens as the slaves were given their free will back. Some began to run away, others fought with renewed vigor. But as the last of that unholy magic left the battlefield, my fellow witches dropped to the dirt. Seven died for us to live. And we would not waste their sacrifices.

A roar of pure rage bounded over the army, echoing all the way from the castle, and I smirked. Belial was pissed.

CHAPTER FORTY-ONE
Gremory

The tide turned on the battlefield as soon as Delphine's witches sacrificed their lives to break the dark magic Belial used to turn his people into zombies, as Tabitha and Michaela called them. Speaking of my little sprite, I turned my gaze to the healers' camp and spotted her bright blonde pixie cut darting between patients. My enhanced vision easily noted the sweat on her brow and the way her clothing clung to her body. It still unsettled me that she was here, but Delphine had insisted it was the right decision. Her insistence only enhanced my worries.

Many of those freed by the witches fled the field, but they would be caught and questioned. We did not murder those who surrendered, but I'd be damn sure they meant it before letting them go free. Never again would I let such a disaster happen. We deserved peace and happiness in Tellisa.

My senses tingled, anticipating a new danger. I whipped around just as Foras dropped out of the sky before me.

"Hello, traitor," Foras sneered.

He was a slimy piece of shit before, and that clearly had not changed, nor had his power status. I smirked. "Foras. Still licking the boots of your superiors, hoping one will look your way?"

The power-hungry hybrid dropped into a fighting stance, two whips with sharp spikes unfurling in his hands. He hissed like a pissed off cat, snapping the whips at me, but I didn't move. Foras was an opponent I could handle. He may have been conniving in certain circles, but I had spent years training for war and perfecting my ability to understand my enemies. Foras could create illusions, and every move I made would draw me further into whatever false scene he conjured.

"Aren't you going to fight me, former general and all that?" Foras taunted, attempting to draw me out.

I stood on the balls of my feet, ready, but unmoving, a smile playing at my lips. It infuriated him.

Foras snapped his whips in my direction, but I caught them easily, fire coated my hands and I sent the flames back down the vines. He cried out in pain, too slow to drop the whips before my flames reached him. Now that he was distracted, I rushed at the fucker, stellatium blade in hand. His eyes widened in fear, too scared to even use his power as I snarled with rage, unleashing my daemon and driving the dagger into his chest. His screams died the moment I pierced his heart.

Looming over him, I snarled in his pathetic face. "For all the pain you caused, you deserve a more prolonged death. Perhaps a few rounds with Morax for threatening his mate. Even so, you're not worth the effort."

Foras died, alone and snivelling. No illusions, only death.

A surge of power drew my attention back to the battle. I flew across our army, barking out orders to stay in formation, splitting the enemies into more manageable sections. Unfortunately, that powerful blast was all too familiar. The Obscuritas Kings were entering the battle. Belial was still hidden, but we'd draw him out eventually. Laszlo Blackbyrn sent a blast of frigid air laced with icicles sharp as blades into the sky where I hovered. The asshole might have been strong, but I was born in this life and easily shielded against the onslaught. A few creatures near me were not as successful, their cries filling the sky as they dropped to the earth, bloodied and in need of care. Others pulled them away instantly, carting them to the healers.

I set my sights on Laszlo. The Princes requested their fathers be left alive until their arrival, but I wouldn't waste an opportunity to maim them a little. Morax dove from the opposite side of the field, his dark wings blotting out the sun and eyes shining with power. Samuel Delano shot a net of thick vines at him, trapping his wings. The daemon prince roared in fury, and Michaela's voice rang out in alarm on the wind.

The distraction of my comrade falling from the sky and his mate charging onto the field worked all too well, and pain lanced through my side when a spear of ice pierced a lung. My power faltered, and I fell heavily to the earth, quickly urging my body to heal. But it wasn't quick enough. Laszlo was on me in a second. His power clearly favored water, and the cold-hearted bastard was using ice to lock down my limbs. I pushed fire into my veins to melt the frigid ice anchoring me to the ground.

"Looks like I caught a rat," Laszlo purred in that flat voice I loathed. "I always knew there were traitors in our midst. But you stood by while we tortured so many pathetic creatures. That must weigh heavily on your soul."

He wasn't wrong. While undercover, before I rescued Tabitha and fled, I looked on as the Kings committed horrible acts of violence against so many. And I would carry the weight of it for eternity.

"I will avenge all who were ruined at your hands when I kill you and the scum who follow your lead so willingly," I snarled at him. But my bite was not quite hitting its mark.

Laszlo smirked, his black eyes shining with power. "That spear was tipped with stellatium. You won't be healing so well, daemon trash. I will enjoy snuffing out the rebel army's general."

A pain-filled grunt escaped my lips as the ice covering my body suddenly speared into my flesh, tiny ice picks digging into my skin. I couldn't heal and fight it off at the same time, not with the wound from the metal so dangerous to daemons and lumens. Fear pulsed in my chest as Laszlo stalked closer, a stellatium sword glinting in the sun, and aimed at my heart.

Before he could take another step, Delphine dropped from the sky, her magic crackling with her fury. "Over my dead body, false king."

My heart flooded with love for this woman, and true fear followed right behind it as my mate battled Laszlo. She produced her own sword, parrying his with ease, as if she could anticipate his moves. I imagined she could, to an extent, with her abilities to see flashes of the future.

Laszlo taunted her, called her filthy names and threatened to enslave her for his pleasure. The thought of it sent renewed power through my veins, burning away the ice digging into my flesh. I was nearly free when a scream of terror pierced my heart. Craning my neck to the right, I saw daemon dogs attacking the healers. These devil animals were a fucked-up creation of Belial's. He stole them from the forest and altered them in horrible ways. I'd only encountered them once and had hoped to never do so again. But now the rabid monsters were nearing Tabitha. Leona was with her, blades in hand, fighting, but my mate was not so well trained.

"Nuriela!" I bellowed her name.

The lumen launched off the field where she was fighting off ten daemons, her eyes instantly going to Leona and Tabitha. But she was too damn far.

I snapped my attention back to Delphine. She wasn't tiring to the untrained eye, but her movements were imperceptibly slower. My mates needed me. They were fighting battles they could not win alone.

With their safety at risk, my power flared, the ice hissing as it turned to steam, finally freeing me. I attempted to stand, only to be jumped from behind by three daemon traitors. One had a stellatium blade, and the other two held me down as the blade-wielder stalked toward me, straddled my waist, and brought the blade to my throat.

Panic set in, but I was too weak in this moment to change my fate. Time seemed to slow as the crazed fucker pressed the sharp edge to my skin.

"My loves, forgive me," I murmured the words, sending my last thoughts out to Delphine and Tabitha.

The daemon on top of me suddenly started screaming, his eyes bugging out, and he jumped off me. The other two followed, clawing at their chests. I turned my gaze to see Delphine whispering furiously and watched as the daemons burned from the inside out.

Tabitha screamed, and this one was truly terrifying. A daemon dog launched into the air and knocked her to the ground, his sharp teeth aiming for her throat.

Delphine bellowed words I didn't quite understand, but I could feel her power woosh out of her and toward Tabitha. A jewel around her slender neck glowed a brilliant green, and just before the beast could rip into her throat, a blast of magic threw the feral thing away. It slammed into a tree and to the earth with a thud.

Relief filled my chest, but it was short-lived. When I turned back, Delphine was in Laszlo's grasp, the tip of his blade resting over my mate's heart. Her eyes were sad, and neither of us could even shout before he shoved the blade into her chest. Laszlo tossed her away and leapt into the sky. I scrambled over to her, sensing Tabitha running for us. She shouldn't have been, but I was too focused on Delphine in my arms to stop her.

"It's all right my love, you'll heal," I murmured softly. "Please stay with me."

Tabitha dropped to the ground beside me and took Delphine's hand. "Please don't leave me. I need you." Tears ran down her cheeks, and the green jem on her necklace now glimmered with magic.

Delphine's magic.

My mate smiled softly. "I love you both. My heart. My soul. Be happy. For me."

Her heart stopped, and a piece of my own shattered. She was mortal. Delphine used every bit of her magic to save Tabitha. She was on this fucking field because of me, saving me when I should have been saving her.

I roared in anguish, a rush of power sweeping out of me and knocking down the dozen or so creatures closest to us. Tabitha cried, her body shaking with sadness.

Nuri was beside us now, kneeling gently next to me. Morax and Michaela joined her, and they both bowed their heads, a thick cloud encasing us.

Mor eyed the necklace around Tabitha's throat. "Did Delphine give you that?"

Tabitha nodded, sniffling. "Just before going to fight. She said it was to protect me when she couldn't."

"She was mortal when he stabbed her," Nuri whispered, awe coloring her words. "Her magic now lives in that stone. It's been ages since I've seen anything like it."

Morax laid his hand on my shoulder in comfort. "We need to move her. And get back to the battle. The witches will be faltering with their leader gone. We must push forward."

He was right, I knew he was, but my heart was in pieces, the mate bond dim without Delphine's fierce soul on the other end. Morax pushed healing power into my body as I stood with Delphine in my arms. We moved quickly, taking her body to the healers' camp, now devoid of the beasts.

Leona waited for us, her gaze fixed behind us and seemingly far away. "It's time to go to the castle."

CHAPTER FORTY-TWO

Seraphina

So far, this stupid mountain was a bust. Not even a dragon or hidden treasure. Sure, there were creatures, bats almost as big as my torso and other creepy crawlers. They didn't attack, just eyed us cautiously as we passed them by.

"We've been under this fucking mountain for a decade," I complained for the tenth time. "And I don't feel any different."

"You can feel it, though, can't you?" Dev asked quietly. "We're getting close."

I huffed in irritation. He wasn't wrong. There was *something* down here. We were definitely going down, and it was warmer, not colder like I expected.

"Let's play another round of twenty questions," Levi chimed in too enthusiastically. "Whoever wins gets to suck my dick."

A laugh escaped my lips before I could stop it. "How about whoever wins gets to eat me out?"

Ty's muscular arms lifted me off the ground in one effortless sweep. "I don't need to win a game to do that, pet. Your delectable cunt belongs to me."

Desire pulsed through my body at his words. "I need orgasms. Can we find somewhere for a quickie?"

A tremor suddenly flooded the tunnel, the mountain shaking around us. We stopped, waiting, Ty still holding me tightly in his arms. A soft blue light glowed in the distance, too far to make out what it was, but the light was most definitely new.

I shoved off Ty, walking toward Andras and Phen at the front. Both men stood with arms crossed, staring down the tunnel. "Well, seems like we should check it out?"

Andras nodded curtly. He was, for maybe the second time in his life, not wearing a suit. My dark prince wore simple cotton blend navy pants, a long-sleeved crewneck shirt, and boots. Still hot as hell, but more practical for wartimes.

The others were in similar attire, dressed for battle. Because at some point, we'd be joining the others on the field. And I hoped to the gods we wouldn't be too late. Michaela was still alive. Phen said he could sense Morax, and I was certain if she were fatally wounded, I'd feel that, too.

Taking Andras and Phen's hands in mine, I pulled them forward, Levi, Dev, and Ty following close behind. We needed to get this soul-searching shit over with.

When we finally made it to the blue light, the tunnel came to an abrupt end and stone steps led down into a massive open cavern. The blue light came from a body of water. The how wasn't readily apparent, but the water was definitely glowing a soft, silvery blue, similar to my hair color.

"Where is the light coming from?" Levi whispered, awe in his voice.

Steam rose from the water, and I itched to submerge my tired limbs in the pool. "Think it's safe?"

Phen snorted. "Probably not. But won't know until we test it out, eh?" He winked at me.

Andras held fast to my hand, though, not letting Phen pull us closer to the tempting hot spring. "Perhaps we look around a bit and study our surroundings, hmm?" he said, squeezing my hand tightly when I rolled my eyes. "And remember that most who have ventured beneath this mountain never escape it."

My shoulders dropped. "Why do you always have to ruin the fun?"

The words barely left my mouth before Andras grabbed my throat and shoved my body against the nearest cavern wall. The rock bit into my skin, and he squeezed my neck, cutting off my ability to speak. "Sweetheart, I will allow that sass because you are tiring, but snark at me again, and you will be punished."

I grinned. "Well joke's on you, because I love to be punished."

Andras grabbed my wrist with his other hand, bringing my arm up over my head and pressing his body against me. He pinned my hand against the sharp, rocky wall, and I hissed when it cut into my flesh. Several drops of blood dripped to the ground, and another tremor raced through the mountain.

The others gathered near us, and we waited for it to subside, but this time, it only grew. The air became thick with magic. I knew the guys could feel the electric charge in the air just as I did.

We watched warily as something rose from the center of the pool. The water moved as if it were alive, swirling and bending until the shape of a woman's curvy body floated just above the center of the pool.

"The royal blood summons," the water spoke, the voice echoing around the cave.

"Okay then. What now?" Levi whispered on my left. No one responded. We waited for whatever this was to continue. And it did. The creature began to hum, chanting a rhyme.

> *Those who come to seek what's mine,*
> *Their darkest shame they soon will find.*
> *To mend the bonds that once were broken,*
> *Their souls must offer that which is unspoken.*

I absorbed the words, taking in their meaning. "So. Spill your dirty little secrets to the creepy water thing and then we can leave?"

Andras sighed. "I doubt it will be so easy." At his words, the water woman continued.

> *A goddess of this earthly plane*
> *Requires only your deepest pain.*
> *Submerge your souls beneath my depths,*
> *If they be false, we shall claim your every breath.*

"And there it is." Phen rolled his eyes. "Lots of naughty souls in that water, I'll bet."

Andras frowned. "It's not just those who are naughty, Phenex. You must give your greatest shame, your deepest pain, as an offering. If that offering proves to be unworthy, you won't come back out of the pool."

"Water is a wicked power." Phen nodded in agreement. "I bet it will know if you try to offer up something less than that."

"Which explains why so many creatures fail," Dev added. "It's not easy to face something you fear the most. Something you never want to see the light of day."

"We all know you love sucking cock, Dev. It's not a secret anymore." Levi punched Dev's shoulder playfully.

A smirk played at the corners of my mouth. "Well, we've come this far. No point turning back now." I began undressing, and my princes did the same.

Holding hands and moving as one, we descended the uneven steps leading into the water. It was blessedly warm and instantly soothed my muscles. The smell of dewy grass and lavender reached my nose. I inhaled deeply, trying to relax, but that was proving to be difficult.

What was my darkest shame? I'd killed many people, bad people, over the years, and didn't feel sorry about it. Perhaps it was the death of Leona's baby sister? Guilt still gnawed at me for that. But no, it didn't feel like that was it. Would the water know and show me?

Dozens of questions buzzed through my head. When the six of us were neck deep in the water, I sucked in a breath. The mate bond hummed within me, not fully connected, but I could feel my princes just enough to make me ache for more. By the looks on their faces, I could see they could feel the connection too.

"I'm guessing that is purposeful," I mused. "So we can feel each other when the big bad secrets come out."

Typhon nodded. "No hiding. No more secrets between us."

"Here we fucking go." I shrugged and sucked in a breath, dipping below the surface.

A scream rocketed through my mind, and suddenly, I was back in the manor where the Obscuritas Kings held my sister and me captive. I floated above the scene like a ghost, observing. Joseph Bronwen, my father in name but not in blood, was on his knees before me, and I was about to kill him.

Whispers filled my head as I watched.

What did you feel the moment you knew you had to murder your father?

He wasn't my father.

Pain seared through my chest. Wrong answer.

What did you feel the moment you knew you had to murder your father?

Mad.

The pain increased. And I knew my body was drowning back in the pool.

What did you feel the moment you knew you had to murder your father?

This was my greatest shame. Because I wasn't sad, or even sorry. I was mad. But not just mad that I had to do it.

I was mad that he left me behind. Even then, when I knew he had to do it. I wanted someone to pick me. But he didn't. And when I stabbed him, I wasn't sorry. I...wanted to do it. I wanted him to be alone and afraid. And the last thing he saw was me, smiling.

The pain subsided, and even in the water, I could feel the tears burning my eyes. I was the worst fucking person in the world. The worst daughter.

We accept.

CHAPTER FORTY-THREE

Andras

I attempted to keep my eyes open to watch over the others, but it was impossible. And pointless. As soon as I was fully submerged, the visions took over and the secrets of my brothers flooded my mind. Our bond gave us just enough access to witness each others' offerings.

Seraphina's broke my heart. Not because I judged her, or that it was wrong. Because she was a lost and lonely girl desperately looking for the family she was ripped away from. For ten years, she was alone. How could I judge her for not regretting killing the man who left her behind?

When the goddess began whispering in my mind, I already knew what she would show me, what I would offer to my mates.

The ritual that killed Seraphina's sister and mother was not actually the first attempt at capturing them. Even then, while part of me wanted to please my father and gain the power the Kings taunted us with, part of me wanted it all to end, for them to fail.

On one reconnaissance mission, I happened upon a girl who could pass for Seraphina. She was the right age. She had two sisters, and none of them looked alike. I discovered they were adopted. The Obscuritas Kings had them kidnapped and brought to the manor. When it was discovered they were not the powerful creatures our fathers sought, we were punished.

Laszlo Blackbyrn ordered me to torture and kill the girl who could have been Seraphina. She was terrified, and only mortal. And I did as he ordered. She screamed so horrifically, lasted much longer than I anticipated. My father watched me work, made sure I didn't go easy on the girl. Only when he was gone did I vomit.

How did you feel when you tortured and murdered the child?

Relieved. That it wasn't Seraphina. That it wasn't the family my father needed. I didn't vomit because I was appalled at what I did. I was appalled at myself for not caring about what I'd done at all.

At my confession, a weightlessness entered my body, and I had the sense that I was floating and no longer fighting for air beneath the surface of the pool. My brothers were given their own punishments that night, and we shared bits of what we endured, but never had I shared the extent of mine.

The visions continued, and I realized the next was Leviathan's. His story always broke my heart, the things he endured. Samuel Delano had the ability to influence the mind, and he taught Levi similar skills. My brother was also a beautiful man. He grew into his muscular figure as a teen, with those alluring navy eyes and soft lips. And his father used it. Used him. Levi was forced to use his body to gain powerful allies. To coerce men and women, old and young, to join our fathers' secret society. We knew of it, but Levi would never talk about it. Never tell us what he did or how many people he was forced to perform for.

Give us your shame. Tell your brothers who it was that broke you.

The voice echoed in my mind, and I waited to hear Levi's response. The silence lasted longer than I expected. My brother was resisting. He did not want to share, to burden us. I sent courage and acceptance through the bond, letting him know he could do this. We would never reject him.

The scene finally emerged, and bile rose in my throat. Darren Radnor, Typhon's father, was thrusting his disgusting cock inside Levi. He couldn't be more than seventeen. Darren was whipping him with a paddle, taunting Levi, breaking him. He ordered Levi to stroke his cock and come, to enjoy it.

Why did you hide this from your brothers? From yourself?

Levi's shattered soul called out to my own. *Because I couldn't bear to tell Ty. And the only way I got through it…was pretending it was Typhon instead. I wanted Ty to be my first.*

I expected Typhon's rage to rattle our bonds, but in this moment, he surprised us all. Ty filled the mate bond with love and acceptance. With compassion.

We accept.

CHAPTER FORTY-FOUR

Phenex

The stories of the Princes were difficult to watch unfolding. There was so much drama between them. So many secrets. But there was also love and bonds forged since birth. I knew these secrets unveiled would not break them apart. Seraphina's was more in line with my own. My acceptance into this bond was not the secret the goddess would ask of me.

No, that one had settled after spending time with Seraphina, and the others. I was certain the six of us were meant to be together.

The bonds of your mates are not the first ones you've broken.

Yeah, yeah.

It wasn't a secret they would find particularly interesting. This news wasn't related to them at all. But it was the biggest one I'd ever held close, and if anyone deserved to hear it, it was Morax.

True mate bonds share all. Who can say what may come of your admissions.

Cryptic words for a creepy mountain goddess. If I could roll my eyes, I would. The memory rushed through my mind, images flashing until one single moment stood out. It was the moment I led King Corson, our father, to his fate. I helped Belial become the monster he is now.

Belial and Morax both grew into clever and important figures in our father's court. But me, he never cared for me. I was too wild, too independent. He never spoke of my mother but once, when he said I had her eyes. And he looked at me with such hate.

Soon after, Belial told me he planned to force our father from the throne and take it for himself. Said it was for us and we would build a new world together. Even then, Bels was too clever, and a touch sadistic. I didn't believe him, but I wanted our father punished. My eldest brother needed a book of dark magic and sent me on a mission to find it.

It was my fault Belial enslaved our people. With the book, he sought out power in other worlds. Found Laszlo Blackbyrn. All the awful things we'd endured led back to the decision I made to ruin my father. Perhaps I should beg for forgiveness from them all.

No one will want me now.

Andras's dominant energy thrummed down the bond. *We cannot know the effects of our actions. Only new action will help us overcome the wrongs we have committed.*

Having one of my new brothers, my true mates, stand up for me in this moment meant everything. I could feel the others, including Seraphina, agreeing with Andras. Hope burned through my veins, filling me with a yearning so fierce, it nearly cast my soul to the stars. I would make this right. I would bring down Belial and build a new world with Seraphina and my mates.

We accept your vow.

CHAPTER FORTY-FIVE
Devon

Having left the stupid Obscuritas and the other Princes behind once upon a time, this bonding experience was a little overwhelming. I knew what mine would be. Andras seemed to have a similar situation. When his secret emerged, he accepted his fate instantly, knowing what this goddess would reveal. I was jealous of how effortlessly he handled it.

Even Levi's revelation was okay, in the end. It was horrible, and I was happy all over again that Darren was fucking dead, but the way Ty showed up for him through the bond, that was worth everything.

And now it was my turn. Time to reveal myself to them.

The night that I shot Ty and Levi. The scene played out in my mind, and so in theirs. My mind was a mess of my own jealousy, insecurity, and hate. The Kings didn't put those feelings there, only amplified them to an extreme degree.

Tell your mates what you did to them.

Sinking into my memories, I remembered the night of the party. How in love with Sera I had been, even then. The Kings poisoned my love for her with doubt and used my distance from my brothers to feed my jealousy. I was ordered to set the trap and bring them in. Shooting Levi and Ty was not part of their plan. I shot them because I wanted to. When I saw Sera in Ty's arms, believing him, siding with him, I lost my shit.

And the bullets. The shot you took.

Damn this fucking truth shit. They were stellatium. I…I was aiming for Ty's heart. I missed.

Guilt burned through my veins. And shame. I didn't deserve to be here, to be with Seraphina or mated with my brothers. If they couldn't forgive me, so be it.

CHAPTER FORTY-SIX
Typhon

The secrets of my brothers and Seraphina bubbling to the surface were dark and twisted, and not the kind I enjoyed. Andras and Seraphina's stories brought my vengeful beast to the surface, but Levi's and Devon's…their secrets were blackening my soul to the point of no return. My own fucking father brutalized my Levi. He was mine to love and fuck and feel things for that I only ever felt when Seraphina first walked into my gym. How could he look at me? How could he stand to be near me?

As early as middle school, people commented on how akin to my father I was. Our relation was indisputable. Did Levi's heart break when I fucked him, got rough with him? Because his secret was breaking mine.

Then Dev. Fucking hells, my own brother truly wanted me dead, and nearly succeeded.

I could feel the bonds linking us all beginning to fray as my own soul unravelled.

It is not your secret shame that we desire. But your forgiveness.
Fuck you.

Pain filled my lungs as the water rushed down my throat. It was nothing compared to the shattering of my fucking heart. I was never certain I had one, until now when it cleaved in two.

Mate bonds are sacred, and only your truest selves can rise again.

More than anything, I wanted the bonds of my brothers and my woman restored. It was my greatest desire, my deepest hope. But in this moment, my soul was unmoored and alone.

The sliver of a thread connecting me to Seraphina glowed with power, tugging me back.

You will never be alone again, Typhon. Come back to us.

Seraphina's words echoed down the bond, a whisper, but it was enough.

My father, the fucking bastard, was dead. I was not him, and never fucking would be. I loved Levi, and I would never let him forget it. And Dev, the little prick. I'd kick his ass again, but forgiveness was his. We deserved forgiveness.

At my final words, the pain subsided. The mate bond pulsed with life. Suddenly, I could feel them all, every emotion flooded through me, but one echoed through us all, joy. A radiant, happy-as-fuck joy.

We did it, motherfuckers. I sent the words down the bond just as control of my own limbs returned. Kicking to the surface, I swam across the pool and wrapped Levi in my arms.

"I wish he was alive, only so I could kill him again," I growled into his neck, biting and marking his flesh.

Levi melted into my arms, tugging my hair free of its tie and threading his fingers in it. "I have never seen him in you. Every inch of your flesh, every piece of your soul, belongs to me, just as I belong to you. I love you, Ty."

His words filled my heart with relief. I knew they were true because of the restored mate bond, but hearing them from his lips was something I didn't know I needed.

A petite figure squeezed between our bodies, and my dick jumped to attention at the naked goddess now wedged between us.

"If you're fucking, we're fucking," Seraphina whined. "Did anyone else get horny as hell the second the mate bond returned?"

Seraphina faced Levi, and he was currently eye-fucking the shit out of her. I wrapped my hand around her throat, holding her in place. With our souls connected and finally freed from the weight of our secrets, it was past time for us to fuck each other into oblivion.

I spotted Dev over Levi's shoulder, hanging back. But not for long. Phen wrapped his arm around Dev's shoulders and dragged him toward us. "No more hiding in corners, brother," Phen gripped the back of Dev's neck. "Don't need the crazy mountain goddess stealing our bonds away."

We were still in the water, but close enough to the stairs for us to stand in waist-deep water. Seraphina moaned in my arms, and I smirked, eyeing Levi's hand between her legs, teasing her.

"Speaking of stealing bonds away," Andras cut in, and I knew I'd rage against his next words. "We don't have time for orgasms. The bonds may be restored, but that doesn't mean they can't be taken away."

Dev nodded, as much as one could with a daemon prince wrapped around him. "Andras is right. We need to get to that battlefield."

At his words, Seraphina wiggled out of my arms. "Yes, let's kill the bad guys, celebrate with orgasms after."

CHAPTER FORTY-SEVEN
Leona

My body was flooded with adrenaline after fighting off those psycho-ass dogs. There were too many fucked-up creatures in this world, and I didn't have nearly enough information or firepower to handle fighting them. The battle was raging, with our side finally winning. If only because of Delphine's sacrifice. Tabitha worked beside me, helping the healers while her own bloodshot eyes remained filled with tears.

I didn't know Delphine all that well, but I knew what it felt like to lose someone who held a piece of your heart. The girl was a badass in my opinion. After everything she'd been through, all the bullshit life threw her way, and now losing one of her mates, it was insane she was still standing here.

If I'd endured all the shit Tabitha had, I'd probably have fucked off to a beach somewhere and never talked to another human again. But we weren't on Earth, or surrounded by humans. There were some. Good guys from the Umbra Noctis, who I met over the years because of Nuri's involvement, and the handful of slaves fighting for the bad guys. They were dying fast. Falling at the hands of their own as much as ours.

The daemons and lumens fighting for Belial didn't care who they killed. The ones that stuck around after the witches freed their bonds, they were vicious as hell. And yet, they were no match for Gremory. That daemon was in serious beast mode after gently placing Delphine's body in one of the healer's tents. He was a fucking devil in every sense of the word. He used the elements, weapons, wings, and claws to maim and kill anyone who stood before him. His fury was infectious, and our own people were fighting with renewed energy. The Kings had retreated to the far side of the field, attempting to take down Morax. But Michaela had joined him, and together they were a fucking force.

I was impressed with the girl. She appeared frail and slender, but clearly packed a punch. And she was a quick study, fighting with her lumen powers with ease. Maybe I was a little envious. Not having any kind of magic like the witches or elemental power like the daemons and lumens put me at a serious disadvantage.

A sudden shift in the air caught my attention, and everyone else's. The enemy army started cheering, and I craned my neck to see what was happening. One of the injured lumens stepped up beside me, looking out on the field.

"Belial has left his castle." The lumen spoke, fear coloring his words. "We're fucked."

I scanned the sky for Nuri. She was fighting near Grem. They both paused long enough to notice the new player on the field. I didn't want her to go after Belial. Of course we had to defeat him to win this fucking war, but if she faced him and lost, I would be completely alone.

She was my only friend, the only creature in the universe I trusted.

It's time, little one. Come to me.

I nearly stumbled when the voice echoed in my mind. He'd been silent for ages, and the absence of his possessive promises had built a longing in me I didn't care to admit to.

Where are you?

In the castle. Locked away. Listen to her wings.

I had no fucking clue what that meant, but someone else might. And I would need help getting into the castle.

"Nuri!" I shouted into the sky, knowing she would hear me even a mile away.

She dove out of the sky, landing before me, covered in gore and looking like some kind of ancient warrior. "What's wrong?" Her eyes raced over my flesh with concern.

I shook my head. "Nothing, really. But we need to go to the castle."

Nuri pursed her lips. "And why is that?"

Planting my feet and squaring my shoulders, I prepared for her reaction to my next revelation. "I've been hearing someone in my head. I thought maybe I was going insane. He's trapped in the castle. He says I can free him. I think it's important and might help us win the war."

Nuri fisted her hands at her sides, her dark-blue eyes glowing with power. "And you have no idea who this is?"

I shrugged. "It sounds insane…but I think it could be King Corson." Nuri sucked in a breath, but I continued before she could interrupt. "He said…listen to her wings."

Nuri's eyes flashed, and an unreadable expression crossed her face. "Let's go while Belial is distracted. Michaela is putting on a show, and the brute can't resist. He's always coveted what he cannot have."

CHAPTER FORTY-EIGHT
Nuriela

Listen to her wings. The words sounded off in my head over and over, like a beacon calling me home. Every night since we returned to Stella Terra, I dreamt of Lailah. At first, they were memories. Moments of happiness from our childhood. Learning to use our powers, teasing smiles and delicate touches. And the night we mated. It wasn't a truly solidified mate bond. We didn't consummate it, but we declared our feelings and shared a kiss that has lived like an imprint on my lips every moment since.

Now, within the castle walls, I could almost taste her power. She was gone, but if her wings were here, they would hold a whisper of what she once was. Rage boiled the blood in my veins at the thought of her magnificent white wings displayed in this rubble. Belial mocked me with such a display. He wanted my Lailah, and this was all he could have of her. But no more.

Lo walked just two steps behind me, mirroring my movements. She'd come so far since I found her half dead in that fire. The burn scars that I couldn't heal she now wore like armor. They were painted over with tattoos, but the design didn't hide them. The tattoo artist worked with the lines of her scars to turn her pain into a work of art. Most of it was covered now in her fitted catsuit and the vest I gave her. It was sewn with stellatium, making it strong enough to stop an average blade from piercing her flesh. There was only so much I could do to protect her.

The castle was mostly empty, with only a handful of soldiers in our way so far. I dispatched them easily. But I refused to let my guard down. That was becoming increasingly difficult the further down we went into the castle. Lailah's scent was in the air and driving me mad.

Nuri.

I gasped, bracing myself against the wall as Lailah's melodic voice caressed my soul for the first time in over a decade.

"Nuri?" Lo touched my forearm softly. "Are you all right?"

So many emotions burned through me, but "all right" was not one of them. "Let's keep moving."

Lo nodded, following me as before until we reached a set of massive, stellatium doors. She immediately moved ahead to open them, knowing they would burn my skin. The chamber within was dimly lit, with no furniture, save for the massive bed at the center. It was less of a bed and more of a coffin, considering it was encased in glass. Power radiated around the thing, and I knew it would be nearly impossible to break it. My power wouldn't be enough.

A rush of Lailah's power reached me, and I spun around to see her perfect wings fastened to the wall. I choked back a sob, fury in my soul at the callous display. Belial's two treasures, his father's soul and the last spark of Lailah's power, locked away for him to admire at his leisure. Well, no longer. I was taking them both.

After an hour of trying every damn thing I could think of, Corson remained locked away. We were able to get Lailah's wings down, and they were now lovingly wrapped in fabric and strapped to my back.

"Is he speaking to you?" I asked Lo once more. She was likely going to punch me.

"No, damnit," she huffed. "How the hell are we supposed to get him out if I can't even get him to speak again?"

I sighed, voicing my growing concern. "Maybe it wasn't Corson speaking to you."

Lo shook her head vehemently. "It's him. I can feel it. It's like my soul is attempting to leave my body. I would start licking the damn coffin if you wouldn't judge me, that's how strong the pull is."

A chuckle escaped my lips. "It does sound like you're experiencing the beginnings of a mating bond. How that's possible, I have no idea. Humans don't mate with daemons or lumens."

"Says who?" she challenged.

I rolled my eyes. "Says all of our history. So unless you've got magic in your blood, it's impossible."

"Aren't you forgetting something?" Lo snarked, tapping her temple. "I could have creatures in my bloodline."

She wasn't wrong. We don't know her full lineage. But the chances that I happened upon the mate of King fucking Corson is wildly unlikely.

Nuri. Help her.

Lailah's voice caressed my ear, and I shivered.

"Let's try your blood."

Before I could make another move, shouting from down the hall caught my attention. Peeping out, I spotted over a dozen soldiers heading our way.

"Shit." I slammed the doors shut, my skin burning against the deadly metal, then conjured several logs to brace against it and keep the soldiers out. Depending on their power levels, we could only have minutes before they broke through.

Lo whipped out a dagger and wasted no time. She cut into her palm and pressed it against the wards on the glass. The castle shook with the force of an avalanche, power crackling in the air. The plan worked, and the glass shattered, turning to dust. But Corson remained prone on the bed.

The doors shook, the metal starting to give. "Lo, we need to go."

I turned back, and my mouth dropped open.

She was straddling the damn king. "Wake up, Sleeping Beauty!" She slapped him across the face, but he didn't budge.

Just know, my heart is yours. It's always been yours.

All I could see in that moment was Lailah. Her pink lips, her soft blue eyes. Her voice filled my mind, and time began to slow.

The doors burst open, and daemons flooded into the room. I whipped out my blades and attacked the soldier closest to me. Within minutes, I was surrounded, fighting off several at once. These daemons had minimal power levels compared to my own, but the sheer numbers were going to overwhelm me.

Make of your power a gift and come to me.

Lailah's words were wrapped up in purest love. For years, I wanted to die. I wanted to end it and meet my mate once more, but she never responded to my pleas for her approval. How could I do such a thing without knowing if she still wanted me? This life, the things I'd done, they were terrible. I'd killed and tortured countless creatures. Lailah would never have done such things.

I know your heart better than even you, Nuriela.

Maybe I was the one going insane, but it was time. And it was the only way to save Lo. She deserved happiness and the chance to find her mate. If it was the king, then I would be the one to give her that chance. I closed my eyes and sent out a massive blast of wind, knocking the daemons away. There was no time to explain what I had to do, so instead, I leapt over the soldiers to Lo's side and snatched her wrist. I used my dagger to carve a symbol into her skin at her wrist.

Lo didn't move, didn't speak, only watched. As soon as it was finished, I carved one in my own flesh. The powerful connection hummed with life as soon as I finished.

What comes next will be important, and only you can save her.

Flashes of the last days I had with my mate filled my head. All the hints she gave me then were coming together now.

I squeezed Lo's hand gently. "Be happy, Lo. I know you're meant for great things. Don't waste your life living with hate and anger."

Her eyes widened. "What are you doing, Nuri?"

Remember Lo. She's the key.

The night Belial nearly captured Lailah and killed me, he bound my life to the daemon king's with dark magic. I nearly forgot about it, until the memories flashed before my eyes. This was why I survived, why Lailah needed me to be here, without her. It was finally time for me to see her again, and save Lo's life in the process.

Smiling at Lo, I glanced at the trapped king. "Give Sleeping Beauty a kiss. Then give those fuckers hell. I'm off to meet my girl."

Before she could respond, I turned back to the daemons. I blasted the shit out of them with everything I had. "I'm coming home, Lailah," I whispered, feeling my power leaving my body and transferring to Lo's. My soul flickered like the dying flame of a spent candle. Only a single spark remained, but it was enough to get me to her. "I'll meet you in the stars, Lailah Valdis."

The night sky was all around me, and stars burned so bright I had to shut my eyes, my last thought only and always of her.

CHAPTER FORTY-NINE
Michaela

The earth shook with so much force, I nearly stumbled to my knees. Morax caught my arm, and we scanned the horizon with wild eyes. Everyone on the battlefield looked to Zamina Castle. A brilliant white light shone into the sky, and a ball of blue fire shot up and away.

"What is that?" My voice was filled with awe at the sight before us. "That can't be something of Belial's. It feels…good."

Morax squinted, his eyes seeing more than mine could. My own senses were heightened, but he had way more practice with it. "It's not my brother, or a daemon. It's a lumen death. I think…I think it is Nuriela."

Horror and fear flooded my nervous system, and my wings snapped out. "No!" I shouted into the wind, ready to fly to her aid, but Morax caught me around the waist.

"You cannot save her, *mae domina*." His voice was soothing as he held me. "She is gone. But the war is not over yet. Let's make her death worth it."

Angry tears bubbled over, and I wiped them away with the back of my hand. Morax was right. "It's past time for Belial to die. Let's do this."

With power humming in my veins and rage in my soul for the ones we lost, I gathered all the air power at my disposal and created a massive vortex, sending it through the battlefield straight for the eldest daemon prince.

Belial's claws raked across the throat of a soldier, and he spun around just in time for my power to knock him out of the sky. He recovered quickly, but Morax was there, ready to take him on. My mate and I fought the arrogant daemon as one unit, using our bond to anticipate the other's moves. Our power worked in tandem, attacking him from all sides.

I could see Belial's fury at being beaten by his own brother, and triumph edged forth within me. But I should have known it wouldn't be that easy. Too focused on the evil asshole, I didn't notice the daemon zooming through the sky at my back. He slammed into me, and we fell to the earth. Morax shouted in alarm, and his moment of fear for me made him vulnerable. Belial slammed a dagger into Mor's side, and I screamed as his pain shot through our bond.

Belial pulled the dagger out with a dark grin, my mate's blood oozing from the wound. Relief coated my thoughts when I saw the dagger was only steel. Mor would heal faster than if it were stellatium.

I wrestled the daemon who knocked me down, searching for a weak spot in his moves. His hand was coated in thorns when it delivered a punch to my side. I wasn't fast enough to dodge him completely, but the slim armor I wore beneath my shirt saved me.

The daemon snarled at me, his eyes red with power and lust. "Belial wants you alive, so I can't kill you. But I can make it hurt. Surrender, lumen whore, and I'll be gentle."

His words were meant to scare me, but I'd been a captive of the Obscuritas Kings and my soul was strong enough to handle this male.

The corners of my lips slowly turned up into a feral grin, and the daemon hesitated. "I will never be someone's prisoner again. And I will not surrender to weak men."

Giving him no time to recover, I leapt into the air and feigned right, forcing the daemon to protect his left side from my sword, leaving his right exposed. Using the element of water, I summoned a dozen icicles and shot them into his side. He screamed in pain, dropping to his knees and melting the ice so he could heal, but I was not going to offer mercy. Stellatium sword in hand, I rushed the daemon, piercing his chestplate and driving the blade into his heart. Wide, unseeing eyes looked up at me as he fell to the dirt, dead in an instant.

My victory was short-lived. I turned to see Mor bleeding from a dozen wounds and losing the fight against his brother. Just as I was ready to join him, Laszlo and Samuel appeared on the battlefield before me.

"Michaela Valdis," Samuel cooed, his voice smooth and enticing. "Won't you come and play with me? I promise you'll enjoy what I offer you, more than what Darren had planned."

I could feel his power of manipulation attempting to coax my mind into compliance, but I was stronger now and shook him off, locking my own mind down with steel doors to keep him out. "Your parlor tricks don't work on me anymore, Samuel Delano. You seem weaker. Perhaps all those stab wounds from my sister are still giving you trouble?"

Samuel snarled, his face turning ugly with his true emotions on display. "Your slut of a sister will pay for that. I will break her so thoroughly, her mind will never recover."

Laszlo held out his palm, a ball of ice hovering above it. I filled my own with fire just as he shot the ice at my feet. It splintered into hundreds of spikes, circling me. A dome of air rose over my head, blocking me from flying away. The two false kings worked together to trap me. I threw my power at the cage, rattling it, but it wasn't enough to break through.

"Michaela!" Morax shouted my name, attempting to run for the Kings, but his brother caught him by the throat with a blade.

"They won't kill her." Belial grinned, his face a vicious mirror of my mate's. "I need her alive for now. But she can watch you die. Know that everything that was yours, dear brother, will be mine."

I screamed as Belial's blade started to break the skin of Mor's throat, and everything suddenly slowed. It was as if I'd paused time itself. Every single creature on the battlefield was moving in slowest motion. A drop of Mor's blood oozed behind the blade, and my heart shook with fear. Power unlike I'd ever unleashed coursed through me and pulsed through the air, slowing until it stopped time entirely.

The energy it took to stop time was draining my power like an unhinged faucet. My limbs shook with the effort to maintain it, and I wasn't going to be able to hold it much longer.

Michaela, stop. You'll die if you don't. Mor's voice echoed down our mate bond.

No. I can hold it. Get away from Belial, and I'll let go. I ground my teeth, sweat coating my brow.

I love you, mae domina.

No. Don't you dare say goodbye. We can do this. Don't fucking give up on me.

Never, my queen, my soul. But I refuse to be the cause of your death, and this power is too strong, it will kill you.

His words rang true; I could feel it. The Sight was more than just visions, it was this raw energy that could stop time itself, but even Lailah had only managed to pause a handful of seconds when she saved Nuri. Wave after wave of energy rushed out of my body as I held the entire battlefield at a standstill.

But I couldn't live without him, I wouldn't live without Morax. There was no life for me without him. I closed my eyes, ready to unleash the full force of the energy within me. I would die, but so would everyone else.

It's you and me forever, Morax. I'll see you in the stars.

Sucking in my last breath, I counted down the seconds. Three. Two.

And then the vision hit me. No, it wasn't a vision. It was real. Seraphina had come.

CHAPTER FIFTY

Seraphina

The scene unfolding below us was fucking insane as we flew over the forest, the crumbling castle in the distance, and the craziest battlefield in between.

"Why is everyone frozen?"

"Look, there." Phen pointed toward a cage of ice in the middle of the barrens. "I think your sister is doing this."

Phen was right. Michaela was trapped in some kind of icy cage, and Morax was at the mercy of Belial. A blinding light coated my sister's body, and I could see her limbs shaking with effort. She was going to fucking kill herself.

"Seems like we arrived just in time," Levi called out to my right. He reached over and pinched my side affectionately. "Let's go give them hell, shall we?"

His navy eyes glowed with power, and lust zipped through my body. His cheeky smirk turned feral as he registered what I was feeling through our mate bond. Having all my men returned to me was a heady feeling. Before, when we were first mated, the bonds were more like a caress. I could feel them, but there was still a barrier. We had all been harbouring our own secrets then, carrying shame and guilt and anger from our past. But no longer. We freed ourselves of those shackles, and

I'd never felt more powerful than I did now. The blood of my daemon father and lumen mother sizzled with power beneath my flesh. It ached to be unleashed. And I knew just the devils who deserved the full extent of my wrath.

My black wings carried me through the air as we soared together through the sky, dropping to the bloodied earth like six beasts unleashed from hell. Now fully embracing their power, my princes looked every bit the daemons they were. It was not only Phen who sported horns and claws, but all five of my mates. They were monsters of the most glorious variety. Andras's wings were jet black and feathered, similar to mine. Levi's were deep red and scaled like a dragon. Typhon's were more batlike, with sharp talons and a shimmer of dark green in the sunlight. And Dev's wings were feathered, a deep charcoal with an almost silver hue to them. Each of my mates was beautiful and terrifying in their monstrous forms, and I loved them all the more.

If only someone was recording this, because our descent to the battlefield must have looked cool as hell. As soon as my booted feet hit the ground, I cast a fire hotter than lava over the ice trapping my sister. It sizzled away into a cool mist.

"Miss me?" I teased, and her eyes widened in relief.

"Morax." She sobbed the word, and I whipped my gaze to her mate, but Phen was already there. He snatched the blade away from Belial just as Michaela let go of her hold over the others.

Shouts of fear and confusion rumbled through the hundreds of creatures, and then the fighting resumed. But it was the shocked and fearful faces of Laszlo and Samuel that had another zip of lust rushing through my veins.

"Seraphina," Andras growled. "Why the fuck are you getting turned on whilst staring at my father?"

I laughed, biting my lip. "Look at the fear on his face? And Samuel, did you miss me? I've come to poke more holes in your weak flesh. Just the thought of the bloodbath to come is making me want to fuck my mates' brains out."

Andras slapped my ass, and I yelped. "No more lusty thoughts, sweetheart. It's time to end this."

Seeing him so animated was doing things to my heart. Andras grinned, his sharp black horns glinting in the daylight, and those chocolate brown eyes I loved winked with devious intent.

"I agree with Andras," Ty purred, his wolfie eyes winking at me. "If I feel one more wave of lust coming from you, I will fuck you until you scream right here on this battlefield."

"ENOUGH," Laszlo bellowed, causing everyone within earshot to turn their attention to him. "Surrender now, or face unimaginable fates."

I rolled my eyes, tossing my hair over my shoulder. "Bring it on, bitch."

And then he did. Laszlo was no weak mortal. He wasn't actually a daemon or lumen, but he was trained enough in dark magic, and with Belial's help, almost as powerful. As soon as the fighting resumed, Morax snatched my sister and rushed out of the fight. She was kicking and screaming, but I was cool with their retreat. They both looked drained, and I'd rather they recoup some strength before joining back into the fray. Besides, this was my fight. The vow I made to destroy the fucker who murderer my mother and my sister. Who forced me to kill my adopted father, Joseph Bronwen, who only ever tried to love us. The fucking dicks who assaulted my sister, my friends and even my mates. And me. Laszlo Blackbyrn did everything he could to break me, and failed. Now it was time for him to die.

We split up into pairs. Andras and Dev taking on Laszlo, while Ty and Levi went after Samuel. I joined Phen with his attack on Belial. The piece of shit daemon prince was definitely the strongest of our enemies, but this time, I was prepared.

Ignoring the distraction tactics he attempted, Phen and I fought him with coordinated attacks, giving Belial no time to pause.

"I see you've mated, Phenex," Belial taunted. "Not male enough to keep her all yourself, though. The whore had to find four other dicks to suck because yours just wasn't enough."

I sent a blast of fire at the asshole. "Sounds like someone is jealous. Whip your dick out, Belial. I bet it's pathetic. Where's your mate? Oh right, no one wanted you."

Phen chuckled, his emotions unbothered by his brother's taunts. The bond between us hummed with confidence and strength. "Your mind games won't work on me any longer, big brother. I have found my family. The ones who truly make me feel alive. Something you will never know."

Belial roared in fury, and we used the opportunity to bring him down. He was strong, though, unnaturally so. Every hit that connected seemed to heal even faster than the next. The fucker was still drawing too much power from his source.

CHAPTER FIFTY-ONE

Leona

When my sister died, I vowed never to care enough for anyone ever again for it to hurt me if I lost them. And I hadn't. No men in my bed, no friends, nothing. Except Nuri. At first, we were just two broken souls working together against a common enemy, but eventually, and against my will, we became more than that. She was the only true friend I had. Someone I felt I could trust completely. I needed her; she was a crutch, a block against everything else I was too afraid to face alone. With her, the monsters stayed away.

And now she was gone, leaving me to walk this miserable world alone once more. Tears blurred my vision for the first time since my sister's death. The brilliant light that appeared with Nuri's final act began to fade, and her lifeless body rested on the floor, surrounded by dozens of dead soldiers.

The mark she carved into my wrist had healed, surprisingly fast. And something strange hummed in my veins. It crawled under my flesh, as if seeking something, or testing its new owner. I didn't know how I knew it, but this entity was Nuri's power. Her final act in this world was to gift me what made her a lumen. I closed my eyes and tried to wield it, but nothing happened. Her power didn't answer to me, not yet.

It was eerily quiet in the castle now. Sighing, I turned back to the king, still lying on the stone bed, but now he looked more alive and less like a statue.

Moving carefully, I climbed on top of him again and noted his features. He might have been the most beautiful creature I'd ever seen. And damn, he was massive. My legs could barely straddle his waist. This daemon king had to be seven feet tall. His thighs were the size of tree trunks, and his arms were nearly as thick as my waist. He had similar facial features to his sons. They all had olive-toned skin, sharp jawlines, and jet-black hair. The king's was longer and wild, even more so than Phenex's. His lips were full, and I licked my own, staring at him.

With her final breaths, Nuri told me to kiss him. Pretending the idea wasn't something I fantasized about after his filthy promises in my head was futile at this point. Voices called out in the castle, far away, but not far enough. The battle was raging again, and if I was caught in here, no one would be saving me. And since the power in my veins was resisting me, waking Corson was my only option.

I just hoped he was mine, like he professed, and not an evil psycho like Belial. Leaning down slowly, I caressed his cheek, the sharp stubble tickling my palm, and pressed my lips to his.

Wake up, daemon king. I sent the thought out, and within seconds, the monster beneath me stirred.

A deep growl built in his chest. His eyes snapped open, and I gasped at the stunning colors swirling in his irises, greens and golden browns, like a wolf. His clawed hands snatched my hips, squeezing tight, the sharp points digging into my flesh, but not enough to draw blood.

I held my breath, staring down at the beast, and waited to see what would happen next. He inhaled deeply, and my thighs itched to squeeze together. His nostrils flared, and a dark grin touched his lips, the glint of fangs displayed in a show of dominance.

"Hello, little one," he purred. "I knew you'd find me."

Words escaped me in that moment, and I licked my parched lips. His eyes tracked the movement predatorily. His large hands squeezed my waist. Corson rolled his hips beneath me, and I could feel the hard length of his dick pressing against his pants.

The soft leggings I wore were about to be soaked with my arousal if he kept doing that.

Corson groaned. "Your scent is intoxicating, nearly as breathtaking as your beauty." He lifted my shirt and traced the tattoo-covered scars down my left side. He snarled. "Every inch of you is perfect, little one, never forget that. But I will make the ones who did this to you writhe in pain before they die."

His hand against my bare skin made me shiver, and my mind barely registered the fact that I was letting someone touch me without losing my shit. I still hadn't spoken a word, and Corson didn't seem troubled by my reactions.

He cocked his head, rolling his hips again so I could feel him. "My son is still draining my power with the perverted bond he forced on me. It can only be undone by my mate. We need to consummate our bond, my beauty."

My brain finally caught up with my mouth, only to blurt out the first thought I had. "You mean we have to fuck right now?"

Corson's dark chuckle turned into a seductive purr as his hands roamed over my thighs. "So crass. So slender in my arms, but I can see you are fierce. Yes, mate. We need to fuck for our bond to break the dark magic my son used to bind my soul to his. Only you can do this, by becoming my mate, or killing me. The choice is yours."

A ridiculous laugh escaped my lips. For over a decade, I had sworn off sex and anything intimate with anyone. And I'd killed often. You'd think the choice would be simple. Kill the king, save everyone. And yet, this beast, who could easily overpower me and take whatever he wanted, was giving me a choice. His life was in my hands. I could sense the hint of a bond between us, and maybe it was the power hiding in my blood or I actually had gone insane, but I didn't want to kill him.

Actually fucking him, though, still seemed terrifying. And I was incredibly inexperienced. He likely had hundreds of partners over the years. What could I even offer?

He seemed to read my inner turmoil as if my feelings were written plainly on my face. "I will not force you, little one. But know, you were made to be mine, and there is nothing within your dark and broken soul that will scare me away."

Fucking hell. He was really good with words. Fuck it.

"I don't want to kill you." I spoke slowly, my face flushing with embarrassment at what I needed him to do.

His wolf-like eyes filled with lust and pulsed with tempered power. Corson rolled his hips again, his dick feeling even thicker between my legs. My leggings were absolutely soaked.

"It's going to sound fucked up, but I need you to do it." I whispered the words, barely able to say them out loud. It was shameful, but after the way I was introduced to sex against my will, it's what I needed. Wanted. Desired.

"Do not hide your desires from me, mate. Give me your most depraved thoughts, and I will bring them to life for you," he purred, a devil smirking up at me.

I leaned forward, slowly gliding my hand up his chest until I wrapped it around his neck. Well, not really. His neck was thick and muscular, just like the rest of him. "I need you to force me."

Power hummed around us at my admission, and before I could blink, Corson had switched our positions, my back now flat against the stone bed he'd previously been trapped on. He continued to purr and growl, the deadly sounds doing things to my insides as he ripped my clothes from my body until I was naked and on display for him.

I squirmed under his gaze, but Corson gave me not an inch of space to move. His arm snapped out and easily wrapped around my throat, holding me in place but still allowing me to breathe.

With his other hand, he undressed. His chest had a smattering of black hair, covering chiseled abs and the most delicious hips with that V-shape you only saw on models in porn magazines. He oozed raw power and masculine energy. And his fucking dick.

"Oh god. Oh fuck," I whimpered as he pressed the head of his huge dick against my bare pussy.

Corson grinned, his dark horns spiraling out of his long hair, and looked over every bit the daemon king he was. "No god. Only me."

He didn't give me time to change my mind, to resist, to move. Corson sheathed himself fully within me, and I screamed at the intrusion. He was so fucking huge, I thought he'd tear me in half. Corson roared, pounding into me over and over like a wild animal.

"Mine," he snarled, his eyes glowing as his power returned to him. "You are fucking mine. And the world will burn for keeping me from finding you sooner."

I moaned, my back arching as he took and took from me. The pain subsided as pleasure unlike anything I'd ever experienced flooded my system. His hand squeezed my throat, and the lack of oxygen brought the pleasure to new heights. My senses exploded as the mate bond tying me to this beast grew stronger.

Corson loomed over me, his hand letting up slightly so I could suck in a breath, the relentless thrusts of his hips continuing. "Open your eyes. They're glowing like emeralds, filled with a dark lust that matches my own."

Staring up at this beast, I knew I'd made the right decision. The bond between us hummed with power the closer I got to pure bliss. My blood sang with Nuri's gifted power, seeking out the daemon king's soul that was slowly tethering to my own. I could feel him within me now.

"Leona. My Leona," Corson purred, my name a prayer on his lips. "Come for me, mate of mine."

And then he was on me, his sharpened canines biting into the soft flesh at my throat, latching on to suck the lifeforce right out of me. This new combination of pain and pleasure sent me over the edge, and I screamed as my first real orgasm that didn't come from my own hand sailed through my body with the force of a hurricane. My pussy clamped down on his cock, and Corson groaned, his own desire peaking with mine as he filled me with his seed.

The moment he bit me, the mate bond burst to life and Corson's mind opened to me. Every feeling he had I could now feel. The bond pulsed with energy and was overwhelming my senses.

Corson pulled away, lapping at the wound he made on my neck. "Now take my blood, my lifeforce, and let our bond be sealed for eternity."

My daemon mate pressed one of his sharp claws to his bare chest, just over his heart, and blood welled over the cut. He leaned down, his cock still inside me, half hard and throbbing. He rolled his hips, groaning as I lifted up on my elbows and licked the blood from his chest. Corson grabbed the back of my head and forced my mouth onto the wound.

"Bite me," he commanded. "Mark me with your teeth and claim my soul for yourself."

His words filled me with a heady power. I could feel my teeth sharpening as I bit into his flesh and drank from him. It was absolutely insane, and felt right all at once.

Mine for eternity. As I am yours.

His words boomed in my mind, and his possessive need filled my soul.

CHAPTER FIFTY-TWO

Leviathan

A possessive snarl escaped my lips when I saw Seraphina leap at some daemon scum and wrap her legs around his face, stabbing him in the head. "Seraphina! Get your perfect pussy away from that fucker's mouth!"

The daemon in question dropped to the dirt, blood pissing from his head and my girl straddling him with a grin. I snatched her arms, pulling her off of him, and cupped between her legs like a domineering animal. "The only mouths that are allowed so close to your pretty pussy are your mates'."

She laughed, tousling my shaggy hair and rolling her hips against my hand. "I didn't really think the plan through. I just thought, how can I kill this prick and have fun at the same time?"

Ty landed next to me, his leathery wings folded at his back. His horns were curled and ribbed like a ram, and all I could think about was gripping them while he fucked me into oblivion.

He winked at me, a knowing smirk on his face, then turned and set the body of the daemon Seraphina nearly face-fucked on fire. "No more cunt-to-face ninja moves, pet. Or I'll be forced to get out the paddle."

Seraphina leapt into the sky to rejoin Phen in his fight with Belial. "Don't threaten me with a good time."

The battle was officially in our favor, but our biggest threats needed to be turned to ash. I clamped my hand on Ty's shoulder. "Shall we go kill my father?"

My brother-in-arms and mate for eternity grinned like the daemon he was, and we stalked Samuel Delano through the bloody field of bodies. Gremory was off to our right, his fighting more ferocious than ever. Delphine was not on the field, which was concerning, but perhaps she was with the healers. Since our arrival, we hadn't had much time for small talk.

I watched from several feet away as my father dispatched a member of the Umbra Noctis with ease. James, Ty's gym manager and friend, rushed Samuel, and I heard Ty cry out as the man attacked my father. We started to run, refusing to let the villains of our lives take another creature we cared for from this world.

Samuel was seconds away from bringing James down when Ty lashed a whip around my father's neck and yanked hard. He cried out, falling to his knees, but recovered quickly. James nodded to us and moved on to find a new opponent.

"Well, if it isn't my disappointing son and his dim-witted bodyguard," Samuel taunted, bringing air into his palms and preparing to fight. "When will you ever learn to fight your own battles? Can't take me on your own?"

Once upon a time, his words held more weight. He manipulated me, taunted and dragged me with his words, and I let them hold power over my actions, my soul. But no longer.

Fire burned through my veins, coating my skin in a deadly heat. I relished the fire, as it was always my fascination, and became my sanctuary. The flames listened to my every command, and now they would burn the man I should have destroyed sooner.

"That's always been your problem, Samuel." I smirked at him, unaffected. "You've never known true companionship. I could kill you on my own, but why deprive my brother, my mate, of the privilege of causing you pain?"

Samuel's eye twitched, a subtle sign of his discomfort. "You're too weak to even try. Go on, send the dullard away and face me like a ma—"

His words were cut off by Ty whipping him again and again until the man's flesh peeled from his bones and blood coated the dirt at his feet. Samuel snarled and fought, finally catching one of Ty's legs with a whip of air and sending him flying. But I wouldn't give him time to recover. I grabbed my father from behind, holding him in an unbreakable hug.

"Come, father, no more words. I want to hear you scream," I purred into his ear, letting fire consume us both.

I'd mastered the elemental power of fire more quickly than any other, and it was stronger than the air power he favored. Samuel screamed as he tried to break free of me, but I was his reaper and he would not escape this battlefield alive.

Ty returned, rage in his eyes and a smug smile on his face. My flames would never harm him, and he stepped up to my father, a stellatium blade in hand.

He peeled away the scraps of clothing still covering Samuel's body. The flames licked at his flesh while he screamed. "This is for every time you forced horrid experiments on us." Ty stabbed him in the chest. "This is for thinking you could take Seraphina from us." Ty stabbed him in the gut. "And this is for letting vile beings rape Levi to help you gain power." Ty snarled the last words and sliced my father's dick clean off.

The high-pitched scream that left my father's lips was one of pure agony and gave me an unholy amount of satisfaction. Blood pissed from his mutilated junk, his belly, and his chest. His skin was bubbly and charred. The pain of it all was clear on his face. I shouldn't have enjoyed this, but I did. Samuel Delano was one of the worst people I'd ever known. And his cruelty was at an end.

When the screaming stopped, Ty and I smiled grimly at each other. "Finally," I sighed. "Thank you, brother."

Ty pulled me into his arms and hugged me fiercely. "I wish I could bring him back and do it over and over again. Killing him once wasn't enough for what he put us through. For what he did to you."

I shook my head. "Once was enough. The real treat will be to move on with our mates, together, and never think of him again."

Ty nodded, and we turned to the others, only to see Andras and Dev battling Laszlo with everything they had. Three kings down, one to go.

CHAPTER FIFTY-THREE

Andras

Taking down the Obscuritas Kings was never going to be easy, and I knew from the start of our plans to wipe them out that my father would be the most difficult.

Devon and I fought him with cold precision. My brother might have been more emotionally inclined than I was, but with our mate bonds fully intact, we worked in perfect coordination. My father didn't speak. He didn't try to taunt me as I overheard Samuel attempting with Levi and Ty. Laszlo Blackbyrn raised me to be as cruel and calculating as he was. Which meant he knew I would never fall for a trick like that. And by the sound of Samuel's screams, neither did they.

Devon, however, was not above taunting the devil. "Sounds like you're the last cult king, Laszlo," he sneered, almost happily. "And you will die just as they have. Alone."

Laszlo created a shield of ice in front of him to block our attacks. "Not unlike your father, Devon. Although he died begging for his life. The traitor. He thought we didn't know about his secret daughter. I will say, I took pleasure in letting him know, just before the end, that she was mine now."

"Fuck," I mumbled, seconds before Devon launched himself at my father. Which was exactly what he wanted.

Devon, damnit, get out of here. He's going to kill you.

My brother's rage was only surface level, though. Laszlo assumed Devon had lost control, but when he pulled down his shield to spear him in the chest, Devon's own earth power turned the spear to dust and launched his own blade at my father instead. It was an impressive move, but not quite enough. Blood trickled down Laszlo's cheek for only several seconds before the wound healed. He was healing too fast, even for his level of power.

We discovered much over the last year, and Laszlo Blackbyrn was doing everything he could to become immortal. It was more than just gaining daemon power, he wanted to become a god.

"Where is my sister, you piece of shit?" Devon snarled.

Laszlo smiled, his clothing still impeccably clean for being in the middle of a war. "She's tucked away in the castle. Did I forget to mention, I've tied her life to mine? I'm sure that cut you dealt me just now felt much worse for her."

"You're lying." Devon spat the words, true anguish reaching him now.

"Tell me, son, do I lie?" Laszlo mused, his black eyes glittering with malice.

"You're the biggest lie of them all, Laszlo." I held his gaze, unafraid. "But you're also cruel, and I have no doubt what you say is true. If only to hurt as many people as you can before we end you."

"And you could have been my greatest accomplishment. A true Obscuritas Prince." Laszlo's fury colored his words, the cool demeanor faltering. "Instead you succumbed to baser emotions like love. It will be your undoing, son."

Icy rage built within me, and I itched to fight him, but without truly knowing the state of Dev's sister, I hesitated.

Devon. Take Ty and Levi and go find your sister. I'll handle my father.

Devon frowned at me. *Alone?*

Thanks to you and Seraphina, we are never alone. Go, brothers. I've got this.

Wasting no time, Devon and the others launched into the sky and raced away for the castle ruins in the distance.

Laszlo smirked at me. "Sent your playmates away? I would've enjoyed an audience."

My father was unravelling. I could sense the slightest hint of unease beneath his cool facade. But where his fear was coming from, I wasn't sure. At least, until we heard Belial's bellow of rage.

Seraphina dropped from the sky at my side, smiling as if Santa Claus just appeared with gifts on a snowy Christmas morning.

"If I believed in Santa, then yes, totally," she sassed, hearing my thoughts as clearly as I could hers. "Belial's reign of zombie terror is coming to an end."

I arched an eyebrow at her. "Is that so?"

She nodded, turning her back on my father and focusing her attention on me instead. It was a bold and calculated move, and fuck if I didn't love her more for it. Seraphina was truly fearless, and in all her years, never gave my father what he coveted most. Her.

His careful mask vanished, and his lust and demented envy for my mate clouded his normally dead eyes. "That's impossible."

Seraphina didn't even turn around. Instead, she wrapped her arms around my neck and reached up on her tiptoes to smash her lush, red lips into mine. A ring of fire bloomed around us, cocooning us in this moment of bliss on the battlefield.

Breaking from the kiss, I stared into her ocean eyes with nothing but pride and adoration. "I love you, angel. More than anything."

Her eyes glowed softly, and I could feel the emotions down our bond mirroring my own. "And I love you, Andras." She cocked her head at me and smirked. "Perhaps we think of changing your name, though. What about Valdis? Way cooler than Blackbyrn."

I chuckled and kissed her forehead. "Are you proposing to me, Seraphina Valdis?"

She scoffed and rolled her eyes, earning her a smack on the ass, which of course she loved. "We are so beyond husband and wife, Andras. Unless we make it weird and pass around a cup of blood or something cool like that."

This time, a full-on laugh escaped my lips. "I would gladly take your name and be rid of the Blackbyrn family once and for all. And drink your blood, too. Anything you want, you shall have it."

The fire Seraphina erected around us sizzled when my father's ice finally breached her power. I had a feeling she let him. My mate's power was beyond anything we'd known. With the bond restored, I could feel the endless well of it living within her. Seraphina had yet to unleash her full power.

"Did your mate tell you how she knelt at my feet and sucked my cock, son?" Laszlo drawled. "Did she tell you…how much she enjoyed it?"

Shame trickled down the mate bond, and five very angry snarls reared up around her.

Don't you fucking dare fall for that shit, pet. Ty sent his rage-filled response through our connection.

Phenex chimed in next. *You are a fucking queen, Seraphina Valdis. Make him bow.*

Give him hell, mera dil. *For all of us.* Dev added, sending strength down our bond.

Levi's emotions were laced with vengeful fire. *I'll burn his balls to ash. Unleash the beast within,* diabla.

Seraphina stared up at me, letting the initial reaction to my father's words fade away and keeping close the love and strength of her mates. I brushed a lock of silvery blue hair from her face.

"Reclaim your power, Seraphina," I whispered into her ear. And then I knelt before her, both knees on the ground, so she could look down at me and see that no one was above her in her quest for revenge against my father. "I bow for my queen, my mate, and the most powerful creature in this world."

Laszlo scoffed, but his jealousy was obvious. "You whimpering fool. She's already had her mouth filled with my cock. And I will have the rest of her before this day ends."

My father charged at us, and I leapt to my feet, ready to protect her, but she didn't need my protection.

Seraphina turned to Laszlo as if she had all the time in the world and held up one hand. "Stop."

She spoke the world softly, almost melodically, and Laszlo froze. His eyes nearly bugged out of his head. "You little—"

"Don't speak," she commanded, her voice still carrying that lilt. "It's over, Laszlo Blackbyrn."

I watched her in awe, ready to defend if needed, but she was finally freeing her invisible shackles, her ties to her past shame and regrets. Her skin glowed with a silver light, and her wings unfolded, black and glittering with the ends colored red and orange as if they were on fire.

We've got my sister. She's knocked out now, but she's okay. Devon's voice was filled with relief.

Levi chuckled. *And Seraphina was right. Some crazy shit went down here.*

More like crazy fucking. The daemon king is more feral than I am. Ty snarked.

Their joy was infectious, and I was eager to join them, but first, my father needed to be dealt with.

CHAPTER FIFTY-FOUR
Seraphina

With the unbridled love and trust from my mates, I deliberately clipped the ties binding my energy to the guilt of my past. My actions were not always noble, and I could never repay the debt of life I owed to those who died for my family, for my need for revenge, but I could make amends the only way I knew how. One final act of vengeance.

Laszlo Blackbyrn had tried to break me from day one. He murdered my family, my friends. Tortured and brutalized the people I cared for. But no more. Power bloomed within me; the blood in my veins carried the magic of two royal bloodlines. I closed my eyes and embraced all of it, my daemon heritage, my royal lumen family, and even my mortal father, a sacrifice I would never forget. The elemental power crashed through my body with the force of a tsunami. And something more.

Cancatiers are what humans think of as sirens. A creature who can lure others to their call with a song.

I'd been quietly practicing this strange power since I heard of it while being held prisoner. It was difficult to do when you also didn't actively want to take away someone's free will. But damn was it cool. With just a few words, Laszlo now belonged to me.

Slowly, I circled his rigid form, sniffing out his fears. This power could also taste the emotions of those around me, and while Laszlo was still angry and arrogant, fear was creeping in.

"How did you bind yourself to Devon's sister?" I asked, using the song-like voice to force his response.

Laszlo ground his teeth, as if the answer was being ripped from his lips. "There are stolen manuscripts in the castle, taken by Belial from witches and creatures from other worlds."

"And what else were you doing with these books? I know you weren't planning to be Belial's lapdog," I taunted.

The dethroned king growled. "Never. I called on the gods. And I was going to bind one to me, stealing his power and immortality."

Andras stepped up to my left side. "You called? As in, there is already a god under your thumb?"

Laszlo ignored his son, but I wasn't having any of that. I sang out the words, compelling him to answer.

The man's eyes were so furious, I nearly laughed. "No. I managed to open a way to bring the god to Earth, but he was too strong. I lost him."

Andras arched an eyebrow, and we exchanged shocked expressions. "Well shit. Didn't realize there were literal gods wandering around."

My other mates returned, Devon carrying his sleeping sister in his arms. Several healers ran to us and took her to safety, but the battlefield was silent. Only Belial remained, and he was about to face a gnarly reunion.

It was time for Laszlo Blackbyrn to die. With my mates at my sides, I rose up several feet from the ground and glared down at the man I vowed to end.

"Laszlo Blackbyrn," I stated loud enough for all to hear. "You have committed horrible acts against my friends, my family, and mankind. You deserve to die."

His fear filled me with a heady satisfaction, and I continued. "You and all that you built will be ripped to shreds, stricken from this world and every other. No one will remember you. You will die here and never be thought of again."

Laszlo's body raged, but with my power commanding him, he could not speak. In his final moments, he could do nothing but watch and wait to die.

Ty laughed, a deep happy sound. "Do you smell that? Blackbyrn's pissed himself."

The others grinned, and a smirk touched my lips, knowing that in the end, he was alone and afraid. I called on all the elements, building a tornado of power, surrounding him completely. Because I was still a little sadistic, I gave him the ability to scream. And he did. Boy, did that piece of shit know how to scream. We could hear his terror through the wind as the elements tore him to shreds. The powerful storm dissipated, and there was nothing left of the once Obscuritas King, Laszlo Blackbyrn.

Andras hugged me from behind, kissing my neck softly. "Thank you for freeing us of him. *Tu es magnifique, mon ange.*"

His words fed the unfettered happiness building within me. I could feel the others through the bond, a wild joy overtaking each of us. The Kings were finally gone. I looked across the field at Phenex, the final piece of the puzzle and much needed mate in our little family. He and Morax had Belial caged, with Michaela's help. My sister was using her crazy Seer power to slow Belial's movements so he couldn't fight. She was a fucking badass.

We joined them, lending our own power to Belial's cage so my sister could rest. She looked a little rough, and I was concerned she'd bottom out with so much power flowing out of her.

Brushing my shoulder against hers, I checked her for injuries. "Hey, sis. See you've been out here kickin' ass today."

She smiled, but it didn't fully reach her eyes. "Yeah. We couldn't save everyone, though."

I was about to question her when a monster of a fucking daemon dropped from the sky with a petite human in his arms. The face of the daemon in question was all too familiar. King Corson looked a hell of a lot like his sons, but at least a full size bigger. He was like a damn bear. And the tiny human at his side, who was definitely radiating some not-so-human powers, was Leona.

"What in the fuck is going on?" I gawked, unable to hide my surprise. We'd heard from Phen and Mor that Belial's connection to his father broke, but how that happened was still a bit of a mystery.

Ty snickered at my side. "Little Lo bagged herself a daemon king."

Levi grinned. "Yeah. He nearly took our heads off when we went into the castle. Phen saved us."

Phen winked at me and waggled his eyebrows, as if I didn't know all the dirty promises he was already sending down the mate bond.

"My sons." Corson spoke, his voice deep and commanding. "Belial. How did it come to this?"

Belial was like a feral cat, snarling and raging in his cage. This was one beast who would never be tamed. It was plain enough for us to see. If we let him go, he would do everything in his power to destroy us and continue his plans for domination.

Corson explained, in short, how his son had stolen away his free will with dark magic. It began more subtly, influencing the King's decisions until he thought he was going mad. When he realized something was wrong, it was too late, and Belial sent Corson into a deep sleep.

Pain and sorrow speared my heart as Phen fully understood the weight of his father's words. Corson was not the monster Phen and Mor thought he was. Belial, their twisted eldest brother, was the true devil hiding in their midst.

CHAPTER FIFTY-FIVE
Michaela

Morax, my mate and husband, was struggling with the revelations of the evening. The sun was setting behind the castle, and stars glittered above us as the moon rose into the sky. We sat together, staring up at the stars, as the events of the day settled in. I squeezed his hand.

Since the end of the fight, Morax refused to let me go, and I didn't mind one bit. There were several moments today when I thought we might lose each other. Just as my visions predicted, Seraphina and her mates arrived and turned the tide of the war in our favor, but not before we lost a few of our own.

Hundreds of daemons, lumens, witches, and humans lost their lives in this final battle between good and evil. Because in the end, that's what it came down to. I knew our side had also made some bad choices, but we saved countless lives, too.

"Should I be feeling bad that I don't feel bad about my sister murdering Laszlo Blackbyrn?" I mused out loud, knowing what his response would be.

"Absolutely not," Morax growled, pulling me into his arms. He lifted me effortlessly until I was straddling his hips, facing him, our bodies melting into each other. "I would have killed him myself, given the chance, for what he did to you. It wasn't murder, little lumen. His death was a deserved punishment for his crimes."

I nodded, but Morax continued before I could respond. Cupping my chin, he forced me to look into his eyes when he spoke next. "You, my gentle wife, must not waste any more feelings on the Obscuritas Kings, or anyone else undeserving of your attention."

He was right, of course. They didn't deserve our attention, or our mercy. "What about you, are you okay with Belial's punishment?"

Corson couldn't bring himself to kill Belial, so for now, the evil prince was locked away in an impenetrable cage. My sister insisted on being present and making sure it was secure. I trusted her, and for now, the prince lived.

Mor sighed, and his golden eyes dimmed. "It is difficult to understand my feelings. For most of my life, I believed my father was the villain. He was horrible to us. To our people. But it was Belial all along. That is a lot to reconcile. And my eldest brother's actions played a major role in all the pain and suffering of your family. If not for his choices, you may never have been harmed the way you were by that ridiculous cult."

The traumatic memories of what Darren Radnor and the other Obscuritas Kings did to me were locked away in a vault. Not because I was afraid to face them, but because they didn't deserve my time.

"And if not for Belial, perhaps I would not have summoned you, and we would not be here, in each other's arms," I murmured against his lips. "I will always carry heartache for the ones we have lost, but a life without you, Morax, would have been no life at all."

My mate smiled at me, some of that golden power returning to his beautiful eyes. "Aren't you wise, mate of mine?"

I nodded. "Oh yes, I am very wise." I wiggled against him, and Morax growled.

Mor nipped at my lips. "And asking for trouble, sassy princess."

Voices carried to us, and Morax lifted me into his arms and stood in one graceful movement. He carried me toward the growing crowd, only setting me on my feet when we got close enough to hear our friends sharing their stories of the day.

A giant pyre had been erected, with several bodies of our friends carefully wrapped and laid on the logs.

Delphine. She sacrificed her life to save Gremory and Tabitha, and countless others. Gremory and Tibby were huddled close together. Neither had spoken much since the battle ended. Mor shared the news of his father and brother with Gremory, and he only nodded, accepting the information without giving much away.

Nuriela had done something similar. Only, while Delphine channeled her magic into a stone for Tibby to carry and use when needed, Nuriela had done something even most daemons and lumens had never heard of. The lumen mate of my eldest sister had somehow transferred her lumen power to Lo. It was unheard of, considering Lo was a human, or so we all thought. It was supposed to be impossible for mortals to become daemons or lumens. The mechanics of that entire scenario were still being worked out.

My sister stood close to Tibby, offering her support to one of the only friends she'd made over the last ten years. Gremory wasn't letting anyone close to his mate, but Seraphina was the exception.

Phen carried another body onto the pyre, stating the daemon's name as he laid the body with the others. The young male, Elgo, was the one to lead my sister and her mates to the mountain. He'd arrived to join us in battle, letting us know they successfully entered. And then Elgo had been one of the first to die by Belial's darker creations. Elgo joined a group of truxens fighting in their animal forms. The truxens fought more fiercely than any, taking on the monstrous creatures in Belial's army, including those crazy devil dogs. Only after they started dying did we realize they were once daemons and lumens. Belial's dark magic had forced them into animal form permanently.

The sins of the daemon prince were long and varied.

Phen took the young daemon's death quite hard. Seraphina pulled him into her arms when he stepped away from the pyre.

The gathered crowd waited in silence, the air heavy with loss. Seraphina cleared her throat, and we looked to her as one.

"I'm not exactly the speech-giving type," she began, almost shyly. "But I wanted everyone here to know how much it means to me that you fought at my side. That you came together after so long to finally free yourselves, this world, and my own from tyrants and would-be kings who encouraged only hate and submission. I don't know what the plan is now, but I know I will do whatever I can to help restore what was lost."

Murmurs of agreement flitted through the crowd. Several louder voices mentioned the Valdis name, the royal bloodline.

Phenex spoke up next. "Seraphina is the one the prophecies whispered about. The one with power unlike our world has seen for centuries. The one who would change what was and bring about a new age for all daemons and lumens. She is my queen, my mate, and I would kneel for her, now and always."

Phen's declaration had the murmurs growing even louder, several people looking to their neighbors to see if any would kneel, but my sister stopped them.

"While I love having my mates on their knees, I have no desire to be queen in any true sense," Seraphina declared, holding up her hands in surrender. "I'll be your champion, your muscle, whatever you need, but I'm no ruler. And if I had to choose one, it would be my sister, Michaela."

"What the…" My words failed me at her announcement. My cheeks turned hot with the hundreds of eyes now staring in my direction. King Corson remained silent, a giant in the shadows with his new mate.

Morax brushed his hand against my back, reassuring me before he stepped forward. "Perhaps I am biased, but I too believe Michaela Valdis would make a just and compassionate queen. Do we need a royal to lead us? I cannot say. Today is not the day to decide. Let us mourn our dead, celebrate their accomplishments, and cherish the time we shared with them."

I loved him so completely, so thoroughly, I thought my heart might burst from it. And Seraphina. These people believed in me so fully, it was the most loved I'd ever felt in my life. Tugging his arm, I pulled Morax to me for a soft kiss. I really wanted to attack him with several inappropriate kisses, but now wasn't the time.

Later, mae domina. *Later I will worship my queen.*

Seraphina used her power to light the pyre, and we looked on in respectful silence. The stars above us twinkled and glowed brighter than normal, as if they too were welcoming the souls of our fallen friends. One particularly bright star with a hint of pink to it shone above the others. I gasped when a new star joined it, a soft blue color emanating from it. How I knew, I couldn't tell you, but I was certain those stars were the souls of Lailah and Nuriela. While my heart wished they were here with us, I was happy to see them finally together again.

CHAPTER FIFTY-SIX

Seraphina

The celebrations that occurred among my people were fucking wild. These creatures truly knew how to party. And the number of orgasms my body could take had reached a new record. Having the privilege of five sexy-as-fuck mates with soaring libidos was really doing things for my self-esteem. But it wasn't just for me. The six of us were one family, always there for each other. Even in my darkest, loneliest moments, I wished for this. For a love that refused to break, that could survive any hardships. And with my princes, I found that kind of love.

Devon joined me on the balcony of the truxen palace. We'd traveled back to their city, finding it more appealing than the castle with Corson and Lo. It was crazy as hell that Lo was now some kind of born again lumen and mated to Phen's father. *Did that make her my mother-in-law?*

Well, sort-of. The six of us had collectively decided we didn't need a ceremony. Being called a wife just wasn't my thing. Instead, we got really drunk on each other's blood, with the cup and everything, like I told Andras I wanted. Then had each of our love bites permanently marked onto our skin.

Ty, as promised, had his on my ass. And I got mine on his dick. Phen also begged Ty to pierce his cock so they could be twins. Then Phen convinced me to let him pierce my nipples. It hurt like a bitch, but the orgasms from Levi's wicked mouth just as the needle entered my flesh made up for the pain. And of course they were so pretty I couldn't stop staring at them. I walked around topless constantly, which maybe was also the reason I continued to have endless orgasms.

"How are you, *mera dil*?" Dev inquired, wrapping his arm around my waist and resting his chin on my bare shoulder.

I wore a navy-blue, silk, halter-necked gown with nothing underneath. His fingers danced over the fabric across my abs, teasing and keeping my lust-filled thoughts active.

"Enjoying the view and the company." I smiled, staring out at the starry sky. "How are you? Given any thought to what we do next?"

Devon shrugged. "Where you go, I follow. My sister is doing well here, with the truxens. I believe she wishes to stay for a while. But that doesn't mean we must stay."

We were deciding as a family what our next moves were. None of us had any real desire to return to Earth. Michaela and Morax were staying on Stella Terra. Grem and Tibby were headed to Earth, with plans to go to New Orleans. Delphine had left them with a few wishes, and one included finding a witch in New Orleans that would need help.

I was happy they had each other and hoped having a mission of sorts would also help my dearest friend and her mate find some kind of happiness, even with Delphine's absence.

Corson abdicated as king of the daemons, and was now fully invested in Lo's well-being. The power Nuri gave her hadn't fully settled, and he was concerned. They were going to some entirely different planet for assistance.

And I was maybe more interested in a similar path. My time on Earth, and even here, was colored with bad memories, loss and pain. It wasn't all bad, seeing as this world also returned my mates to me and restored our bonds. But I was leaning on some otherworldly travel. For ten years, my entire life centered on revenge, and now that quest was over. I was free. We were free to live however we liked. And a vacation with my mates to a faraway land sounded pretty fucking cool.

A few moments later, the other four princes joined Dev and me on the balcony. Ty pulled me from Dev's arms and spun me around. He lifted me off the ground and sat my ass on the balcony ledge, spreading my legs so he could plant himself snugly between them.

Ty growled, tugging the ties at the back of my neck until the top of my dress fell away. The cold air nipped at my pierced nips, and his growl turned possessive as he captured one peaked bud in his mouth. I moaned and closed my eyes, enjoying the attention.

Levi waved a hand, and suddenly we were surrounded by fog, blocking out the party and any prying eyes. "So, are we going on adventures?"

Ty released my right breast and continued over to the other. His hand drifted up my thigh, teasing me with gentle touches that were much too slow. I grabbed his wrist and shoved his fingers against my bare pussy.

My monster man chuckled. "My pet is a greedy little slut these days, aren't you?"

A whimper escaped my lips when he slid two fingers inside me, teasing with slow, curly motions. "Yes."

The mate bond flooded my veins with lust at the single word I uttered for my princes. Andras spoke next, making the decision, as always. "We are going. The six of us deserve some time to ourselves."

Dev nodded. "I'd enjoy somewhere quiet with less males gawking at Seraphina."

Phen tousled Dev's hair. "Are you jealous, baby? They're staring at you, too. Those bright-green eyes are truly mesmerizing."

Dev shoved Phen away and blushed. He pretended not to enjoy the attention, but Dev adored Phenex. And their bond was adorable. I needed everyone to be in less clothing. My orgasm was building and there wasn't even a single dick on display.

"Dev," I panted. "Take off your pants and let me stare into those pretty eyes while Phen fucks your tight ass."

This time, it was Andras's turn to laugh. "So demanding. You heard her, boys. Do as our queen commands."

Even if I hadn't taken the throne, or any of the titles offered to me, I would always enjoy my princes treating me like a queen. And they would be my kings. Now, and always.

EPILOGUE
Seraphina

Noircoeur was completely packed with creatures. Daemons, lumens, mortals, and others. But the burlesque lounge I enjoyed performing at was no longer owned by the Obscuritas Kings. The club now belonged to the Umbra Noctis. Once an underground group of dissenters, the Umbra Noctis was the new society of creatures united in their efforts to protect all creatures and expand their reach to new worlds.

We returned to Earth after a few nights of celebrations on Stella Terra. Tibby and Gremory were with us as well, and seeing her smiling was filling my heart with happiness.

"Can I tempt you into joining me on stage, Tibby?" I sang out to my friend, with no power, only a pleading tone. Tibby was one person I would never use my ability to influence minds on. Not after the years she spent under Laszlo and Samuel's influence.

Her bright-blue eyes sparkled when she smiled, tucked between Gremory's thighs where he sat at the bar. "Absolutely not. My voice can't hold a candle to yours."

I waggled my eyebrows. "Who said you had to sing?" Gremory arched an eyebrow, and I grinned at him. "Did you know your girl is a talented pianist?"

Tibby flushed bright red at the compliment. "I'm really not. I just dabble."

Gremory wrapped his arms around her slender waist and rested his chin on her shoulder. "Seeing as you have an exceptional talent for downplaying your abilities, I'm going to need a demonstration."

I reached out and squeezed her hand encouragingly. "Come on, my friend. Before we part ways, let's give them all a show."

Tibby smiled softly and nodded. I tugged her out of Grem's arms and away to the stage. We sauntered past the VIP booth where my mates were lounging, and I gave them a wink. I may have changed into the tiniest bodycon dress and thigh-high red boots since ducking into my dressing room. Several growls and horny snarls from the booth had a few heads turning. Tibby and I laughed, skipping away.

Fucking hells, pet. You look good enough to eat. And I will be having a taste when you leave that stage.

I am so fucking turned on right now. Can we have an orgy in this booth? Do the curtains close? Phen was like an eager puppy, and his excitement at experiencing the club for the first time was infectious.

Oh, they sure as fuck do. But I don't think there's room for an orgy. Let's go back to the Towne House and play hide and seek. First one to find Seraphina gets to fuck her mouth. You game, diabla?

Desire stirred low in my belly at his words. *I'm in. Just because I love your dicks doesn't mean I'm going easy on you, though. No rules.*

Shall we have teams? Andras mused. *Perhaps Dev can assist with the cock sucking.*

If you want your dick in my mouth, Andras, all you have to do is ask. Dev sassed back, and for a moment, we were all silent.

Raucous laughter from the booth caused dozens of heads to turn, and I couldn't keep the grin from my face. My mates and I had come so far in our relationship with each other. The last time I sang on this stage, the Princes were still unaware I was investigating each of them. But while I thought I was sneaking into their lives to ruin them, these fuckers were digging their claws into my black heart. We never stood a chance. And if I could do it all over again, I would. Despite the pain, and the loss, we found each other in our darkest moments.

This life was not for the faint of heart, but it was ours.

"So, my friend, what song do you have in mind?" Tibby asked, seating herself behind the piano on the stage.

With lust pulsing through my veins, I knew just the one. "Let's do 'Heaven' by Julia Michaels."

Tibby began fingering the keys with extra finesse. She played beautifully. I spied Gremory in the crowd laser-focused on his mate. My gaze turned to the booth with my own mates, and their hungry eyes melted my insides. It was our last night on Earth before we set out for worlds unknown.

The song ended to a standing ovation from the crowd, and I had a new game in mind for us. Leaping off the stage and running for the exit, I cast one last look back at my mates.

Catch me if you can, boys.

THE END

ACKNOWLEDGEMENTS

OMG THE SERIES IS OVER?!!!! HOW DID THIS HAPPEN??! First, my editor Andrea for being honest and always pushing me to be my most creative self, thank you for making this series even better than I could have done on my own. And to my PAs, Nikki and Holly, loves of my life, my OGs. Thank you so fucking much for all that you do to keep my shit together. I would be nowhere without you.

To my beloved street team. SO MANY of you were here from the very beginning, taking a chance on a new baby author, and that you're still here with me, loving these characters and hyping me up, I will be forever and ever grateful.

THE READERS. When I first put out ARC signups for Retaliation, Book One, there were 300+ signups. I was absolutely floored. That so many of you stuck around for the entire series means everything to me. I love how emotional I can make you (yes, I collect your tears like a dragon hoards gold). Thank you for being here until the end.

THE AUTHORS. Could never have come this far without having a gang of fellow authors cheering me on, offering advice and just bouncing ideas around with. You all are one of my favorite things about being an indie author.

And last but CERTAINLY NOT least. My bestie, Marissa. You are the best fucking hype bitch (as a Leo, no one is shocked) ever and I love you forever for being there for me from the beginning until infinity.

This is not the true end, as I have so much more to share, including stories in this world. Grem and Tibby deserve a little something, don't you think? (I'm sorrryyyyy).

Anyway, thank you to every single human who helped me turn this fever dream of a story into the explosive series that it became. I. LOVE. YOU.

www.ingramcontent.com/pod-product-compliance
Lightning Source LLC
Chambersburg PA
CBHW070545120726
47909CB00007B/2240